PRAISE FOR
THE SCRAPBOOKING MYSTERIES
BY LAURA CHILDS

"Childs rounds out the story with several scrapbooking and crafting tips plus a passel of mouthwatering Louisiana recipes."
—*Publishers Weekly*

"The heroine is a plucky, strong, and independent woman who takes charge when necessary as she is the original steel magnolia."
—*The Best Reviews*

"If you are a scrapbooker and like to read, then Laura Childs's Scrapbooking Mystery series is for you! These books are so great that I just couldn't put them down! I just can't wait for the next one to be released."
—*BellaOnline*

"Scrapbook aficionados rejoice! Ms. Childs creates a charming mystery series with lively, quirky characters and plenty of how-to . . . Serving up some hors d'oeuvres of murder and mystery, creativity and fashion, she has a winning formula to get even the laziest of us in a scrapbooking mood."
—*Fresh Fiction*

"Like her Tea Shop Mysteries . . . Childs's Scrapbooking series is an entertaining read. The author mixes French Quarter charm with eclectic characters and witty drama."
—*Romantic Times*

"An entertaining who-done-it."
—*Midwest Book Review*

"Perfect reading."
—*Romantic Times* (four stars)

"Childs does an excellent job of weaving suspense with great tips for scrapbooking and crafting aficionados."
—*I Love A Mystery*

D0043271

·LAURA CHILDS·

Eggs in Purgatory

BERKLEY PRIME CRIME, NEW YORK

THE BERKLEY PUBLISHING GROUP
Published by the Penguin Group
Penguin Group (USA) Inc.
375 Hudson Street, New York, New York 10014, USA
Penguin Group (Canada), 90 Eglinton Avenue East, Suite 700, Toronto, Ontario M4P 2Y3, Canada
(a division of Pearson Penguin Canada Inc.)
Penguin Books Ltd., 80 Strand, London WC2R 0RL, England
Penguin Group Ireland, 25 St. Stephen's Green, Dublin 2, Ireland (a division of Penguin Books Ltd.)
Penguin Group (Australia), 250 Camberwell Road, Camberwell, Victoria 3124, Australia
(a division of Pearson Australia Group Pty. Ltd.)
Penguin Books India Pvt. Ltd., 11 Community Centre, Panchsheel Park, New Delhi—110 017, India
Penguin Group (NZ), 67 Apollo Drive, Rosedale, North Shore 0632, New Zealand
(a division of Pearson New Zealand Ltd.)
Penguin Books (South Africa) (Pty.) Ltd., 24 Sturdee Avenue, Rosebank, Johannesburg 2196,
South Africa

Penguin Books Ltd., Registered Offices: 80 Strand, London WC2R 0RL, England

This is a work of fiction. Names, characters, places, and incidents either are the product of the author's imagination or are used fictitiously, and any resemblance to actual persons, living or dead, business establishments, events, or locales is entirely coincidental. The publisher does not have any control over and does not assume any responsibility for author or third-party websites or their content.

PUBLISHER'S NOTE: The recipes contained in this book are to be followed exactly as written. The publisher is not responsible for your specific health or allergy needs that may require medical supervision. The publisher is not responsible for any adverse reactions to the recipes contained in this book.

EGGS IN PURGATORY

A Berkley Prime Crime Book / published by arrangement with Gerry Schmitt & Associates, Inc.

PRINTING HISTORY
Berkley Prime Crime mass-market edition / December 2008

ISBN: 978-0-425-22495-3

BERKLEY® PRIME CRIME
Berkley Prime Crime Books are published by The Berkley Publishing Group,
a division of Penguin Group (USA) Inc.,
375 Hudson Street, New York, New York 10014.
BERKLEY PRIME CRIME and the BERKLEY PRIME CRIME design are trademarks of Penguin
Group (USA) Inc.

PRINTED IN THE UNITED STATES OF AMERICA

10 9 8 7 6 5 4 3

This one's for the hometown folks.

Acknowledgments

Many thanks to Tom Colgan, Sandra Harding, Sam Pinkus, Pat Dennis, and all the fine designers, writers, and publicity folks at Berkley Prime Crime. Thanks also to Jennie, Bob, and Dan. And to all the folks I've known and loved who served (sort of) as inspiration for my characters.

·CHAPTER 1·

SUZANNE Deitz didn't set out to start the Cackleberry Club, the whole thing just sort of happened. The ramshackle whitewashed building with the tangle of wild roses and stack of antique egg crates out front actually began life as an unassuming Spur station on Highway 65, just outside the small town of Kindred. Truckers stopped there to buy diesel, empty their bladders, and stock up on Slim Jims. Underage teenage boys tried to wheedle six-packs of Schlitz. And on Sundays, folks from the Journey's End Church of Ultimate Repentance came by after morning services for ice cream. Probably, raspberry swirl and peppermint bonbon brought cooling relief from a sermon rife with hellfire and brimstone.

But then Suzanne's husband, Walter, died, and Burt Lemmings, the district manager for Wanamingo Oil and Gas, got a bug up his fat ass and decided to jack up fuel prices and add a hefty surcharge for delivery. In the middle of interviewing for a new manager, Suzanne found herself caught between that proverbial rock and a hard place.

"Walter died, you know," Suzanne told Lemmings,

standing out by the pumps that had finally run dry. She was lean and brown from the sun, her hair a silvered blond, eyes a deep cornflower blue. "Four months ago. Pancreatic cancer." She pushed the toe of her cowboy boot into the dust and stared at the turquoise leather steer head on her left ankle and tried not to let her lower lip quiver. Walter, who'd been one of the town's doctors, had given her those boots two birthdays ago. Back when the damn dots on his damn X-ray had just looked like specks of dust.

Burt Lemmings sucked air through his front teeth and stared across acres of waving green soybeans and undulating pasture that seemed to stretch from southern Minnesota to the nether reaches of Missouri. "I got increased costs," he told her, his beady eyes carefully avoiding hers. Lemmings wore shitty double knits, a wonky tie, and possessed not an ounce of sympathy.

Suzanne wasn't born yesterday. And now that she was on the far side of forty, she didn't have much trouble spotting an asshole from a mile away. Maybe, Suzanne thought, teaching school and overseeing the Spur station wasn't really in the cards after all.

Then her best friend Toni's husband took up with the floozy bartender from the American Legion, and Petra's husband got so bad he finally had to go into the Pine Manor Nursing Home. And like planetary aspects lining up in a once-in-a-thousand-year cycle, the three women came together. Middle-aged, semi-desperate, with more grit than you could shake a stick at.

·CHAPTER 2·

Three Months Later . . .

"WE are officially out of wild rice sausage," Toni announced. She stood behind the lunch counter, hands on skinny hips, wearing an AC/DC concert T-shirt and tight jeans, her reddish blond frizzled hair pulled on top of her head like a show pony. All around her forks clacked noisily against plates, coffee was slurped loudly, and the gaggle of men hunched at the counter watched her surreptitiously. For Kindred and the surrounding area, Toni was pretty hot stuff.

"I'll grab another package from the cooler," Suzanne told her, moving quickly, pushing her way into the kitchen.

It was nine in the morning, and the mercury had already hit eighty, the heat gathering momentum, building into a steamy midwestern August day. Toni, as waitress supreme, was handling the morning rush with aplomb, if you could call eight men perched at an eight-stool counter a morning rush. Petra was short-order cook, rattling pots and pans, making magic at the grill, slipping in a few strips of turkey bacon here and there, doing her small part to help keep their patrons from suffering cardiac infarctions before they hit fifty.

Suzanne, as one part inventory manager, one part marketing guru, and one part majordomo, ran herd on the rest of the place.

The rest of the place, the Cackleberry Club in toto, was a homey, crazy-quilt warren of rooms that almost defied description.

There was the café, of course, the counter and a half dozen battered tables that turned into a tea shop in the afternoon. The whitewashed walls were decorated with antique plates, grapevine wreaths, old tin signs, and turn-of-the-century photos. Vintage hats hung from pegs, wooden shelves were jammed with ceramic chickens and forties-era salt and pepper shakers.

The small Book Nook across the hall carried CDs and boasted a fairly decent children's section. Toni led the book club on Tuesday nights. Their first few meetings had started out academic and scholarly, the women discussing writers such as Jane Austen and Charlotte Brontë. But after someone brought along a jug of wine and everyone had a glass or two of sweet, jammy Shiraz, the women pretty much admitted that bodice-busting romances were really top of mind.

Next door was the Knitting Nest, a cozy corner filled with overstuffed chairs and stocked with a veritable rainbow of yarns and fibers. Petra taught Hooked on Wool classes Thursday nights. This was a slightly more crunchy-granola crowd, distinguished by their nubby sweaters and Swedish clogs.

The adjoining bakeshop sold fresh-baked breads, potato rolls, corn muffins, and apple and strawberry pies. Locally grown produce was also carried in season, inventory being what folks trucked in that morning. Today the shelves held blueberries, plums, tomatoes, green beans, and honeydew melons, as well as rhubarb jams and native grape jellies made by Petra in the same double boiler her grandma had once used. The small, secondhand display cooler offered wheels of organic blue and cheddar cheese produced by Mike Mullen, their neighbor down the road who owned a herd of long-lashed, doe-eyed Guernseys. And there were fresh eggs, brown, white, and the speckled variety, from local poultry producers.

Eggs were the morning specialty at the café. Puffy golden omelets bursting with sautéed mushrooms and molten with pungent Gruyère cheese. Monte Cristo Eggs Benedict served with a sidecar of sour cream and strawberry jam. Slumbering Volcanoes, a concoction of baked eggs, pepper jack cheese, and roasted garlic atop grilled artichoke hearts. Toad in the Hole with pork sausages surrounded by a flaky golden crust of baked eggs. Plus Scotch Eggs, Eggs on a Cloud, and Huevos Rancheros. Hence the name, of course: the Cackle-berry Club.

SUZANNE wasn't surprised when, at half past nine that morning, Bobby Waite came ambling in. Bobby was Kindred's most popular attorney, a nice enough fellow who always had his polo shirt tucked neatly into his khaki slacks and wore well-buffed Cordovan leather loafers.

As Suzanne's lawyer, Bobby had been a gentle guiding force through the myriad death certificates, probate red tape, and other documents that the banks, courts, and Social Security Administration had required.

"Got a few more papers for you to sign," Bobby told her. He slid onto a just-vacated stool and shoved the documents across the counter.

"More government stuff? They sure love to poke their nose in a person's business," said Suzanne, fumbling for the pen tucked into her jacket pocket, finding it wasn't there. Then again, neither was the jacket. These days she was comfortable and unapologetic in faded blue jeans and a white shirt tied at the waist. Serious jewelry traded for silver earrings and a simple turquoise bracelet that some-how looked exotic against her suntanned skin.

Bobby reached into his briefcase, fished out a silver Bic. "Here. Use mine."

As Toni was wont to do, she sidled over. "Whatcha want for breakfast, honey?" she asked Bobby.

He shook his head. "No time. I'm on my way into the office, then I have to drive over—"

"You gotta have breakfast," cut in Toni, who wasn't about to let him off so easily. "It's the most important meal of the day. Fortifies the body and the spirit. Maybe you want to take somethin' with you?"

"Okay, sure," Bobby relented, a grin on his face. "Your Eggs in Purgatory then." Eggs in Purgatory was Petra's version of baked eggs swimming in lethal Tabasco and chipotle-laced tomato sauce. Besides being delicious, you were assured of getting your capsaicin fix.

"You got it," said Toni, with the enthusiasm of an insurance salesman who'd just landed a major account.

Suzanne scrawled her signature where Bobby had affixed little plastic tabs with red arrows. Idiot-proofed it, she told herself, for people like her who needed a professional to deal with the nits and nats of legal documents. So she could focus on more broad-concept topics. Like . . . eggs.

"Got another call last week," said Bobby. "About your land." Suzanne owned a two-hundred-acre portion of land nearby. Well, actually, it had been Walter's land, an investment of sorts when he'd signed on as doctor at the Westvale Clinic. Now the land was hers, and she continued to lease it to a farmer named Ducovny who produced corn and soybeans from the rich, black soil.

"A serious offer?" she asked. "Beaucoup bucks?"

Bobby shrugged. "More like a casual inquiry from an agent. You still not interested in selling?"

"I'll think about it," Suzanne told him. But she knew it wouldn't be top of mind. She was noodling lots of plans for the Cackleberry Club. And maybe even a sister restaurant that offered fine dining. Suzanne had a real passion for cooking and food concepts, especially when it involved fresh ingredients that were locally sourced. And Kindred, with its dairy farms, boutique cheese makers, and organic farms, was a rich source.

"Well, let me know," said Bobby. He stashed the papers back inside his well-worn briefcase and then fumbled for the white plastic container that Toni slid across the counter.

Suzanne thanked Bobby again, then grabbed an order book and threaded her way through the cluster of wooden tables where two more groups of customers had made themselves comfortable.

It was crazy, she decided. The Spur station had done a reasonable business, had been a good investment. But this place, the Cackleberry Club, was going gangbusters. Suzanne still wasn't sure what the magic charm was that drew folks in. It could be the home-cooked angle. Men loved Petra's breakfasts, and women adored their tea service in the afternoon. Or maybe it was the eclectic mix they'd stumbled upon: the food, the books, the yarns. Whatever it was, business was good. In fact, three months after launching, they weren't just eking out a living, they were edging toward making a profit, a difference that didn't sound like much, but was immense in the scheme of things.

"BOBBY Waite is sitting out back," Teddy Harlingen told Suzanne some twenty minutes later. He slipped onto a stool and winked at her. Teddy Harlingen was a World War II vet who'd served with George Patton in the Battle of the Bulge, got bayoneted in the gut, and never let anyone forget it. Unfortunately, Teddy's mind had slipped a few cogs since his glory days with the hard-charging general.

"What are you talking about?" asked Suzanne.

Teddy giggled as he tilted his head sideways and rolled his eyes. A three-day stubble covered his wrinkled cheeks, and his eyes were a transparent blue, as though he'd been gazing out to sea too long.

Suzanne knew that Teddy always showed up the day after his Social Security check arrived, ordered a humongous breakfast of scrambled eggs and sausage, then caromed off down the road on the balloon-tired Schwinn bicycle his son had outfitted with training wheels. Probably, Suzanne figured, that vehicular arrangement neatly offset Teddy's penchant for splurging on a pint of Mad Dog 20-20, then following it up with a night of beer and bull at Schmitt's bar.

"Did you do something to Bobby's car?" asked Suzanne. Teddy was known for his practical jokes. He'd once jammed firecrackers and fresh cow manure into the tailpipe of Joe Dumar's milk truck. That had caused a big stink in more ways than one.

"Didn't do nothin'." Teddy shrugged. "Just walked by, saw Bobby sittin' there."

"And what did Bobby say?" asked Suzanne. Her eyes slid over to meet Toni's, who was doing her darndest to ignore the old coot. Toni shrugged. An I-don't-know-what-the-heck-that-old-geezer's-talking-about shrug. But Suzanne was suddenly aware that Baxter, her aging Irish setter, was barking his fool head off out back. Baxter, who napped out there pretty much every day, was rarely disturbed by anything, save the occasional Harley-Davidson that rumbled into their parking lot or a lone jackrabbit that poked its furry nose out of the fringe of woods the property backed up to.

"I'm gonna go out back and check on Bobby," Suzanne told Toni. "Sounds like he might be having car trouble."

But Toni was suddenly busy, trying to explain the subtle but critical variances between Eggs Florentine and Eggs Neptune to a customer at the counter.

Suzanne pushed her way back into the kitchen, where she was once again enveloped in a rich cocoon of aromatherapy-like smells. Pepper jack cheese melted on sizzling eggs, mettwurst sausage and cinnamon French toast fried on the grill, blueberry scones and ginger muffins baked in the oven.

"Hey," said Petra, who was handling the grill like a jolly maestro, flipping cakes and prodding sausages, then spinning deftly to plate each breakfast. Already in her fifties, Petra was smart, intuitive, and a calming influence. With her bright brown eyes and kindly, square-jawed face, she was always quick with a smile. And though her body was full-figured, it was still curvy in all the right places.

Suzanne couldn't resist snatching a piece of turkey bacon from the grill, then pulling open the oven door for a quick peek. "Lookin' good," she declared. Petra was also baking one of her trademark carrot cakes.

"No you don't," warned Petra. "Remember what happened when you snuck a peek at my pineapple upside-down cake? Poor puppy went flat as a board."

"Not my fault." Suzanne grinned. "That was due to a barometric imbalance in the stratosphere that produced gobs of humidity."

"Oh you are so full of it," laughed Petra, as Suzanne eased the oven door closed then slipped out the back door.

Baxter's barking could mean the coyotes were back, Suzanne decided. She'd seen one last week when she was hauling out garbage. A small female, skinny and mangy. She'd felt so sorry for the miserable little thing that she'd tossed it a hunk of chicken. Now she wished she hadn't. She'd probably just encouraged the little pest to pay a repeat visit.

Off in the distance Suzanne could see a hawk circling lazily in the sky, probably zooming in on a nest of field mice. She winced inwardly, suddenly thinking of the shrieking intrusion that would come cannonballing out of the sky, the tiny lives lost. Since Walter died, she thought about death a lot. Yesterday, she'd set a little red spider outside rather than swat it.

Suzanne crossed the back lot, a patchwork of hardpan,

grass, and struggling violets. A slight breeze had sprung up, and she felt it instantly dry the tiny beads of sweat on her forehead. Her silver dangle earrings fluttered gently, caressing her throat like butterfly wings.

"Hey, Baxter," Suzanne called. "What's going on, fella? What's got you so hot and bothered?"

Baxter, his brow furrowed, his muzzle starting to go white, pulled himself up to greet her and give an answering woof. Although Baxter didn't seem particularly upset now, something had gotten him riled up. And Bobby Waite's shiny black Ford pickup *was* parked over there by the old shed. If he was hunting around in there for tools, he was out of luck. There was nothing in there now except a sputtering Toro lawn mower and a few bags of fertilizer that were probably well past the statute of limitation on germination.

Car trouble? Suzanne wondered as she crossed the backyard. She figured maybe Bobby had phoned Lou Marcy at the Conoco station, then didn't want to wait around for the tow truck to show up. Maybe Bobby had caught a ride into Kindred with one of her customers. He was a busy lawyer, after all, with a meeting to go to.

Suzanne edged up to the truck. With the sun tasering down in a cloudless blue sky, it was hard to see in, lots of reflection off the glass. She had to press her nose up against the passenger side window.

And then wished she hadn't.

Bobby Waite was in there, all right. Along with his take-out order of Eggs in Purgatory. The whole shebang was splashed across the dashboard and up the front window. Gobs of sauce obscured the speedometer, dripped off radio dials, and soaked Bobby's shirt. In fact, it looked like a damn ten-gallon can of industrial-strength tomato sauce had exploded in there. Except, Suzanne realized, some of the red stuff was blood.

·CHAPTER 3·

NEWS traveled fast around Kindred. By twelve noon every seat in the house was taken and a line stretched two deep outside the Cackleberry Club, all the way past the now-defunct gas pumps.

Sheriff Roy Doogie and his two deputies had gotten there first, of course. Light bars pulsing, sirens blatting, they'd speed-balled to the scene of the crime, responding to Suzanne's frantic 911 call. Once they'd hopped up and down, giving a darn fine impression of the Keystone Cops, they'd settled down a bit, surveyed the scene, and properly expressed their dismay. Hats had been removed, foreheads mopped, pink scalps had been scratched. All that heavy exertion had led to only one conclusion. Better call in the state crime lab.

Those boys were a whole lot cooler. Arriving in shiny black vans, they swaggered around in their dark blue knit polo shirts emblazoned with the words Crime Lab. After all, another dead body was no big deal to them. They were the A-team versus Doogie and his boys, who were more accustomed to collaring the county's speed demons and dealing with invading raccoons who knocked over garbage cans and terrorized small dogs.

Sheriff Doogie pulled it together, though, and while the state guys were snapping pictures and filling plastic Baggies, he attempted to interview darn near everybody in the tri-county area.

Now they were all hunched around Suzanne's largest table, mumbling in low voices and eating lunch. Nearby tables were filled with locals straining to catch snatches of their conversation.

Suzanne didn't know how they could eat after dealing with all that blood. Discussing it, photographing it, taking samples of Lord knows what, then putting Bobby's poor, wrecked body in that super-sized Ziploc bag or whatever it was. She personally didn't think she'd be able to consider food for at least another day.

"Suzanne." Sheriff Doogie pushed back his chair and stood up, choreographing a quick hitch of his pants at the same time. "You remember who was hanging around here this morning?" He adjusted his wide black belt, which seemed to have a gun, cell phone, nightstick, keys, and handcuffs hanging from it, giving the impression of an at-your-ready Swiss army knife.

"Most of 'em I know," said Suzanne. "They're pretty much regulars. You want me to make a list for you?"

Sheriff Doogie pulled out a spiral-bound notepad. "Just tick off the names."

Suzanne gave Doogie the names while, all around her, tables were cleared, new places set, and another shift clambered for seats. Everyone was oddly fascinated by the killing, the first to occur in Kindred in more than sixty years. Everyone wanted to dine at the scene of the crime, so to speak. Go figure.

"What about people you don't know?" asked Doogie.

Suzanne cocked an eye at him. "You mean strangers?"

Doogie nodded at her, and his jowls sloshed slightly.

"Then I wouldn't know their names, would I?" said Suzanne.

Sheriff Roy Doogie was dogged in his persistence. If it was in his power, he was going to run this murder investigation strictly by the book. "What about credit card receipts?" he asked.

Suzanne gave a slight snort. "It's breakfast, Roy, not the tasting menu at the French Laundry. Our most expensive entrée is Eggs Balderdash, and that's only seven ninety-five. The thing of it is, most folks don't slap down their American Express card for breakfast. Most people just *pay* for their eggs versus financing them."

"You don't have to be so doggone touchy," Sheriff Doogie admonished her.

"Sorry," said Suzanne. Finding Bobby had rattled her. "It's just that . . ." She swept her arms outward in an expression of futility. "We're awfully busy."

"So are we," said Sheriff Doogie. And for the first time, Suzanne saw the worry and fear behind the look of earnestness on his doughy face.

"So . . . ?" said Suzanne, her natural curiosity suddenly surpassing her aversion to blood and death. "Bobby was, what? Shot?" She was pretty sure that's what had happened, but she decided she could really use some honest-to-goodness details. After all, it had happened right here on her property.

Sheriff Doogie gave a grudging nod and made an accompanying sound that approximated a "Yup."

"I take it a gun was not left behind at the scene of the crime?"

"Nope."

"Do you think it could have been some sort of a weird accident? Whoever did it panicked and fled the scene?"

"We don't know that yet," said Sheriff Doogie.

Suzanne stared at a point slightly to the left of Sheriff Doogie's head. "Probably shot with a handgun," Suzanne mused. "But I never heard a sound." She turned toward Toni, who was carefully placing silverware atop folded paper napkins on their round, six-top table. "You were in and out of the kitchen all morning, Toni. Did you hear a shot out back?"

Toni shook her head slowly as she wiped a knife blade against her denim apron. "Uh-uh." She'd already been questioned, had already told the sheriff that she hadn't seen or heard anything unusual.

"We assume the suspect used some kind of silencer," Sheriff Doogie volunteered to Suzanne.

"A silencer," said Suzanne. Suddenly it didn't sound like Bobby's death had been any sort of accident. Now it sounded suspiciously like murder. "That's kind of a fancy gun accessory, isn't it?" she asked.

Roy Doogie suddenly fixed her with the stare of a slumbering rattlesnake. He knew he'd said too much.

"I mean," continued Suzanne, her words tumbling out. "A gunman with a silencer implies it might have been planned. That it was some sort of . . . hit." She almost let the words *contract hit* escape her lips but pulled back at the last moment.

Sheriff Doogie closed his jaws so hard, Suzanne could hear his mandibles click. "Why do you have to say something like that?"

Suzanne held her ground. "Because, given the circumstances of Bobby's death, it just seems like a very real possibility."

"Look," said Sheriff Doogie, obviously trying to nip Suzanne's harebrained theory in the bud, "Bobby Waite was just a small-town lawyer. He wasn't involved in anything that would remotely constitute what you'd call a hit. That stuff only happens on TV. It especially doesn't happen to folks in places like Kindred."

"I'm just saying," said Suzanne.

"Well, do me a big fat favor and don't say too much, okay?" Sheriff Doogie's face was developing a series of radiating red blotches. In fact, it looked like a hornet had just stung him dead center on the forehead.

"Sure," said Suzanne. "Okay. Take it easy. Don't go having a coronary."

Sheriff Doogie stomped back to the table where the state crime scene guys were finishing their slices of country apple pie, and Suzanne scurried over to clear another table.

She hadn't been trying to be a wiseass or spin a far-fetched theory. She was just genuinely shaken by the murder of Bobby Waite. He was a friend, after all. He'd been there for her when Walter died, easing her through probate and insurance settlements and all that other legal crap, not that it was completely wrapped up even yet.

And nothing this violent had ever happened in Kindred before. Not that she could recall, anyway.

When Suzanne was a kid growing up here, Kindred had been a dozy little town. A Norman Rockwell knockoff with a downtown full of yellow brick buildings and a calendar of charming community events that included band concerts in the park, church raffles, bake sales, and Fourth of July parades where old soldiers dressed in moth-eaten uniforms and kids decorated their bikes with red, white, and blue crepe paper. Time-warpy stuff.

Suzanne realized that her childhood had been an almost idyllic experience; the little town in the valley was practically surrounded by acres of hardwood forests, a slice of natural prairie left over from the eighteen hundreds, the high bluffs of Cottonwood Park, and a meandering trout stream known as the Catawba River. Because the bluffs were limestone and the water moved constantly, there was no scourge of mosquitoes, either.

The past eight to ten years, however, Suzanne had come to think of as the mushroom years. New stores, new people, new everything springing up all over the darned place. With all that growth had come an influx of problems, too. A sprawl of strip malls, a trailer park, more traffic, the big

Save Mart out on Sealy Road that sucked customers away from Kuyper's Drug Store, the Ben Franklin, and Hanson's True Value Hardware.

Along with all that unplanned growth had come higher taxes, zoning issues, even a few reputed meth labs farther out in the country. Because the town coffers stretched, split, and ran dry, Kindred bid on and won the contract for a new state prison. Now that monstrosity of cement and razor wire was hunkered a few miles south of town.

The bike trails, parks, towering bluffs, and pristine trout streams were still there, of course. But those scenic wonders just drew more people. Stately old homes were being rezoned and yuppified by new people who wanted to turn them into trendy B and Bs. People who had fled big cities trying to escape big-city problems.

Kindred, the slumbering little midwestern town perched on the winding ribbon of I-90, had morphed. And with the murder of Bobby Waite this morning, it had been seemingly changed forever.

·CHAPTER 4·

LUNCH ran well past two o'clock this Tuesday. Petra was kept bottled up in the kitchen by the influx of customers—luncheon gawkers, really—who'd heard about the murder and been drawn to the Cackleberry Club.

Like blowflies to a body, Suzanne had decided. She was buzzing about in the Book Nook, straightening the children's section. For some reason, a lot of today's extra traffic had spilled over into the narrow aisles. Now the little nook with the faded oriental carpet and saggy, rump-sprung chairs looked like an F-5 tornado had cut a swath through it. Volumes of Harry Potter and Blue's Clues were scattered on the floor, a couple of sci-fi books were mixed in with the romance section, and Danielle Steele had somehow made her way into the cookbook section.

Hastily gathering books and putting them back on their rightful shelves, Suzanne glanced up and found herself staring into the earnest brown eyes of Vern Manchester.

Vern was a local real estate developer who'd put up a nice-looking string of town houses on the south side of town. Bridgeview Estates they were called, although no actual bridge was there for viewing. Vern had also served on the planning committee along with Walter when Claiborne Corrections Corporation had first come in and pitched the idea of a privately owned prison situated in Kindred. Walter had been hesitant, not because it was a prison but because for-profit prisons had a nasty reputation. Vern had thought it would be good for the town. They'd partner on construction costs, and the prison would provide work for local contractors as well as jobs for area residents. All that extra income would increase the town's tax base. Vern had claimed it would be a win-win situation for the entire town.

"Afternoon," said Vern.

"Hey there, Vern," Suzanne replied.

"Heard you had some excitement here this morning," said Vern. He said it casually, but like everyone else, he seemed breathless for details.

Suzanne sucked in a quick breath then blew out steadily. This was probably the way it was going to be all week. Folks dropping by to cadge as much information as possible.

"A sad situation," Suzanne replied. She decided if she kept her answers brief, almost to the point of abrupt, people might get the idea she really didn't want to talk about it.

"I just stopped by to pick up a book for my wife," said Vern. "Lenore was pretty hot to get that new Rachael Ray cookbook, and I had Petra order it. But, just now, when I ran into Tim Waverly in your parking lot, he filled me in on the bad news about Bobby Waite! Shocking. Just shocking." Vern shook his head in disbelief, and his expression actually was one of shock. "Has Sheriff Doogie come up with any sort of suspect? Or, for that matter, a motive?"

"No," said Suzanne, "but for what it's worth, Doogie seems to be working hard on it."

"Well . . . good," said Vern. "This whole thing has just . . . stunned me. Knocked me for a loop. You, too, probably."

"I found Bobby," said Suzanne. She wasn't sure why that little factoid suddenly popped out of her mouth.

Vern's eyes opened so wide you could see all the white surrounding his irises. "Must have been awful for you!"

"It was pretty bad," Suzanne told him. Although she could think of worse.

SHERIFF Doogie stopped back again, generating yet another flurry of excitement at the Cackleberry Club. This time he slumped at a table with one of his deputies, writing in his notebook, looking more than a little frazzled. Even though they were offering afternoon tea service, Suzanne hastened over with a pot of coffee.

"Not sure how good this is," she said, splashing coffee into two brightly colored ceramic mugs for the men. "It's been sitting awhile. Could taste like diesel fuel."

Doogie looked up at Suzanne and pursed his lips. "Do you think Teddy Harlingen might have been hanging around here before he came in for breakfast?"

Suzanne blinked. "What? Is Teddy a suspect now?"

The young deputy shifted in his chair. He looked barely twenty-four. Probably fresh out of the two-year criminal justice program at Darlington College over in neighboring Jessup. "Please just answer the question, ma'am," he said.

His words slammed Suzanne right between the eyes. She'd been ma'amed. A hit-and-run ma'aming. The worst kind. "Just you be polite," she told him in a voice that bordered on stern. She raised an eyebrow and stared at Sheriff Doogie. "Is he?"

"Teddy has guns," answered Doogie. "He was in the war." He lifted his mug, took a long slurp of coffee.

"Gimme a break," snorted Suzanne. "That was sixty-five years ago. Poor Teddy can barely find his way down a single-lane highway let alone mastermind a murder. Besides, what motive could he possibly have?"

"Not clear yet," said Doogie, digging in a little.

"No way is Teddy your guy," said Suzanne. She slid into the empty chair across from the sheriff, ignoring the young deputy, whose face had turned tomato red. "Are those crime scene guys running ballistics tests on Teddy's guns?"

Doogie nodded. "Course they are."

"There you go," said Suzanne. "Those tests are gonna come back negative, and then your whole investigation's gonna be back at square one. Meanwhile, some asshole will have a one-day jump on you guys."

The deputy threw her a curious look. "What do you know about investigating?"

"Hey," she said, tapping a finger on the table. "I watch *Law & Order* and Court TV. I know how it's done."

Doogie drained the rest of his cup loudly, then set it down. "Except it ain't nearly that glamorous. Or easy."

"I cancelled book club tonight," Toni told them. The three of them, Suzanne, Toni, and Petra, were collapsed on the old sofa in the Knitting Nest, cradling mugs of tea. Darjeeling, a nice bright estate varietal.

Things at the Cackleberry Club had finally settled down to a dull roar. The café was officially closed, there were lots of empty shelves in the bakery section, and just a handful of people lingered in the bookshop.

"Well, not exactly cancelled," continued Toni. "I just moved it to tomorrow night. Okay with you?" She looked at Suzanne, who was, as they always joked, their CEO: chief executive organizer.

"Sure," said Suzanne. "No problem. Whatcha guys been reading?"

Toni assumed a slightly guilty countenance. "I'm afraid

we sacked Cormac McCarthy and now we're into Nora Roberts."

"Now there's a lady," said Petra, who had her nose stuck inside the *National Inquisitor*, studying an article on plastic surgery gone wrong, "who knows how to write a love scene."

"I don't want to bum anybody out," said Suzanne, "coming on the heels of today, but things are probably gonna be crazy again tomorrow."

Petra nodded. "I'm sure they will." She hesitated. "But you should take a gander at our receipts. I kind of hate to say this, but we had our biggest day ever."

"That's pretty bizarre," muttered Toni, who had grabbed Petra's *Inquisitor* and was now perusing an article on botched Botox injections. She placed an index finger in the center of her forehead and pushed up. "No," she muttered to herself.

"We drew a lot of new customers," said Petra, "who'll hopefully keep coming back."

"So there's an upside to Bobby's murder," sighed Suzanne.

By the time Suzanne loaded Baxter into her Ford Taurus and drove to her little home on Laurel Lane in the north side, the oldest part of Kindred, it was well past six o'clock. She poured a mixture of kibbles and low-fat cottage cheese into an aluminum dog dish, then dropped in a Rimadyl tablet to help combat Baxter's arthritis. Suzanne filled another aluminum dish with fresh, cold water, then set everything down on the kitchen floor on top of an old gingham place mat.

"There you go, sport," she said, dusting her hands. "*Bon appetit.*"

Baxter dug in with relish, something Suzanne wasn't quite feeling yet.

After discovering Bobby Waite's bloody body earlier, she hadn't felt like eating all day. She still didn't.

That, however, didn't preclude Suzanne from having a glass of wine. A liquid refreshment was always good for relaxing at the end of a perfectly strange day, she told herself.

She went upstairs to the big front bedroom she and Walter had shared, shucked out of her clothes, and pulled on her black silk kimono. What she'd always thought of as her lovemaking kimono. Big wide sleeves afforded easy access, the tie belt was easy to undo, and the silken fabric slipped seductively off her shoulders.

Now she put it on when she wanted to feel close to Walter.

Padding back downstairs, she pulled open the EuroCave wine refrigerator that kept the wine at a perfect fifty-six degrees. Walter had been a real wine aficionado, regularly buying cases of French and California estate Cabernets and Bordeaux. His taste had rubbed off on her, and now Suzanne pulled the cork on a Trefethen Vineyard Reserve Cabernet and poured two fingers' worth into a crystal Riedel Vinum Cabernet glass.

She carried her wine into the living room and set it on the glass coffee table. Grabbing the remote for her Bose system, she pushed Play, then Shuffle, and sat back in the big aubergine-colored chair and tried to find comfort in the fact that the day was drawing to a close.

Just like that, one of her favorite songs came on. An old Nina Simone ballad that she and Walter had made their own.

Suzanne takes you down to her place near the river . . .

Nina Simone's voice was a mellow caress. A little husky, too. Like maybe she'd just had sex and was curled up with her lover, sharing a smoke. The way she and Walter always had. Their one guilty pleasure.

And she feeds you tea and oranges . . .

Don't, Suzanne warned herself. *Don't look back too much.* But she let the music wash over her anyway. How could she not?

And then the tears came, streaming hotly down her face, even though Suzanne wasn't sure who she was crying for: Bobby, her dead husband, Walter, or herself.

CHAPTER 5

JUNIOR Garrett stomped across the wooden floor in his pegged jeans, tight white T-shirt, and battered cowboy boots, posturing like an overage juvenile delinquent.

"You sicced the police on me!" he shrilled at Toni. Junior's lackluster forelock hung down over his face like a dark semicolon. His olive complexion bloomed, chameleon-like, into an ominous, blotchy red. Ordinarily, Junior Garrett wasn't a bad-looking guy, but this morning he was positively menacing.

"I did no such thing," Toni yelled back at the husband she hadn't seen hide nor hair of in three whole months.

Conversation came to a screeching halt at the Cackleberry Club. Heads turned, and chairs creaked as they were turned to more advantageous angles. The men seated at the counter shifted nervously. Junior and Toni going at it was tantamount to a domestic disturbance of the first magnitude. Kitchen crockery could go airborne, punches could be thrown.

Suzanne stepped in quickly to referee. "You want to take

this outside, Junior? Because whatever your problem is, we're really not interested."

"She sent Sheriff Doogie after me," said Junior, pointing an accusing index finger at Toni. He'd lowered his voice some, but it still dripped venom, and his face was twisted into a tough-guy expression. "Now the old fart thinks I had something to do with Bobby Waite's murder!"

"Did you?" asked Suzanne, suddenly relieved that Doogie hadn't stayed fixated on Teddy Harlingen.

"No way!" snapped Junior. He glared at Suzanne with righteous indignation but allowed her to take him by the arm and guide him over to the Book Nook, away from prying eyes. Toni trailed behind, angered by her husband's accusations, her curiosity burning bright at the same time.

"You can't come busting in here, upsetting my customers," began Suzanne, once they were all out of earshot. "You gotta learn to keep your cool."

"Not when she's still on my back," Junior snarled, gesturing at Toni, who stood there with her arms folded protectively across her chest. "There's a reason I left home, you know. 'Junior, take out the trash. Junior, do you really need *another* beer with that Krispy Kreme? Junior do this, Junior do that.' "

"Poor you," said Suzanne. "Marriage was just one big imposition, huh?"

Junior flashed a sour look at Suzanne. "Now she's trying to pin Bobby Waite's murder on me." He jerked his chin to indicate Toni.

"You're out of your mind," said Toni. "But now that you bring it up . . ."

"Says you," replied Junior, spinning on his stacked cowboy heels and stomping out of the shop. "I hope you gain fifty pounds."

"You see why I married him?" said Toni. "Who could resist those impetuous, childish ways?" Even though she tried to sound flip, she looked a little shaken.

"You filed papers on Junior?" asked Suzanne. She put her arm around Toni and gave her a reassuring pat.

"Oh yeah," said Toni. "Course I did. The very next day after he left me for that . . . that woman."

"Good girl," said Suzanne. "You did the right thing."

Some five minutes later, life at the Cackleberry Club had returned to normal. Petra was bent over the hissing, sputtering grill, humming the melody to Sheryl Crow's "Live It Up" and cooking two orders of her famous Eggs Enigma, a tasty concoction that included freshly grated Parmigiano-Reggiano cheese and diced pancetta. Toni was chasing back and forth from the kitchen to the café, delivering orders. Suzanne was muddling things around in her head, sticking close to the kitchen.

When Toni came charging back through the swinging door to pick up another order, Suzanne called, "Toni?"

Toni was just loading two hot, steaming plates of pecan waffles and sausage onto her tray. "Yeah?"

"Does Junior have guns?"

"Jeez . . . how come you're asking about that?" said Toni a bit defensively. Then she paused a moment to seriously consider Suzanne's question. "Yeah, a few. A shotgun and maybe a couple of rifles. A twenty-two for sure. Yeah." She nodded. "For deer hunting."

"No handguns?"

"Not sure," said Toni.

Suzanne patted Toni's skinny but well-muscled arm as she slipped past her. "Take it easy," she said. "You're among friends."

As Toni's eyes welled with tears, she fanned herself rapidly with one hand. "Sorry," she apologized. "I've been getting way too emotional lately. Next thing you know I'll be having hot flashes."

"Welcome to the club," murmured Petra, who was a few years older than both of them.

* * *

SUZANNE accosted Sheriff Roy Doogie the moment he walked in.

"What's the deal with Junior Garrett?" she asked. "Why did you tell him Toni tried to pin Bobby Waite's murder on him?"

Sheriff Doogie slid his wide-brimmed modified Smokey Bear hat off his head and stared at Suzanne with rheumy eyes. "I did no such thing."

"But you obviously talked to Junior," said Suzanne. Hands on slender hips, she stared up at the sheriff's khaki bulk.

"That's called following up," said Sheriff Doogie, enunciating each syllable distinctly. "Standard police procedure. Something I do understand, in case you thought I was fixated only on Teddy Harlingen."

"Okay," said Suzanne. "Good."

"Seems Junior had an altercation with Bobby Waite a couple weeks ago at Schmitt's Bar," explained Doogie. "Half the town witnessed it. Well, the half that was still relatively sober, anyway. Junior was crazy mad at Bobby because he'd apparently drawn up divorce papers for Toni. I think they'd been served on him that morning."

"Oh," said Suzanne.

"Oh," said Sheriff Doogie, looking stern.

"But you don't really think Junior Garrett was the one who shot Bobby Waite, do you?"

"Like I told you before," said Sheriff Doogie. "I'm following up. In fact, I got a ton of following up to do. And if you're going to dog me every step of the way, it's going to be a long, shitty process."

"It's just that Junior came storming in here," said Suzanne.

"I'm sure you girls can handle a goofball like Junior," said Sheriff Doogie.

"Women," said Suzanne, correcting him.

"Huh?"

"I think you meant to say we *women* can handle a goofball like Junior."

"Sure. I guess." Doogie's eyes skittered along the back of the counter, past the coffee machine, across golden loaves of fresh-baked bread, finally settling on a plate of sticky buns dripping with caramel sauce and sprinkled with pecans.

"Sticky bun?" asked Suzanne. She grabbed one, slid it onto a plate, and held it up like she was offering a reward to a trained bear. "Coffee, too?"

Sheriff Doogie nodded. "You bet."

Once she got Sheriff Doogie settled at the counter, Suzanne grabbed two coffeepots and threaded her way through the tables. Just as she'd predicted, the place was jumping. Word about Bobby Waite's murder had spread throughout the county, and people were lining up to get a contact high off the tragedy and excitement that seemed to linger in the air at the Cackleberry Club.

On Suzanne's third time past Sheriff Doogie, he reached out and put a hand on her arm.

"What?" she asked him.

He gave her a baleful look. "Did Teddy Harlingen have any kind of confrontation with Bobby Waite yesterday?"

"What? Are you kidding me?" said Suzanne. "I told you Teddy's not your suspect."

"Everybody's a suspect at this point," muttered Doogie.

"Now *that* can't be terribly productive," replied Suzanne.

Doogie just grunted.

"Do they know what kind of weapon was used on Bobby?" Suzanne asked. "I mean the, um, caliber?"

"Forty-five," said Doogie. "Know anybody who owns a forty-five?"

"Not offhand," said Suzanne, "but I could ask around."

"Don't," said Doogie.

Suzanne gave him a bright smile. "Maybe the Cackleberry Club could host one of those gun trade-in deals, like police in big cities have. Call it something catchy . . . maybe guns for griddle cakes."

"No thanks," said Doogie, trying to soldier on bravely. "Okay, so here's the deal. The tire treads those crime scene guys took impressions of are standard on a Chevy van. You know anybody who drives that type of vehicle?" He pronounced vehicle like all law enforcement officers do: three distinct syllables, hard on the middle one.

Suzanne actually did know someone whose van fit that description. Charlie Pepper, one of her egg producers, drove a Chevy van. "Maybe Charlie Pepper," she told the sheriff. Fact was, Pepper had dropped by early yesterday with a delivery. Brown-speckled eggs from his New Hampshire Reds.

Sheriff Doogie opened a black perfectly bound notebook and jotted a few notes. Yesterday, he'd seen one of the state guys use one just like it, and it had seemed like a good idea. Spiffier than his usual spiral-bound books. So he'd purchased one at the Ben Franklin store first thing this morning.

"Was Pepper here yesterday?" Sheriff Doogie asked.

Suzanne nodded. "Sure. Tuesday egg delivery. We like Charlie's eggs because his hens tend to lay double yolks."

"Ever had any problems?"

"With the double yolks?"

Sheriff Doogie sighed. "No, with Pepper."

"Charlie took off on a four-day junket to Vegas last year and ended up staying an extra week. His wife couldn't take care of the chickens and make deliveries, too, so we had to get our eggs from Calico Farms instead."

Doogie shook his head. "That's not what I mean."

"I know what you mean," said Suzanne. "And the answer is no."

·CHAPTER 6·

"I call this my angel afghan," said Petra, "because the wool's so fluffy and light." She was sitting in the Knitting Nest, needles clacking, a puff of woolly afghan draped casually across her lap.

Suzanne fingered the partially knit piece. "Alpaca?" she asked. She knew Petra favored alpaca.

"Seventy-five percent alpaca, twenty-five percent wool," said Petra. "Hand spun by that woman over near Jessup."

"Leticia," said Suzanne. Leticia Sprague was a throwback to an earlier time. A woman who raised her own animals, sheared them herself, spun her own wool, and dyed it. The end result was rich, lush skeins of wool that afforded an almost sensory experience. Once in a while they were lucky enough to offer some for sale at the Cackleberry Club. Of course, the wool flew out the door almost immediately.

"Leticia calls this color sandstorm," Petra told her. And to Suzanne's eyes it did look like a sandstorm. She'd never traversed the Gobi or Sahara deserts, but, studying the way the rich browns and rusts mingled with flecks of gold, she could imagine that earthen-tinged landscape shimmering under the force of the sun.

"I still want to learn how to knit," Suzanne told her. Of course, Suzanne wanted to learn Italian, hike the Appalachian Trail, and ride a zip line through the canopy of a Costa Rican rain forest. But none of that had materialized yet, either.

"It's not difficult," said Petra with a smile. "What I'm doing here is just a vertical drop stitch. And allowing lots of air between stitches to show off color variances." Petra leaned forward, touched Suzanne gently on the arm. "You've had a lot on your plate, dear."

Suzanne nodded. "We all have."

Petra acknowledged her response with a faraway smile. "Donny and I used to sit together at night, him gluing together model airplanes, me doing my knitting. Not talking all that much, but we were still . . . connected. Then, when Donny was diagnosed with Alzheimer's, the knitting's what kept me sane. Sitting in endless doctor's offices, waiting for test results that always seemed to turn out badly."

"I know," said Suzanne. Since Walter died she could barely bring herself to step inside any type of medical office. Walter had been a doctor, and all his medical knowledge still hadn't saved him from getting cancer. Now Suzanne even hated taking Baxter to the vet for his lousy rabies shot. She glanced at the wall, at a small, framed needlepoint Petra had made. It was titled *Prayer of a Breton Fisherman,* and the words read, "Lord, the sea is so wide and my boat is so small. Be with me."

"Even now," said Petra, "when I go visit Donny, I like to think he can hear the gentle clack of my needles and somehow, deep down, make the connection, know it's me by his bed."

"I'll bet he does," said Suzanne.

"Suzanne?" Toni was standing in the doorway. "Gene Gandle is on the phone." Gene was the head reporter, the only reporter really, for Kindred's weekly paper, the *Bugle.*

"Doing a story on Bobby," said Petra.

"Probably," nodded Toni.

Suzanne hurried into the Book Nook, pushed her way into their small office, and picked up the phone. "Gene," she said.

"Hello, Suzanne!" Gene was over-the-top cheery.

Probably, Suzanne decided, that upbeat voice was how he got folks to spill their guts. "Hi, Gene," she said back.

"Just wanted to touch base with you on this Bobby Waite thing."

"It was a murder, Gene, not a thing. Let's give it the proper gravity it deserves."

"Absolutely, Suzanne," Gene replied. "Which is why I wanted to check with you. I understand you were the one who found the body?"

"That's right," said Suzanne. "Lucky me."

"And you didn't see anything fishy around your place beforehand?"

"Not any more than usual."

"Any guesses?" Gene asked. "Any . . . hunches?"

"Nope," said Suzanne.

"You're not being very helpful, Suzanne," said Gene. And now there was a distinct *tone* to his voice.

"Are you writing a story or launching an investigation?" asked Suzanne.

Gene hesitated for a moment. "Well, maybe a little of both."

"In that case," said Suzanne, "you should be confabbing with Sheriff Doogie."

"I tried that," said Gene. "He wasn't exactly forthcoming."

"Sorry I can't help you, either," replied Suzanne.

"Hold on one second," said Gene. Suzanne could hear him talking to someone else at the *Bugle*; then he came back on the phone and said, "Laura wants to know if you'll have next week's 'Tea Tastings' column in by Friday." Laura Benchley was the editor.

"No problem," said Suzanne, knowing full well it was a problem.

"GENE tryin' to weasel a story?" Toni asked once Suzanne reappeared in the Knitting Nest.

"He gave it a good shot," said Suzanne. "But I didn't have anything to tell him."

"Good girl," said Toni. "Hey, you still planning to schlep our receipts to the bank?" She held up a zippered black nylon envelope stuffed nearly to the breaking point.

"On my way," said Suzanne.

"Twelve hundred eighty-seven dollars and thirty-eight cents," said Toni.

"Wow," said Petra. "Big bucks."

"I counted it twice," said Toni, "and made out a deposit slip, but you can do a recount if you want to."

"Nope," said Suzanne. "As I recall, you were the one who got the A in consumer math. I'm the geometry drop-out."

"Tried to put a square peg in a round hole?" asked Petra, a grin on her face.

"Still trying," replied Suzanne.

DOWNTOWN Kindred still retained much of its hometown flavor. Feed store on the outskirts, old railroad depot that had been turned into the Kindred Historical Society, stretch of yellow brick buildings that, even with their tarted-up neon signs, still exuded turn-of-the-century charm.

Suzanne parked her car in front of Root 66 Hair Salon. It was run by Gregg and Brett, two gay guys who still did 1980s-style mall rat hair but were a hoot to gossip with. Gazing through the front window, Suzanne could see two tiny women hunkered down in the red vinyl salon chairs. Both had blue rinses in their hair and were being freshly coiffed for the coming week. This eighty-plus dynamic duo was Minerva Bishop and Cleopatra Sunderd, known to everyone as Mrs. Min and Mrs. Cleo. They were pretty much the closest Kindred came to social dowagers.

Crossing the street, dodging traffic, Suzanne headed for the First Community Bank. She had about fifteen minutes until closing and didn't relish the idea of keeping that much cash in her home overnight. For some reason, Bobby Waite's murder had changed her notion of safety in Kindred.

"Hey! Suzanne!"

Suzanne turned to find Melissa Langston hurrying toward her. Known to everyone as Missy, she was Bobby Waite's administrative assistant and a member of the town council. Missy was a blond, blue-eyed Iowa girl with creamy skin and an old-fashioned, movie-star quality about her. Thick blond hair, worn in a pageboy, brushed her shoulders. She was thin yet managed to have voluptuous curves at the same time. In her early thirties, Missy was still unmarried but was reputedly dating the local undertaker.

"Missy, oh my Lord!" Suzanne greeted the woman with a big hug. In all the furor with the sheriff and the state crime lab and the extra traffic at the café, she'd forgotten entirely about Missy. "Honey, I'm so sorry about Bobby," said Suzanne. They continued to hug each other, nodding, letting a few tears ooze out.

"When I heard you were the one who found him, I was going to call," explained Missy. "But then Sheriff Doogie showed up, and things got so crazy." She relaxed her embrace and straightened her shoulders, trying to look strong.

"You gonna be okay?" asked Suzanne.

Missy managed a smile and nodded her head in the affirmative. "Sure. Of course." She dropped her voice low. "They're releasing Bobby's body tomorrow. Ozzie's gonna take care of it." Ozzie Driesden was the local undertaker, Missy's sweetheart.

"So the funeral's being planned," said Suzanne. She

thought for a moment. "Have you talked to Bobby's wife?" Bobby had a wife, Carmen Copeland, who was a very successful romance writer. Word had it that Carmen had a writing studio in the neighboring town of Jessup where she also taught an occasional creative writing course at Darlington College. With Bobby living in Kindred and Carmen over in Jessup, Suzanne suspected that Bobby and Carmen had fashioned a different kind of marriage. Different, anyway, from the kind she and Walter had.

"I spoke with Carmen on the phone yesterday," said Missy. "But just for a couple of seconds. I think she's in shock. Lord knows, everybody else seems to be."

"That's for sure," said Suzanne. She suddenly wondered if Sheriff Doogie was going to turn his beady-eyed gaze on Bobby's wife. Or if he had any reason to.

"Missy," said Suzanne, recalling Sheriff Doogie's questions about the tire treads, "did Bobby ever have any dealings with Charlie Pepper?"

Missy's front teeth worried her lower lip. "Why are you asking?"

"Because Sheriff Doogie asked about him. And Charlie made a delivery yesterday right before Bobby came by. Not that it means anything . . ."

"There was that Chemco lawsuit," said Missy.

"Refresh my memory, would you?" said Suzanne, more than a little interested now.

Missy glanced to either side of them, making sure they wouldn't be overheard. "Last year this Chemco Fertilizer truck slammed into Charlie's delivery van out on Highway 212. Charlie came to Bobby because he wanted to sue Chemco. His truck wasn't all that damaged, but he claimed the chemicals got all over his truck, and it wasn't fit for deliveries anymore. He also claimed whiplash and bodily injuries."

"So Bobby filed a lawsuit," said Suzanne. "And I take it things didn't go well?" All this had obviously taken place before he'd become their egg man.

"Charlie got his truck fixed," said Missy, "but that was about it. He claimed neck and back injuries, said they were absolutely *killing* him, but nothing ever showed up in the X-rays and medical reports." Missy shook her head. "Then one of the insurance investigators made a video of Charlie playing golf a couple of weeks after the accident."

"Bet that didn't help Charlie's case," said Suzanne.

"Shut it down completely," said Missy. "So Charlie got real upset with Bobby, claimed he didn't fight hard enough. Charlie wanted some kind of jury trial, but the suit got kicked over to mediation." Missy rolled her eyes. "You know, pretend judges."

"I can't imagine Charlie held a grudge over that."

"You don't know Charlie," said Missy.

Maybe I don't, Suzanne thought to herself. The man barely spoke a word to them when he delivered eggs. And they say it's always the quiet ones . . .

Missy drew a deep breath, let it out slowly. "But still, I can't see Charlie committing murder."

"Did Sheriff Doogie ask you about this?" said Suzanne.

Missy nodded. "Oh yeah. And he's gonna come over again first thing tomorrow and go through all of Bobby's files, see if he can glean any sort of information that might point to a motive."

"That's good," said Suzanne.

They stood together in lengthening shadows, each lost in their own thoughts.

"Anyway," Missy said, "I'm sure glad I ran into you." She blinked away a tear. "Like I said, I was going to call . . ."

"If you need anything, just give me a jingle, okay?" offered Suzanne. "Maybe you want to talk or just need someone to help figure things out at the office." Along with Bobby, Missy had been a godsend when Walter had died. Suzanne would never forget her kindness.

"Thanks," said Missy. "That means a lot to me." She sniffled. "You know, Bobby had almost three dozen active clients. They're all clamoring for answers, and I don't know what to tell them."

"What about Bobby's partner?" asked Suzanne.

"Since he's semiretired, he's probably gonna stay that way," said Missy. "I can help clients with *some* things, but I don't have a law degree . . . I'm a paralegal at best." Tears suddenly welled in her eyes. "I've no idea what's gonna happen to his law practice . . ."

Suzanne dug in her handbag for a Kleenex, passed it to Missy.

"Thanks." Missy blew her nose, sniffled, and blew again. "I feel like I'm being pulled in a million directions." Another tear trickled down her cheek. "Carmen's near hysterical, Sheriff Doogie is all over me, clients are calling like mad, and . . . and . . ." She looked up at Suzanne. "I still haven't given you that chocolate chip cookie recipe I promised you."

"Don't worry about it," said Suzanne. "In fact, it's the *last* thing you should worry about."

·CHAPTER 7·

"YOU'RE back," said Toni as Suzanne threaded her way through the now-empty Cackleberry Club. "I already fed Baxter. One cup of dry kibble and a dollop of nonfat yogurt. Was that right?"

"Baxter would eat a carburetor if you drizzled yogurt on it," said Suzanne. She glanced out the kitchen window where Baxter was snoozing again, his muzzle positioned in a small puddle of fading sunlight. "So, how can I help?" The reading groups that had been cancelled last night were reconvening tonight. At least they hoped folks would show up. This was a fairly new event for the Cackleberry Club, and Suzanne hadn't really helped out before.

Toni pulled off her apron and ran a hand through her shaggy mane of hair. "If you could just man the Book Nook for the first twenty minutes or so, that would be great. People get here, they usually browse around, find a couple books that interest them. Then we'll get the two groups going. I'll be leading Romance in the Book Nook, and Heather King's gonna do Mystery in the Knitting Nest. Anyway, once discussions are under way, give it forty-five minutes or so, then set out the scones and tea on the counter. We'll take our break when you give the high sign."

"Sure," said Suzanne. "No problem." She was restless anyway, and puttering around the kitchen always calmed her down. She wandered back, pulled a clean white apron from the cupboard, washed her hands, and then opened the double doors of their large cooler. Suzanne grabbed butter, milk, powdered sugar, and vanilla, measured everything into a saucepan, stirred it over medium heat, watched as it thickened and turned into a nice, creamy icing. Dipping a clean spoon into the mixture, she tasted. Darn near perfect. Okay, now for the fun part. Using a silver butter knife, Suzanne layered a thin coat of glaze onto the three dozen miniature chocolate scones that Petra had baked earlier. She let the glaze drip down in what she thought was a lovely freestyle technique, then arranged the finished scones on a large silver platter and draped a hunk of plastic wrap over the top. So far so good.

When the first book club members began to arrive, Suzanne hustled into the Book Nook to man the cash register. Business was brisk for about fifteen minutes as customers milled about, buying books and asking a few oblique questions about Bobby Waite's murder. Then the book club members broke into their respective groups and settled down to the business at hand.

Suzanne headed back to the kitchen to start her tea. She selected four white china teapots and measured out fresh jasmine tea leaves into two of the pots. She studied the tins lining the kitchen shelf and decided on a black currant tea, a rich, aromatic tea she knew would be a lovely complement to the chocolate, for the other two pots. She took her time, enjoying the aroma of the fresh tea, munching a scone, and chasing it down with a cold glass of milk. She dug out twenty cup-and-saucer sets, carried them out to the counter, then made it all look pretty by arranging them around a vase of daisies.

Finally, Suzanne set her water to boiling. When it was

almost at the stage where bubbles were beginning to form, she poured her hot water gently over the tea leaves to steep. Then she carried the tea and scones out and set it all on the counter.

Even though they were supposedly taking a break, the book club members, ladies mostly, seemed to carry on their discussion while enjoying the refreshments. Suzanne wound her way through the tables, pouring refills, offering seconds on scones, stopping to chat whenever there was a familiar face.

On her final pass, she overheard two women talking about Carmen Copeland, Bobby's wife. Curious, Suzanne sidled over to listen.

"She *already* had her house up for sale," said the first woman.

"House? I didn't know she had a house," said the second woman. "I was under the impression it was more of a writing studio."

"Oh no, it's a great big Victorian thing. Very grand with lots of scrollwork and gingerbread cutouts. She *lives* there." This was accompanied by raised eyebrows and an elaborate eye roll.

Suzanne wandered into the Book Nook, pondering the woman's words. Carmen Copeland was in the process of selling her house? Did she just not need it anymore? Or was she in the process of moving away? And how would Bobby's death affect her plans?

Drifting over to the Romance section, Suzanne ran a finger along the spines of some of Carmen's books. *Love in Peril*, *The Daffodil Queen*, and *Splendor Island*. She noted the back-to-back curlicued *C*s that had become Carmen's logo. Opening her most recent offering, *Fanciful Love*, Suzanne scanned the titles in Carmen's backlist and decided that Carmen probably earned quite a bit of money from her best-selling romance novels. Probably a lot more dough than Bobby had earned. Probably (and Suzanne knew she was letting her imagination run a little crazy here) more money than Carmen would ever collect from any life insurance policy she'd had on Bobby.

Suzanne thought about that for a minute.

She was pretty sure she'd read somewhere that a high percentage of murders were committed by unhappy spouses. In most cases, however, it was the husband doing away with the wife, not the other way around. Of course, there were always exceptions to that rule.

Suzanne stared at a Reading Is Right! poster for a few moments, then shook her head as if to clear it. What evil twist had her mind just taken, anyway? Trying to work up Carmen as a suspect in her own husband's murder? That wasn't particularly fair. Chances are, the poor woman was at home right now, prostrate with grief over her husband's death.

"Sure she is," she whispered aloud. "Any woman would be."

It was dark by the time Suzanne got the kitchen cleaned up and loaded Baxter into the car. She stood for a moment, gazing out across the lush, dark wave of soybeans and caught the occasional flash of tiny, flying beacons: fireflies. Lovely little critters. Overhead, stars twinkled back in solidarity, looking like a great sequined dress draped across the night sky.

Voices raised in joyous song carried faintly on the warm evening breeze. The Journey's End Church was having their Wednesday night prayer meeting.

Suzanne started her car and nosed around to the front of the building. Cars were parked every which way, so she eased out carefully. Just as she was about to pull onto the highway, she saw headlights coming at her from the right. Fast. She did the smart thing and waited.

Like a bullet, a pickup truck flashed by. And right on its tail, a dark SUV, running full bore, its headlights off.

What the heck? The SUV is chasing that truck? Sure looked like it to me.

Curiosity sank its talons into Suzanne, and she tromped down on the accelerator, taking off after them.

She caught up with the racing vehicles about a mile down the road. The pickup had slowed slightly and was slaloming all over the road, weaving dangerously from one lane to the other. The SUV was still hard on its tail.

Suzanne dug in her purse for her cell phone, punched in 911. This was a bad situation. A professional intervention was needed.

Just as the dispatcher at the law enforcement center answered, Suzanne saw red taillights flare, bounce hard to the left, then disappear down a steep embankment. They reappeared a moment later tracing a perfect red arc.

"The truck's flipped over!" she shouted into the phone and to Baxter, who was bouncing like a manic rocking horse behind her, panting, wheezing, hanging his big head over the front seat. Drool soaked her right shoulder, hot doggy breath warmed her neck. "Highway 65, just a mile west of the Journey's End Church!" she screamed to the dispatcher.

A hundred yards from the crash site, Suzanne slammed on her brakes and rocked to a hard stop. Peering into darkness, she saw the dark SUV idling by the side of the road.

Had the driver scrambled down the embankment to give aid to the pickup driver? Had she just imagined there'd been a chase?

She identified herself to the dispatcher, repeated her location, then shoved the gearshift into park. Jumping from her car, Suzanne ran toward the accident scene. Someone needed help!

She'd gone barely ten yards when a sharp crack pierced the night and stopped Suzanne dead in her tracks.

She held her breath, listening, and finally picked up the sound of heavy panting, as though someone might be struggling to crawl out of the ditch. Then heavy footsteps hit the berm, scuffing gravel.

"Hello?" she called out, suddenly unsure. There were no streetlights out here, and the summer darkness seemed thick and oppressive.

There was a dull click and then, like some terrible, mechanized mosquito, a bullet whined past her left ear.

Shooting at me? The notion hit her in a blinding flash and seemed utterly preposterous. But her survival instinct kicked in and telegraphed *Hit the ground* to her stunned brain. Suzanne threw herself facedown on the pavement, grimacing as gravel and grit bit into her palms and stung her knees. Rolling backward a few turns, executing a strange side-kick crawl, she scrambled like mad and came up on the far side of her car.

Baxter was a crazy dog, barking frantically, throwing himself at the windows. Suzanne was fearful the next bullet would be aimed directly at him.

She jerked open the back door, cursing the dome light, and threw her arms around Baxter's furry neck. Fighting him, pulling him to the floor, she crawled in and huddled low, pulled the door closed.

As she lay there struggling with the dog, trying to keep him down, a second bullet ripped into her windshield with a tremendous thunk!

Dear Lord, thought Suzanne, her heart beating a timpani solo in her chest, *not this way. Please, not this way.* Pulling herself into a ball, she fumbled in the safety kit she kept in her car. Her fingers skittered across a small Maglite, then wrapped around a roadside flare that looked like a big firecracker. Could it be used as a weapon?

As her ears registered another faint whine, Suzanne ducked reflexively, certain another bullet would come blasting at her. But it was the whine of a far-off police siren. Sheriff Doogie or one of his deputies was on the way.

At the same time, she heard the SUV's engine roar and then a loud squeal of tires as it sped away.

Suzanne dug into her roadside emergency kit again and grabbed the Maglite. Then she jumped from her car, slammed the door fast on Baxter, and sprinted toward the ditch where she'd seen the pickup truck flip over. Scrambling down the steep, weed-choked embankment, stickle burrs tore at her ankles. But she knew she had to get down there, had to help whoever had crashed.

Slipping and sliding down the dark incline, Suzanne finally hit sticky mud and then a good six inches of water.

She flipped on her flashlight.

The pickup truck lay upside down in the ditch. All was silent save for the chirp of unconcerned crickets.

Crouching down, Suzanne flashed her light into the battered, crushed interior. Teddy Harlingen lay crumpled like a sad marionette whose strings had been snipped. Hopelessly pinned, face pushed into the muddy ditch water, Suzanne could only see the back of his head, dark and sticky with blood.

Hot tears stung her eyes. She figured that even if Teddy had somehow managed to survive his devastating crash, there'd been that coup de grâce gunshot she'd heard. An execution-style shooting.

Suzanne stood up, squared her shoulders, and listened as a squad car squealed to a halt up top.

·CHAPTER 8·

THURSDAY was Foggy Morning Soufflé day at the Cackle-berry Club. Petra's whipped concoction of eggs, milk, flour, grated Gruyère cheese, butter, and Dijon mustard sizzled for a few moments in a frying pan, then was thrust into a hot oven to bring the soufflé up to towering proportions. Foggy Morning Soufflé was a once-a-week special and a real crowd pleaser. So, naturally, they were jammed again.

Toni and Petra had caught the story about the accident on early morning radio, sandwiched between wheat prices and hog futures. When they all showed up for work at seven, Suzanne filled them in completely as they hustled around the kitchen, prepping food, readying the café.

"Amazing," breathed Petra.

"Incredible you weren't killed, too," added Toni.

"I thought for sure I would be," admitted Suzanne. Her brain still carried a residual sense of that bullet whirring past her. If she lingered on it for too long, she told herself, she'd go bonkers.

Instead, Suzanne focused on the intoxicating aroma of

Kona coffee that rose from her mug. It was one of the most expensive blends in the café and served only on special occasions. But what better time to treat oneself than the morning following a high-speed chase, especially one that had ended so badly?

"Did you know it was Teddy at the time?" Petra asked, her hands white with flour as she lined up two dozen greased and floured ramekins on a cookie sheet.

"No," responded Suzanne. "It was way dark, and the truck pretty much flew by. But when that SUV flashed past with its headlights off, I knew something was crazy-wrong." She grabbed a pineapple–macadamia nut muffin, still warm from the oven, and split it open.

"And you just had to see what was going on," said Toni, shaking her head in disbelief. "At least you managed to call 911."

"And get herself shot at in the process," added Petra, her voice trembling slightly. "Girl, you could have been killed!"

"Tell me about it," said Suzanne. She knew how close she'd come to having a bullet crease her scalp.

Toni shook a finger at her. "You were reckless."

Petra looked up from her eggs. "Honey, we can't afford to lose you." Then her voice softened to a whisper. "I can't afford to lose you."

They were all quiet for a few moments, lost in their own thoughts. Then Toni said, "Why on earth would someone want to kill Teddy? He's a harmless old coot."

Suzanne had been muddling that thought around herself. "Not sure. But I'm guessing that Teddy might have seen more than just Bobby sitting in his truck."

Toni glanced up sharply. "Whoa. You think Teddy saw Bobby's killer?"

Suzanne held up her hands, then let them fall loosely to her sides, showing her indecision. "Or someone *thinks* he did."

But Petra gave a thoughtful nod. "Teddy saw the killer," she whispered. "And maybe even his own."

"Do you think—?" began Toni, just as something banged loudly against the back door, causing it to swing open and thwack loudly against the cooler. All three women jumped, then turned in unison as an enormous, square-jawed man in a checkered shirt stomped his way into their kitchen.

"What?" he said, seeing their stricken faces. He had a large crate of eggs balanced on his broad shoulders.

"Sorry, Charlie," said Suzanne. "We're all a little unnerved since Bobby's murder."

"And then poor Teddy last night," added Petra.

Charlie Pepper stared at them, a grim look working its way across his weathered face. He was a man who rarely offered words or smiles, but today he wound up and delivered a mouthful. "Don't I know it!" he spat out. "That's why I'm not coming back to the Cackleberry Club," he said in a harsh tone. "You girls gotta find yourself a new egg man."

"What?" squealed Toni.

"What do you mean you're not coming back?" asked Suzanne. "We love your eggs."

"Double yolks," said Petra, trying to help.

"Oh cripes," said Toni, "Are you selling your farm or something?"

Charlie Pepper's brows knit together, and he let loose a disdainful snort. "Town's changed. T'was bad enough when the strip malls and yuppie town houses started popping up all over and the darn taxes began skyrocketing through the roof. Now we got ourselves a murderer walking our streets. Maybe even some sort of weirdo, psycho serial killer."

"Oh, Charlie—" began Petra, but he held up a big paw to silence her.

"To top it off, that lazy doughnut-eater showed up at my place at dawn this morning, asking stupid questions. The sheriff wants to know my 'whereabouts.' Can you believe that? Just 'cause my tire tracks were in your driveway." Pepper was rolling now, letting loose more words than they'd heard from him in an entire month. "Of course my tracks were here. I'm your egg man, for Pete's sake. But that Sheriff Doogie . . ." And now Charlie sputtered a bit. "He upset my laying hens, my poor wife, and, most of all, me! Impugned my reputation. Nobody needs that kind of crap—or even needs this town. Frankie Pilney always said he'd buy my hens if I was a mind to sell. Well, I just might do that. I just might sell 'em and leave town!"

"Nobody's .questioning your reputation, Charlie," said Suzanne, trying to keep her voice calm, trying to back Charlie down a bit. But Charlie wasn't buying it. He spun on the well-worn heels of his lace-up work boots and slammed his way out the back door, leaving the three women with their mouths hanging open.

Toni was the first to recover. "He can't do that."

"He just did," said Suzanne.

"I can't believe it," said Petra. "I've never seen Charlie so . . . so unbalanced."

"You can say that again," said Toni.

Suzanne listened for a moment, then frowned. "Does anybody besides me hear that banging sound?" She was mildly aware of a pounding coming from somewhere. Then again, it could be inside her own head. So much had happened . . .

"Probably Charlie Pepper loading empty egg crates," said Petra.

"No," said Suzanne. "It's coming from the front door."

"Door's open," said Petra. She was usually the first to arrive in the morning, coming through the front door and never bothering to relock it. The stenciled hours on the pebbled glass read, Open at 8:00 A.M. Hungry townsfolk would sometimes gather early in front of the entrance but would respect the posted hours. No one opened the door until it was 8:00 A.M. on the dot.

No one, that is, except Sheriff Doogie. When Doogie was in a huff, he didn't bother with respect or rules.

"Suzanne, you here?" It was Doogie's voice, and now they could hear him clomping through the café like a moose slaloming his way through a church social.

"Yeah, Sheriff. What?" Suzanne called back. She pushed open the swinging door, confronting him as he plopped his bulk onto a chrome stool in front of their nineteenth-century lunch counter.

"We gotta talk," were his dour words as he propped his elbows on the fixture's marble top.

Suzanne stood behind the counter, while Toni and Petra peered through the kitchen pass-through. They watched carefully, Petra kneading a mound of dough while Toni cracked eggs into a bowl.

"Coffee?" asked Suzanne.

Doogie nodded.

Grabbing a ceramic mug, Suzanne filled it to the brim with dark roasted coffee—not her prized Kona blend—and shoved it across the counter at him.

Doogie took a long sip, then eyed her. "You doing okay?"

Suzanne was heartened that Doogie had the decency to inquire about the state of her mental health. The last time they'd exchanged words was over the crumpled body of Teddy Harlingen. Before that it had been terse conversations concerning Bobby Waite.

"I'm fine," she told him. She knew that compared to poor Teddy and Bobby, she really was fine.

Doogie shifted on his stool. "Got any of those biscuit things with the berries inside?" He pointed to the pastry case that was still only half-filled.

"You mean raspberry scones?"

Doogie yawned. "I'm awful hungry. Been up since four."

"And busy at that," responded Suzanne. She placed a scone on a plate, slid it in front of Doogie. When Toni appeared with a glass dish mounded with Devonshire cream, she added a dollop of it to Doogie's plate and handed him a small silver butter knife. "I understand you were at Charlie Pepper's farm this morning."

The sheriff munched a bite of scone before answering. "Nice thing about living in a small town is you don't have to bother telling folks what you been up to. They already know."

"Charlie's our egg man," said Suzanne. "At least he *was*. A few minutes ago he stopped by, practically frothing at the mouth. Said you came by and asked him a ton of nosy questions. He was so upset that you challenged his integrity that he claimed he was quitting the egg business altogether. Threatened to leave town."

"Did he now?" asked Doogie. "That's interesting, because I specifically told Charlie I didn't want him going anywhere." He poked an index finger into the Devonshire cream, touched it to his lips, and licked apprehensively.

"There's something I don't understand," said Toni. She'd emerged from the back again, this time with a bucket of white daisies. "Why was Teddy driving a truck, anyway?" she asked, as she began arranging the flowers in colorful Fiesta vases.

"The pickup belonged to Garland," said Doogie as he slathered Devonshire cream on a bite of scone. "Teddy's son."

"We know who Teddy's son is," said Suzanne, leaving it at that. They didn't need to drag out the messy fact that Garland had a colossal drinking problem and was banned from every bar, saloon, liquor store, roadhouse, and restaurant, including the Cackleberry Club. Garland Harlingen, stinking drunk, was an unruly lout who hurled insults, provoked fights, and fell down, not necessarily in that order. Teddy, on the other hand, had always claimed to be a *controlled* drinker. Whatever that meant.

"I questioned Teddy last night about Bobby's murder,"

said Doogie. "Apparently, he didn't take kindly to it." He shook his head sadly.

Neither did Charlie Pepper, Suzanne thought to herself but bit her tongue. This wasn't a good time to irritate the sheriff. In fact, there was never a good time.

"Turns out, Teddy took Garland's truck and drove into town," said Sheriff Doogie. "Hung out at Schmitt's Bar for a while, sucking down a couple drinks, reminiscing about the war, blubbering in his beer."

"And he was upset about . . . what?" asked Suzanne.

"Bartender said he talked about Bobby's murder and the unfairness of life."

"Who else was at the bar?"

"Same as always," said Doogie. "Half the town. But pretty much everyone claims Teddy was still *relatively* sober when he left. Even the folks at Schmitt's are starting to follow the new DUI statutes."

"Good," Petra murmured from the kitchen. She was the one who'd insisted the Cackleberry Club donate a small portion of their profits to the local chapter of MADD, Mothers Against Drunk Driving.

"Initial blood tests confirm Teddy wasn't intoxicated," said Doogie. "As much as I can put together, Teddy was at the bar, then stopped by Pilcher's Café to grab a burger. Then he headed home."

"That's when I saw him," said Suzanne. She thought for a moment. "Unless he stopped at some other bar."

Doogie shook his head. "Not that we've figured out. And the weird thing is, Garland didn't even realize Teddy had left the farm. He thought Teddy was watching TV in his little cabin next door. Watching that *American Idol* show."

"Do you have any leads on the dark-colored SUV?" asked Suzanne. "Or have you checked registrations for ones in the area?"

"Was it an SUV, or could it have been a panel truck?" Doogie asked.

"Well . . ." said Suzanne. She'd *thought* it was an SUV.

"And the dark color," continued Doogie. "Dark could mean black, brown, blue, or dark green. Do you know how many of those things there are?" He answered his own question. "There must be a couple thousand in the tri-county area."

Toni set the last vase on a table and ambled over to Doogie. "What about the bullets?" she asked. "Couldn't you find casings and trace them to the gun? And aren't all guns registered? Then, if you find that the gun owner drives a dark SUV—"

The sheriff held up a fat paw. "Stop right there. I've said it before, and I'll say it again: you girls watch entirely too much TV for your own good. Do me a favor and do something else. Take up jewelry making or tatting or whatever it is girls do." Doogie slurped the rest of his coffee in one huge gulp, hitched his gun belt, and stood up. He didn't bother to leave a tip because he hadn't bothered to ask for the check.

"Women," Suzanne reminded him as he was on his way out.

Doogie hesitated at the door, shoulders hunched. "See what I mean?" he snarled. "Back in the day it was okay to use the word girls."

"What day was that?" Toni called after him as he pushed open the door and clumped toward his prowler. "The town's annual Cave Man Day?"

CHAPTER 9

BY 11:00 A.M., every table at the Cackleberry Club had been turned over at least four times. Breakfast customers had thronged the place, the raspberry scones had virtually disappeared, and Foggy Mountain Soufflés were history for yet another week. Thirty-seven skeins of yarn were purchased from the Knitting Nest as well as thirteen mysteries from the Book Nook's shelves. At least five customers asked if the Book Nook carried true crime. If one murder was good for business, two was a bonanza.

"I swear," said Toni, wiping her hands on her apron, "if one more person asks me if I know who the killer is, I will scream. They're all acting as if this is *CSI: Kindred*."

"Time for an affirmation?" asked Petra, glancing at Suzanne and Toni, who were gathered in the kitchen with her. She grabbed a small Red Wing crock and shook it gently.

"Why not?" said Suzanne. Petra was a big believer in affirmations, and the three of them had taken to jotting down quotes, inspirational words, and even Bible verses on little pieces of paper, then throwing them into the crock. Suzanne reached in and pulled hers out.

"Whatcha got?" asked Toni.

Suzanne read her verse. "Shoot for the moon. Even if you miss it, you'll land among the stars."

"Good one," said Toni. "Now me." She grabbed a slip of paper and read, "Always leave room in your life for the angels to dance."

"I love that," said Petra.

"Okay," said Toni, "now you, Petra."

Petra grabbed an affirmation, read it aloud. "A hug is the perfect gift. One size fits all, and nobody minds if you return it."

Suzanne reached an arm out and embraced Petra. And the tightness she'd been feeling in her chest eased up a little. "Hey," she said, "we forgot to do the chalk board."

"Let's git 'er done," enthused Toni.

Each day, luncheon specials were printed on the board in bright pink and yellow chalk. Soups, salads, entrées, baked goods, and desserts.

"Curried Split Pea Soup, right?" Suzanne asked Petra.

"And your Cackling Chicken Salad," said Petra.

"Awright," said Suzanne. Cackling Chicken Salad was one of her creations, a giant croissant filled with a delectable mixture of homemade mayonnaise, sliced free-range chicken breast, pecans, grapes, and diced Vidalia onions. It was also one of the café's most requested specials, but Suzanne knew that, this morning, the Cackleberry Club could serve three-day-old McDonald's burgers, and their customers would be content. For a change, everyone was showing up for the gossip alone.

Suzanne brushed chalk dust from her fingers, then completed her menu. Strawberry Spinach Salad, Ham and Cheese Quiche, Cherry Pie Muffins, and Rhubarb Pie. Then she breezed along the counter, filling each customer's mug to the brim. She figured if they sat there long enough, murmuring among themselves, there'd actually be a little time to relax before the noon rush began.

When the bell over the front door tinkled, Suzanne glanced up out of habit and saw the lovely face of Missy Langston, Bobby's assistant. Missy was wearing a floral summer dress that pulled in all the right places and straw sandals with three-inch heels. It was a casual look, one that probably wasn't great in a law office but pretty much worked for every man in the place.

Scurrying to the nearest table, Missy sat down carefully, then crooked a finger at Suzanne.

Suzanne sidled over and slid into a chair across from her. "Hey," she said.

Missy reached over and touched the top of Suzanne's hand. "I heard about Teddy. Are you all right?"

"I was a little shaken up," admitted Suzanne, "but I'm feeling pretty decent now."

As Missy shook her head back and forth, her lush blond hair brushed sun-bronzed shoulders. "Gosh, Suzanne, for you to be involved in another murder is really weird."

"I'm not actually *involved* in the murders," Suzanne responded. "I just keep finding the bodies, that's all." Her explanation didn't make her feel one bit better.

Missy shivered, then said, "Bobby's funeral is set for tomorrow morning."

"Soon," said Suzanne.

"That's how Carmen wanted it," said Missy, her words tumbling out. "Thankfully, the sheriff's office just released Bobby. I mean his body. I mean . . ."

"Take it easy, honey," said Suzanne. "Slow down."

"I'm just so flustered by this whole thing," said Missy.

"We all are," said Suzanne in a soothing tone of voice.

"Nothing like this has ever happened before in Kindred. It's like . . . oh, I don't know . . . a bad moon is hanging over this town or something."

"You mean like a curse?" asked Suzanne.

Missy shook her head. "I'm not *that* superstitious. More like . . . bad luck." She sat quietly for a few moments. "You think the two deaths are connected?"

It was the same thought Suzanne had been turning over in her head. Last night, when she'd finally crawled into bed and was trying to fall asleep, that same notion had spun around inside her tired brain like a load of clothes going through an endless spin cycle.

Suzanne touched Missy's hand. "Missy, do you know where Bobby was headed that morning?"

"You mean Tuesday? When he . . . ?"

Suzanne nodded. "Yeah."

"I think he said he had to stop by his house. And then he was gonna go somewhere, but I don't know where." She pulled a Kleenex from her handbag and dabbed at her eyes. "But that wasn't unusual. Bobby was a busy guy. He had lots of little errands and unscheduled meetings that I didn't always know about."

"Do you think there might be a notation or something in his appointment book?" Suzanne knew she might be getting a little too involved, but just like Alice in Wonderland had discovered, things were getting curiouser and curiouser.

"Sheriff Doogie already went through everything," said Missy, "but I guess I could take a look, too."

"Do that," said Suzanne. She watched as two customers, a man and his wife, peered about the Cackleberry Club with great curiosity, then headed for a table. She'd never seen either one of them here before. The Cackleberry Club was quickly becoming Kindred's main attraction.

"There's one more thing," said Missy, dropping her voice and looking around to see if anyone was watching them. Everyone was. Or maybe it was because Missy had just crossed her shapely legs.

"What?" asked Suzanne.

Missy leaned forward. "Somebody broke into Bobby's office last night."

Suzanne inhaled sharply, then said, "Are you serious?" Bobby's murder was strange enough; Teddy's death was tragic. Now it seemed inconceivable that a burglary had also taken place. It all felt suddenly ominous. Like a triple witching. Or that bad moon Missy had mentioned.

"The sheriff told me not to tell everyone," said Missy. "And I'm not. I'm just telling you. Because you're, you know, *involved*."

"How did you find out?" asked Suzanne. "You went to the law office and—?"

"No, no," said Missy. "Helen Spivak called it in last night. You know, she lives right downtown above the Ben Franklin store. Poor woman has terrible insomnia, almost crippling. Anyway, she called the law enforcement center when she saw lights moving around inside the law office."

"And someone showed up right away?"

"A sheriff's deputy did, yes. But apparently the thief was long gone."

Suzanne decided there was more going on in Kindred than anyone probably realized. She didn't believe in coincidences or astrological alignments or even black cat–type bad luck. "So . . . was anything stolen?" Suzanne had to ask.

Missy glanced over her shoulder. A few customers were still watching cautiously, but her voice was low enough so it wouldn't carry. "Files from Bobby's private office. Stuff he sort of kept to himself."

"The sheriff knows this?" Suzanne wondered if the files were stolen before Sheriff Doogie had had a chance to go through them.

"I called him, but so far he's only sent that same deputy. I guess Doogie's still dealing with this awful Teddy thing."

"Do you know which files are missing?" asked Suzanne.

Missy nodded. "I can remember a couple that he had."

"What were they?" Suzanne didn't mean to pry. Then again . . .

"Well, one of Bobby's files was marked Neukommen."

Suzanne stared at Missy, slowly shaking her head. "Doesn't ring a bell."

"That religious commune out on Sinkhole Road? Neukommen Following? The man who heads it, Claes Elam, is reputed to be a polygamist." Missy shrugged. "Of course, that's only talk. Nobody knows for sure."

"Oh," said Suzanne. "Sure." It was coming back to her now. Maybe three or four years ago, the group calling themselves Neukommen Following had bought sizable acreage over in Deer County. They weren't Amish, and they weren't Mennonites either, but they affected the same sort of dress and manners. Somber black clothes. Long skirts for the women, vests and slacks for the men. The thing that really set them apart, though, was how supersecretive and unfriendly they were.

So why, Suzanne wondered, had Bobby kept a file on them? Had Bobby had some sort of dealings with them? Had the burglar been looking specifically for that file? Or was it just stolen as a smokescreen for some other files Bobby had?

Missy looked nervous. "Those were Bobby's private files, but the reason I know about the Neukommen thing is because one day Bobby got a call from one of the members. A young woman named Lidia. Spelled with an i instead of a y."

"Bobby could have been doing anything for them," said Suzanne. "Setting up some sort of trust, handling property issues, you never know." Suzanne wasn't sure why Missy was telling her about missing files, unless it was because of her offer to help yesterday afternoon.

Missy continued to stare at her with searching eyes until Suzanne began to get a fluttery feeling deep in the pit of her stomach.

"You said a number of files had been stolen," said Suzanne. "Do you have any idea what the other ones might be?"

Missy's head jerked in a semblance of a nod. "Yes, I do. One of the other files had to do with your husband, Walter."

·CHAPTER 10·

A record number of Cackling Chicken Salads, Cherry Pie Muffins, and slices of Rhubarb Pie were served at the Cackleberry Club over the next two hours, but Suzanne was too distracted to notice. All she could think about was what Missy had told her. The stolen file had something to do with her husband, Walter.

Suzanne had forced herself to smile during the lunch-hour rush. Had laughed at unfunny jokes. Had even remained relatively unfazed when two customers requested ketchup for their Cackling Chicken sandwiches.

With all the extra business, there wasn't a minute to spare, even with fifteen-year-old Joey Ewald showing up to bus tables. Joey, who had a screaming eagle tattoo and more silver in his pierced ears and eyebrows than Suzanne had jewelry, earned minimum wage and probably deserved less. But today his mood was a notch above his usual taciturn teenage angst, and he seemed content to be working rather than skateboarding down Main Street, wreaking havoc with traffic and unsuspecting pedestrians.

"Some crazy shit around here, huh?" said Joey. Dark eyes with surprisingly long lashes stared intently at Suzanne. There was a languid, dusky look about Joey, and he was string bean thin.

"Yeah," said Suzanne, "we've never been so busy."

"I meant the murders," said Joey, wiping his nose on the back of his hand. "Kindred's suddenly become an exciting place."

"Ain't it great," said Suzanne.

"And you," said Joey, his eyes lighting up. "You got to see all the blood and stuff."

"Joey, honey," said Suzanne. "Go in back and wash your hands, will you? And be sure to use the antibacterial soap."

AT the first sign of a letup, Suzanne put a hand on Toni's shoulder. "Can you handle things?"

"Sure," said Toni. She studied Suzanne for a long pause. "You okay?"

"Perfectly fine. I just gotta call Doogie."

"Call him what?" asked Toni. "I can think of a few choice names for you to use. Let's see, there's male chauvinist pig, son of a—"

"I can come up with my own," said Suzanne. "And I'm not calling to harass him. The thing is, Missy mentioned that somebody broke into Bobby's office last night."

"Yipes," said Toni. "That's not good."

"Files were stolen," continued Suzanne, "including one that was apparently connected to Walter."

"You gotta be—"

She didn't let Toni finish. "I'm not."

"Well maybe it's about . . . you know." Toni looked suddenly subdued.

"Bobby already brought me those." Suzanne dropped her voice. "I think this file might have been about something else."

"Then get the old codger working on it," urged Toni.

Suzanne hurried through the Book Nook and pushed her way into their small back office. She plunked herself down at the antique oak library table they used as a desk and sighed deeply. Her lack of sleep was starting to catch up with her. She pawed through the clutter of food orders, bills, recipes clipped from magazines, and recipe cards painstakingly written out in longhand and given to them by well-meaning customers. Finally she unearthed the phone.

Punching in the sheriff's direct number, Suzanne crossed her fingers. But the fates were on her side today, because Doogie answered almost immediately.

"Hah?" he wheezed into the phone.

"Can you come over here?" she asked.

There was a long pause, and then Sheriff Doogie asked, "Who is this?"

"Sheesh, don't tell me the county can't even afford caller ID? This is Suzanne. Suzanne Deitz."

"You've become a real pest."

"I'm certainly not." Suzanne wasn't about to let him intimidate her, especially a man who referred to baklava as "that sticky stuff."

"Everybody in this county wants to know what's going on," said Sheriff Doogie. "But you're like a darned gnat, always buzzing around, always in the thick of things. I'm beginning to wonder why that is."

"Are you saying I'm a suspect?" If Suzanne could have reached through the phone lines and wrapped her hands around his thick, red neck, she would have.

"Let's just say that, for the time being, I see you as a material witness."

"But I've only witnessed two dead bodies," said Suzanne. *Two bodies too many,* she thought to herself.

"Exactly my point," said Doogie. "You're always in the wrong place at the wrong time. And you ask impertinent questions."

"In that case, I'm about to fire away with a few more," said Suzanne. "Do you still think Teddy had something to do with Bobby's murder?"

"Shit, I don't know," said Sheriff Doogie.

Suzanne pushed ahead. "You know that Bobby Waite's office was broken into last night?"

Doogie let out an audible sigh. "I'm trying to get over there. Missy's been calling the law enforcement center nonstop. As you can imagine, my docket's pretty full right now."

"Apparently some files were stolen," said Suzanne.

There was the loud creak of the sheriff's desk chair followed by a loud slam, as though he'd just dropped something heavy on the floor. "How'd you know that?"

"Never mind how I know," said Suzanne. "It's what I know."

"And that is?"

"A folder having to do with Walter was stolen."

"So? Probably lots of things were stolen. Might even be kids looking for video gadgets."

"Just look into it, will you?" asked Suzanne. "This is all getting a little too close to home."

"In case you haven't noticed," shouted Doogie, "I'm pretty darned busy!"

Suzanne's temper flared as well. "Just get on it! Do your job!" She slammed down the phone, feeling more than a little frustrated. Glancing around, she saw a squishy foam stress ball, one with a smiley face, sitting on the desk. It had been a gift from Petra, a silly little thing that was supposed to help release tension. Suzanne wrapped her fingers around the thing, cocked her arm, and threw it as hard as she could against the wall. The stress ball slammed into a tin sign that said, *Coffee, 5 Cents,* then slid down the wall into a sad little heap.

It worked, Suzanne decided. She did feel better.

* * *

"HONEY," said Petra, as Suzanne stepped back into the kitchen. "Will you slide those almond scones out of the oven?"

"Sure thing," said Suzanne. She grabbed the oven mitt, the one with the tiny egg pattern all over it, and pulled open the door.

"Looking golden brown?" asked Petra. She was up to her elbows in cream cheese.

"Oh yeah," said Toni, coming up behind Suzanne. "They're perfect." She checked her green order pad. "And I've got orders for them, too. Plus we have five reservations for tea this afternoon."

"Tea time is really taking off," marveled Petra.

"It is this week," replied Suzanne. Of course, they could probably pour motor oil and still draw a crowd.

Petra glanced through the pass-through. Customers had settled in and seemed to be happily munching away. Joey was doggedly clearing tables. "Ladies," said Petra, slicing a giant chicken-stuffed croissant in half and placing each section on a plate, "a quick nosh for each of you."

Toni jumped at hers like a starving dog. "Wonderful." She took a huge bite, nodded her head. "Oh yeah," she said, her mouth full. "Good."

Suzanne stared at her. She was convinced Toni's metabolism was set at warp speed. The woman never stopped eating yet never gained an ounce. She still weighed the same as when they were in high school together, flunking typing and sneaking Marlboro Lights behind the gymnasium.

Toni saw her watching. "Whatcha looking at?" she laughed, knowing she was probably making quite a spectacle. "Hey, did you catch the story in the *Bugle*?"

Suzanne shook her head no.

Toni stuffed another bite of croissant into her mouth and grabbed the paper off the back shelf. "Gene wrote a long piece on Bobby's murder," said Toni. "Even managed to get in a small sidebar about Teddy."

"No wonder we're jammed today," said Suzanne. "It's like he drew a map to this place."

"Continued on page six," said Toni, turning pages. "Hey, that column you wrote a couple weeks ago is in here, too. Oh, and Gene even put in a photo of Carmen." She held up the page so they could all see it.

Suzanne studied the slightly grainy photo. Besides being a rather stunning woman, Carmen Copeland looked imperious and aloof. "Do you think Carmen Copeland could have anything to do with Bobby's murder?" Suzanne asked, surprising Toni and Petra with her question.

"What?" squealed Petra. "His own wife?"

Toni stared, wide-eyed, at her. "Where on earth did that come from?"

"Just something my crazy mind spat out," said Suzanne.

"That suspicious thought had to be grounded in something," observed Petra. "Did you have a run-in with Carmen or something?"

"Nope," said Suzanne. "I've never even met the woman."

"So what's going on?" asked Petra.

Suzanne shrugged. "I think I'm just getting more suspicious of everyone."

"If Carmen killed Bobby," proposed Toni, "don't you think someone would have seen her creepy-crawling around here?"

"Don't know," said Suzanne.

"Besides," said Toni. "I think women are more into poison as their weapon of choice. Seems to me I read that somewhere."

"Probably the *National Inquisitor*," said Suzanne.

"Yeah." Toni nodded. "They're really on top of important stuff like that."

Suzanne glanced at Petra. "What do you think, Petra?"

Using a serrated knife, Petra sliced a long piece from an uncut loaf of sourdough bread and spread it with a mixture of cream cheese and pureed sweet red pepper. Then she rolled the slice into a long tube and sliced off half-inch rounds so that they resembled pinwheels. "I've met Carmen," said Petra finally. "And I really can't see her killing Bobby or running Teddy off the road and then shooting him execution-style. The woman teaches creative writing, for goodness' sake. She's a published author."

"Authors aren't that balanced," said Toni. "Look at F. Scott Fitzgerald or Hemingway or even Hunter Thompson. There's a possibility Carmen just couldn't stand Bobby anymore. Maybe he was driving her insane." She popped her final bite of sandwich into her mouth. "For whatever reason."

"Today's women don't murder their husbands," said Petra. "They toss them out on their keisters and divorce them. Besides, Bobby seemed like a normal guy. I can't imagine him driving anyone crazy."

"Don't be so sure about that," said Toni. "Men can *look* normal but act nutty. Take my soon-to-be ex, Junior. The man used to slide his jockey shorts off, catch them with his big toe, then flip 'em across the room. Drove me insane. Ya see, that's the stuff that sets your teeth on edge and gets a person speculating about murder. Not big stuff, but stupid little things like jockey shorts or toothpaste caps being left off. Or oil cans in the sink," she added.

"Toni," laughed Petra, "you are *so* off the hook."

"Laugh all you want," said Toni. "But I bet if you visited a women's prison and talked to the inmates, you'd hear tons of stories like that. Wacky, self-centered men who drove long-suffering women to commit cold-blooded murder!"

"Is it caffeine that's got you going?" asked Suzanne, pointing at Toni's oversized mug, "or just the memory of Junior?"

"Both," said Toni.

"No, it's Junior," said Petra. "And I suspect you're still a little hung up on him, if truth be told."

"I'm going to *divorce* him," said Toni forcefully. "I mean, how stupid could I have been to develop a bad-boy crush in my forties? Then I completely lost my mind and slipped into a white jean jacket and bridal veil and *married* the idiot! What was I thinking? What had I been *smoking*?"

"At least Junior can't sue you for alimony," laughed Petra.

"I wouldn't put it past him to try," said Toni. "He's nearly unemployable."

"I thought Junior worked as a mechanic," said Suzanne.

"The garage *fired* him," said Toni. "Can you believe it? You have to be a Neanderthal to get fired from a garage."

"So where's he working now?" asked Petra.

"Shelby's Body Shop," said Toni. She let out a giddy bray, then just as quickly got serious again. "To be brutally honest, there were days when, if I thought I could have gotten away scot-free, I would have murdered Junior."

"Every marriage has days like that," Suzanne admitted, though she knew Petra and Toni wouldn't believe her. The rumor had always been that she and Walter had a fairy-tale marriage. Most days, Suzanne would have agreed that was true.

"With the way the world is," said Petra, "with politics and wars and all, I'm surprised more people aren't locked up in the pen."

"Everybody's anxious," agreed Toni.

"Walter was forever prescribing Prozac and Paxil," said Suzanne. "It used to be folks were embarrassed to take antidepressants. But after nine/eleven, they'd come in and pretty much demand them."

"Instead of vitamins, everyone's popping happy pills," said Petra.

"Maybe people are waiting for the other shoe to drop," said Toni.

"What?" said Petra, looking worried. "You mean like some kind of terrorist invasion?"

"No, no," said Toni, "it's not going to be like that movie, *Red Dawn*, where the U.S. is invaded, and Patrick Swayze has to save the day. But . . . I don't know . . . it just feels like something's going to snap."

Suzanne nodded. "People are a little . . . I don't want to say meaner . . . but more abrupt."

Petra agreed. "The other day at the Save Mart I saw a clerk fighting with a customer. They were standing there all red-faced and angry over cans of tuna and boxes of cereal, actually calling each other names. Five years ago that wouldn't have happened in Kindred."

"Urban renewal," said Toni. "Even though we're a small town, we've got big-city problems."

"Next thing you know, gangs will move in," said Petra.

"Who do you think was selling drugs from that meth lab that got busted out by Keller's Dairy?" asked Toni. "Milk cows?" She tightened her apron around her wasp waist and pushed her way back out to the café floor. She had desserts to serve and checks to distribute.

"Listen to us," said Suzanne. "We sound like a bunch of old harpies, crabbing about everything, when we're really three hot women in their forties!"

"And fifties," laughed Petra, as she arranged tea sandwiches on a three-tiered serving tray. Scones on top, savories in the middle, tiny chocolate desserts and lemon bars on the bottom. "But you're right, still crazy after all these years."

Suzanne smiled to herself; she knew Petra was right. She still had *years* left. Decades.

"It's a good thing we bought these tea trays when we did," said Petra. "Afternoon tea has caught on like crazy. And, don't forget, we're catering that bridal shower tea tomorrow." She peeled off a giant sheet of plastic wrap, let it settle over her tray, and sealed it tight.

"I almost did forget that bridal shower," said Suzanne. "What with everything going on . . ."

"Twenty guests coming," said Petra. There was a certain amount of pride in her voice.

"Who's got twenty guests coming?" asked Toni. She was back to grab slices of Petra's rhubarb pie.

"We do," said Suzanne. "Tomorrow."

"For a bridal shower," Petra added. "Party Animal planned it. Besides running the salon, those guys are really starting to build a successful event-planning business."

"You're talking about Brett and Gregg from Root 66?" asked Toni. "I *love* those guys. They were the ones who did the mystery book fund-raiser for the library. Crooks and Books."

"What did they dream up for tomorrow?" asked Suzanne.

"A spa party," said Petra. "So I'm planning a light menu of tea sandwiches, fruit salad, herbal teas, Perrier, and white wine spritzers. But I'm baking a super-decadent cake for dessert."

"What kind?" asked Toni. "Chocolate?"

Petra nodded, then sliced two enormous pieces of rhubarb pie and placed them on glass dessert plates for Toni to deliver. "It's called Better Than Sex Cake. I found the recipe online, and it really sounds delicious. Chocolate, butterscotch, and pecans."

"Wow," said Suzanne. Those were killer ingredients.

"So," said Toni. "At the bridal shower tomorrow. Any male strippers?"

Petra snorted. "Not for this one. Thankfully."

"We could always ask Junior to stop by," laughed Toni. "Wiggle his skinny butt and do a dollar dance or something."

Suzanne and Petra stared at Toni with stunned faces, waiting for a reasonable explanation. They sincerely hoped there was one.

"Didn't I ever tell you?" said Toni. "That's how Junior

worked his way through vo-tech school. Dancing as a Chippendale."

"What!" shrieked Petra.

"He didn't!" said Suzanne.

"Well, not *exactly* a Chippendale," laughed Toni. "He was the low-rent version. More like a chip-on-his-shoulder!"

CHAPTER 11

FROM the very first day that tea was served, the women of Kindred embraced Suzanne's vision of bringing a touch of culture and European gentility to the town. Loving the idea of bone china, finger sandwiches, and dress-up, the ladies gleaned information from romance novels as well as old British movies and dressed accordingly. They scoured local rummage sales and vintage shops for felt hats with perfect netting, tiny mink stoles with dangling paws and tails, and skirts made of shiny taffeta and herringbone tweed. The same women who might have breakfasted at the Cackleberry Club that morning in jeans and a Bonnie Raitt World Tour T-shirt eagerly showed up in the afternoon looking like an extra from *Gosford Park*.

The Cackleberry Club itself underwent a daily transformation. White linen tablecloths covered battered wood tabletops. A crazy quilt of cups and saucers, small plates, silver spoons, and delicate butter knives were laid out. Tiny vigil lights were placed inside glass tea warmers and topped with chintz-decorated teapots.

Three-tiered trays overflowed with sweets and savories.

Tiny rounds of dark bread were topped with cucumber slices, dilled egg salad, chicken pâté, and basil-pesto cream cheese. Savories also included olive tapenade on toast rounds, Gorgonzola and fig bruschetta, and warmed feta cheese stuffed into piquillo peppers. A dazzling array of toasted pecan tarts, sugary lady fingers, caramel pralines, lemon puffs, and little chocolate cups filled with mint ice cream tempted even the most ardent dieters.

If it weren't for the occasional "My goodness, what is that?" or a "Did she really say clotted cream?" the atmosphere at the Cackleberry Club could have easily passed for a proper English tearoom in the Cotswolds.

"Our guests are going through maple scones like popcorn at a James Bond movie," Suzanne told Petra. She wiped her hands on the linen tea towel that hung from her frilly apron.

"Ditto the fig bruschetta," said Toni as she slid an empty platter into the kitchen pass-through. "Oh, and we need another pot of Darjeeling and probably could use another of mango spice."

"Coming right up," said Petra. She glanced at Suzanne, who was arranging a tea tray for a party of four women who were outfitted in vintage dresses, antique lockets, and veiled hats.

"If our customers keep eating like this, we're going to have to raise our prices," said Petra.

"If they keep eating like this, we're gonna have to widen the doorway," Toni murmured. She grabbed the teapots, turned swiftly, and stopped in her tracks.

A new customer had eased himself onto a stool without bothering to remove his trucker cap.

"Dale," said Toni. Dale Huffington was a behemoth of a man, one of the locals who worked at the Jasper Creek Prison, the private prison run by Claiborne Corrections Corporation that Kindred's town council had hailed as a wellspring for new jobs when it opened a year ago.

Dale barely glanced at Toni. "Coffee and a doughnut,"

he growled. He shifted his bulk so his waistline and every-thing above it overlapped his straining belt.

Toni lifted one eyebrow at him. "It's after two, Dale. We're having tea service now."

Dale frowned. "The heck you are." Then he swiveled his head, eyes darting from table to table, his face suddenly taking on the appearance of a cornered weasel. He only now seemed to realize that small groups of women were seated at each table, talking quietly. An assortment of Royal Doulton and Wedgwood china teapots and silver serving trays sat in front of them; the bright scent of Darjeeling hung redolent in the air. Dale's frown deepened, his face blushed crimson right down to the V in his white under-shirt. "Since when?"

"Since a couple weeks ago," said Toni. "It's a new thing."

"Tea is?" asked Dale. He was befuddled, clearly out of his element.

"Well, not tea per se," said Toni. "But serving afternoon tea with various small sandwiches and savories. We're at-tempting to bring a touch of class to the area."

"No doughnuts?" asked Dale. "Suzanne always has doughnuts." He looked around in vain for her, but she'd gone into the Book Nook. "Sugared ones. Sometimes choc-olate with sprinkles." You had to give Dale credit, he was standing his ground.

"Scones," said Toni. She drew the word out slowly, as though she were trying to teach a key word to someone who had journeyed here from foreign soil. "Scones with lemon curd."

"Curd don't sound too good," said Dale, doggedly re-sisting this newly instituted afternoon menu. He inhaled deeply, and it looked as if the buttons on his shirt would pop off and sail across the room at deadly speed.

Toni delivered her steaming teapots, then came back, plated a scone and its accoutrements, and set it all down in front of him. It was one of the maple scones, baked fresh that morning and drizzled with vanilla icing. "Try one," she urged. "On the house. Who knows, you might like it."

"What's that?" Dale's pudgy finger poked at a small glass bowl with a tiny silver spoon sticking out of it, even as his other hand reached up and surreptitiously slid the trucker cap off his head.

"That's the lemon curd and Devonshire cream," Toni told him. She set a cup and saucer in front of him, poured out a swoosh of hot tea. "There ya go," she said, then walked away, busying herself farther down the counter. Just like the Journey's End Church down the road, Toni believed in converting people.

Five minutes later, Suzanne returned with a book in her hand and smiled at Dale. "How's it going at the prison?" she asked him.

Dale bobbed his head. He'd apparently taken a sudden liking to lemon curd, since there was a telltale yellow smear down the front of his blue shirt. "Okay, I guess. Things have been pretty quiet."

"Well, that's good," said Suzanne. All they needed was a prison riot or break or whatever it was happened in those Clint Eastwood movies.

Dale touched a thumb to his blue windbreaker. "They skimp on real uniforms, though. Make us wear these stupid nylon jackets. We don't look like we have any authority. More like security guards at some darned rock concert!"

"You'd fit right in at a rock concert," Suzanne told him, playing to his male ego.

It worked like a charm. Dale fairly beamed. "You're right. I probably would." Then he added in a cautious voice, "This tea thing you've got going, it's a little weird."

"Women like it," Suzanne told him, as though she was sharing a profound secret.

"Yeah, they must." Dale glanced around. "This place has been hopping, huh? Even with the murders and all?"

Suzanne nodded.

"I figured folks would want to avoid this place, but it looks like they're flocking to it." Dale lowered his voice almost to a whisper. "You got any idea who shot Bobby?"

He waited, but Suzanne didn't respond. Finally he shrugged his big shoulders and said, "I liked Bobby. He handled my divorces."

Suzanne almost smiled but instead said, "Sheriff Doogie is working on things."

"What about Teddy?" asked Dale. "I heard you were involved in that, too."

Suzanne sighed. "Not really. I was just behind his pickup truck when it flipped into the ditch."

"A darn shame about Teddy," said Dale. "He was a stand-up guy. Fought the Nazis in World War II. He was right there at the Battle of the Bulge."

"That's really something," allowed Suzanne.

"Poor Bobby," said Dale. "He was only in the National Guard."

"Yeah," said Suzanne, "I guess he missed the big one."

"Bobby was married to a famous writer," said Dale. "Did you know that?"

"Sure, we carry her books."

Dale went on as if he hadn't heard her. "Her name is Carmen Copeland. My wife Gracie used to read Carmen's books all the time. Romances." He rolled his eyes. "Gracie was one of her biggest fans." He smiled a grin that bordered on being wicked. "She's my soon-to-be ex-wife, anyway. And boy was she steamed when I hired Bobby to represent me. She claimed it tainted her love of Carmen's stories."

It couldn't have tainted her too much, Suzanne figured, because Gracie was still a frequent visitor in the Book Nook, on the prowl for Carmen Copeland's latest releases.

"First time I saw Bobby's wife," Dale confided, "I was sitting in Bobby's office and she just strolled right in. Demanded he go over some legal papers that had just come from her agent in New York."

"I've never met her," said Suzanne. But she was curious. She had glanced at Carmen's picture on the back of her bodice-ripping romances more than once. Carmen's heart-shaped face, aquiline nose, and high brow line reminded Suzanne of a Renaissance portrait. A lady of the manor. What she *didn't* look like was the wife of a small-town lawyer.

"That Carmen Copeland is one fine-looking woman," Dale continued. He took a sip of tea and made a face. "She's taller than a lot of men. And she looks rich, what with the clothes she wears and fancy high heels. You know the kind of rich I'm talking about? That aura that makes a person look real clean, like a speck of dirt never landed on them in their entire life."

"Like a china doll," Suzanne murmured.

"I guess," said Dale. Then added, "Strangest thing. I saw her having dinner just last week. Never thought then she'd end up as a widow lady."

"What are you talking about?" asked Suzanne. "Carmen? Where did you see her?"

"That fancy place over in Cornucopia," said Dale. Cornucopia was a small town some twenty miles away. "You know, the place that Czech couple runs. They got a restaurant and bar downstairs and a B and B upstairs."

"Kopell's," said Suzanne. She'd been there with Walter. They'd enjoyed the restaurant as well as their plush corner suite with the feather bed and gurgling spa tub. Better days.

"That's it," said Dale, pointing a stubby index finger at her. "Kopell's. Their specialty's muscovy duck. You ever eat muscovy duck?"

Suzanne shook her head.

"Nothing like it," Dale rhapsodized. "Tender and juicy—"

"Get back to Carmen, will you?" prompted Suzanne.

"Oh. Yeah. This guy I work with, Stan Heller, we

stopped by the bar to have a quick snort. And that's when I saw her with the prison warden."

"You saw Carmen Copeland with Lester Drummond?" said Carmen. Her voice rose in a high-pitched squeak.

Dale snorted. "That'd be him."

"And they were having dinner?" said Suzanne. For some reason she was having trouble wrapping her mind around this. "And Bobby wasn't along?"

Dale lifted his bushy eyebrows. "Nope. And from the way Carmen was acting, it was probably better that he wasn't." He paused, seemingly reviewing the scenario in his head. "But they didn't order the duck." He shook his head as though they'd really screwed up. "Steak, I think. New York strip."

Suzanne had met Lester Drummond, the prison warden, at the opening ceremony for the prison. Drummond had supposedly worked his way up through the corporation, starting in security when he was fresh out of the Gulf War. Now, in his mid-fifties, he was the warden at Jasper Creek.

Suzanne remembered Drummond's craggy face, lined with wrinkles far beyond his years. His head was shaved and, if Suzanne had allowed herself to gossip about him, she would have suggested the man indulged in steroids. He was pro-wrestler big.

Drummond hadn't impressed Suzanne as being particularly articulate, either. Thus, he hardly seemed the type to share an *aperitif* with Carmen Copeland, a woman of both words and style.

Perhaps, Suzanne decided, Carmen Copeland had been on a fact-finding mission about the prison system. She'd heard rumblings that the romance category was on the wane, while sales of mysteries and thrillers were climbing. Maybe Carmen had her sights set on becoming the next Sue Grafton. Except this time, K would be for *Kindred*, not *killer*.

"Did Drummond seem interested in her?" Suzanne asked. She was curious but a little worried about overstepping boundaries. Drummond was, after all, Dale's boss.

"What man wouldn't be?" Dale said with a grin. "She's as pretty as a sixty-six Mustang." He snatched his hat from the counter and stood up. "What do I owe you?"

"On the house," said Suzanne.

Dale glanced around at the tables of women and the plates filled with tiny sandwiches. "What's the deal here?" he asked. "You pay by the piece?"

Suzanne chuckled. "It's usually prix fixe."

"Huh?"

"A fixed price," Suzanne explained.

"Oh," said Dale, understanding now. "Like Old Country Buffet."

"Right," said Suzanne, allowing herself a good chuckle.

CHAPTER 12

"FEEL this," urged Petra, holding out a soft bundle of yarn.

Suzanne rubbed the hand-dyed skein. "It's so soft and pliable. And . . ."

"Oily?" asked Petra. "That's the lanolin in it." She grinned as she dumped a basket of yarn onto the table in the Knitting Nest. "This is one of our best shipments ever. From an animal-friendly farm up in Canada. Their sheep and llamas live out their days producing this excellent wool and are allowed to die a natural death. They don't end up as . . ." Petra hesitated.

"Kabobs?" offered Suzanne.

Petra nodded as she continued to organize the table. She piled up the skeins of wool and laid out a stack of printed instructions. "We're starting a new project tonight," she told Suzanne.

"Tonight's your special group?" asked Suzanne.

Petra gave a soft smile. "The Baby Lamb Club," she said. "Yes."

The Baby Lamb Club was an offshoot of one of Petra's

knitting groups. They were a small band of dedicated women who knitted tiny hats, booties, and blankets for premature babies as well as critically ill infants. Their tiny knitted treasures were distributed in the neonatal and PICU units of nearby hospitals.

Occasionally, Petra would even be asked by one of the nurses to knit a small burial gown. The last thing on the minds of bereaved parents was finding suitable clothing for their infant, and Petra believed strongly in giving of her time to provide one single item that had been lovingly crafted by hand.

On impulse Suzanne put her arms around Petra and gave her a squeeze. "You are so sweet and giving," she said. "I don't know how you do it."

"I just . . . do it," said Petra. "I don't think about the where or the why, I just put my faith in the good Lord."

Suzanne fingered some of the skeins Petra had laid out. She'd chosen all soft pastel colors in alpaca, angora, cashmere, and lamb's wool. The fact that Petra's knitters poured their heart and their energy into these projects warmed Suzanne's heart. And then to donate the tiny clothing anonymously was truly amazing.

"You're going to stop by and see Donny later?" Suzanne asked. Petra usually dropped by the nursing home on the nights she stayed late.

Petra nodded. "Got goodies for him, too." Tucked next to Petra's knitting bag was a white paper sack filled with the best pastries of the day. "You're going home now?" she asked Suzanne. Toni had left two hours ago.

"Just a few more minutes," said Suzanne. She was winding down, letting the day wash into night.

"You take it easy," cautioned Petra. "You've had a rough couple of days."

"I will," Suzanne promised. "Good luck with your class, and give Donny a hug for me."

"Always," said Petra.

Suzanne walked through the empty café, straightening

chairs and turning off lights, then headed into the kitchen. Everything was quiet and pristine, seemingly at rest after such a busy day. A few baking odors lingered, signaling the success of yet another day. Tomorrow they'd do it all over again. Except, of course, there'd be variables. A new menu, different customers . . . new problems? Maybe not. Hopefully not. Maybe by tomorrow everything would be magically back to normal.

After locking the back door, Suzanne unclipped Baxter from his leash and eased him into the backseat of her car. Then she pulled out her cell phone, punched in a number, and didn't bother to say hello when she heard the receiver on the other end being picked up.

"I'm just wondering if you've had time to—"

"What's going on?" groused Sheriff Doogie. "Suddenly we're best friends? You just called a couple hours ago. Lord love a—"

The rest of his words were lost in a burst of static.

"Hello?" said Suzanne. Was he still there?

"What?" came Doogie's unhappy voice. "Whadya want now?"

"You said you were going to check on those missing files from Bobby's office," said Suzanne.

"I did," said Doogie. "And they're still missing."

"That's not exactly what I meant," said Suzanne.

"What was your question again?"

She thought for a moment. What *was* her question? "Um, you were going to think about a possible connection between the missing files, one of which concerns Walter, and . . . uh . . . the two murders."

"Right," said Doogie. "I'll get right on that." The phone clunked hard, as though he'd tossed it onto his credenza or something.

"Huh?" said Suzanne. *What's going on?*

Twenty seconds later Doogie came back on the line. "Okay, I thought about it and didn't come up with anything."

"You don't have to be rude about it," Suzanne told him.

"You don't have to keep bugging me," Sheriff Doogie shot back.

Suzanne heard a few loud wheezes and then he said, "Tell you what, when I *do* find something, I'll call the *Bugle*. That way you can read about it in the funny papers."

Suzanne winced as Sheriff Doogie slammed down the receiver, but she wasn't a bit put off. *Probably because I want something from him. Like . . . information. Okay, I'll give him a few hours to cool his jets, and then I'll call again.*

She thumbed the Off button on her phone and then, for the first time that day, Suzanne lifted her eyes and looked out across the endless wave of green that stretched beyond her woods. A giant red sun was beginning to ride low on the horizon, and everything—woods, fields, far-off trees, the horizon—seemed tinged in gold. It reminded her of those special roses florists sold on Valentine's Day, the ones dipped in twenty-four karat gold.

"Good night to take the long way home," she told Baxter as she climbed in her car.

Ever since Walter's death, Suzanne had found herself talking out loud a whole lot more. Sometimes to Baxter, sometimes to herself, oftentimes to Walter. She decided she'd start seriously worrying when she started answering herself out loud.

Or if I hear Walter from the great beyond.

That thought startled her. And tickled her in a nice way. Well, what if she could? What if she tuned in, focused all her senses, every single molecule of her being, and attempted to communicate with him? Would he . . . answer her?

Suzanne turned that little nugget over in her mind.

She'd certainly heard stories about loved ones who'd passed on, who'd sent warnings or subliminal messages to their folks here on earth. Ginny Ripley, who was on the library committee with her, swore her grandmother told her where her gold locket was stashed.

Could Walter do that? Suzanne thought hard. In life, Walter pretty much had an answer or quick retort for everything. Why should it be different in the afterlife?

That thought kept her grinning as she started her car. Easing it into first, she nosed past the back shed and onto the narrow dirt road, really a tractor path, that wound its way through the woods and into the farm field. Bumping along, she thought about how she and Walter had come out here a few times and parked. Drank a six-pack of Budweiser, watched for shooting stars.

Last August, when the prognosis hadn't looked good and they were still trying to figure out how to possibly say their good-byes, they'd come out here and witnessed the Perseid meteor shower. That awe-inspiring display of planetary fireworks had pretty much convinced Suzanne that heaven really was a physical place, terra firma, or at least a dazzling firmament.

Rolling down the window, Suzanne breathed in fresh, clean air and instantly felt her soul cleansed, too. *This is good, this is so good.*

When Suzanne reached the farmyard, her farmyard, really, she glanced at the gambrel-roofed red barn jutting against the darkening sky. It no longer housed livestock and, once again, she toyed with the idea of getting a horse. Keep it here, close by, take a nice quick gallop whenever she felt like it.

Then she turned and saw Reed Ducovny bent over his Allis-Chalmers. One of the tractor's wheels was off, and he seemed to be wearily pitching wrenches into the dirt.

She glided closer to him, rolled to a stop. "Evening, Reed," she said. "How's it going?"

He glanced up and gave a wry grin. "Got a flat. Always somethin', huh?"

Reed Ducovny was sixty, slat thin, and tough as nails. Suzanne loved that he seemed to take pride in the land, even though it wasn't technically his.

"How are the crops?" she asked.

"Crops are good," said Reed. "Prices should be okay, too."

"Maybe you should just buy this whole parcel," suggested Suzanne. "I'd give you a good price."

He came over and leaned on her window. His grin was contagious. "I know you would, missus. You'd be more than fair. But every autumn the notion of retirement sounds better and better."

"You're too young to retire," she told him. "Besides, if you bought this place, I'd know it was in good hands."

"Thank you, missus, but it's just possible your land might be worth more to a developer than to a farmer."

"I hope not," said Suzanne. More and more of the local farmers seemed to be selling out. She'd hate to see Kindred ending up as a town with lots of people and a suburban sprawl but no one to grow food for them.

"I've been toying with the idea of buying an RV," Reed told her. "Just take off and see the good old U.S. of A. Visit Yellowstone Park, see the Grand Canyon, maybe even stop in Roswell."

"New Mexico?" said Suzanne with more than a note of skepticism.

"Sure," said Ducovny in an affable tone now. "Area 51, where the aliens landed back in the forties."

"I don't think they ever really proved that," said Suzanne, smiling.

But Ducovny turned suddenly serious. "That stuff isn't completely made up, you know. There are sightings all the time. Fact is, the other night I looked out my window and saw strange lights floating across this very field." He swept an arm to give a general indication.

"What kind of lights?" asked Suzanne. She leaned forward a little and looked out toward where he'd indicated.

"Not sure. But they sure made me think of UFOs. The lights were bouncing around like crazy, then shot straight across the road, right near where your café's at."

"Probably just headlights," said Suzanne.

"Maybe," said Ducovny, scratching his chin thoughtfully. "But just when they were really active, they disappeared." He dropped his voice to a conspiratorial whisper, and a twinkle shone in his eye. "Just hope I don't come out some morning and find crop circles."

"I don't think you have to worry about that," Suzanne told him.

"Maybe so," said Ducovny, "But I heard about a farmer over near Jessup whose entire cornfield was destroyed by crop circles."

"I think it was proved that a gang of teenagers did that. Some kind of homecoming prank."

"All I know," said Ducovny, "is I don't want to be part of any experiment. And I sure as heck don't want to get probed." He winked at her and stepped back from the car.

Suzanne fought to hold back laughter. "Take care, sir. Stop by the Cackleberry Club, and we'll fix you something special. We whip up a pretty wild Eggs Benedict."

"I'll do that," agreed Ducovny.

That's all we need right now, thought Suzanne as she drove off. *Toss a bunch of little green men into the mix and really make things wacky!*

CHAPTER 13

BUSTLING around her kitchen, Suzanne prepared a fast dinner for one in the dream kitchen she'd recently renovated. It was a cook's toy store. Wolf gas range, Sub-Zero refrigerator, granite countertops, copper pots and pans. A forty-eight-inch double gas range might be overkill for a single poached egg, but hey, it always turned out to be one heck of a poached egg.

Cooking and entertaining had always been one of Suzanne's passions, and she explored it to her heart's content. Hopefully, the Cackleberry Club would someday have a sister restaurant. One where locally sourced organic goods made their way onto a creative, contemporary American menu.

In fact, Suzanne had already begun to noodle around that dream menu. Starters might include risotto with lobster or seared ahi tuna with avocado puree. Entrées might be chicken breasts stuffed with goat cheese and sautéed peaches, poached wild trout fillets, or wild sea bass medallions crusted with toasted pecans.

A couple of months ago, the *Bugle* had asked Suzanne

to write a small tea column. So far, that column consisted only of tea time tips. But they were urging her to expand into recipes and write about the importance of fresh ingredients, local artisans, flavoring with herbs.

"You are such a lucky dog," Suzanne told Baxter, who was waiting patiently at her feet. "I'm fairly positive there are going to be table scraps."

"Grrrr," was his reply.

Suzanne's meal tonight was fairly simple. A sweet corn chowder with freshly shucked kernels, sautéed red peppers and onion, organic butter, a little half-and-half. A simple Boston Bibb salad with heirloom tomatoes, curls of Parmesan cheese, balsamic vinegar, and extra-virgin olive oil accompanied the chowder. Her drink of choice was a chilled glass of Chardonnay.

Plating her food, she set it on the butcher block kitchen table and slid into a chair. As if on cue, Baxter pulled himself up onto the chair across from her. He'd taken to sitting there every night, as if he knew "amusing dinner companion" was part of his canine job description.

"Good boy," she told him, and Baxter ducked his head and gave her a look she swore was a smile. A toothy smile.

When Suzanne was finished with dinner, she cleaned up quickly, then sat down again to work on her column for next week. She wrote steadily for about twenty minutes, then paused to read what she had so far:

There is a wide repertoire of teas that promise an added touch of tranquillity for your languid summer afternoons. Keeman (or Keemun) is a small-leafed tea grown in China's Anhui province that has a sweet, mild taste and lovely orchid bouquet. Lung Ching, also known as Dragon's Well, is a Chinese green tea that delivers a delicate flavor and plenty of sweet top notes. It is also known for its slightly cooling effect. Ti Kuan Yin, an oolong tea from China's Fujian province, is also known as the Iron

Goddess of Mercy, but don't let the tough name fool you. This fragrant amber liquid is very "peachy" and appealing to the palate.

Of course, there are also herbal teas and infusions that make for elegant summer sipping. Rose hips, hibiscus, lavender, and chamomile are all highly pleasing. And there are an infinite number of rich black teas that have been blended and flavored with dried orange peel, apple bits, berries, or even flower blossoms. Jasmine is the oldest and most famous of these teas, dating back to the eleventh century.

Suzanne hesitated. It sounded credible, but she needed a good way to finish her column off. She thought about it for a few moments, then added one line:

But what's a spot of tea without great food to accompany it? Here, for your sublime enjoyment, is a recipe for buttermilk scones.

Excellent, Suzanne decided. She'd add a scone recipe to round out her column. Laura at the *Bugle* had been pestering her for actual recipes.

Carrying her wine into the living room, Suzanne sat down and thumbed through the latest copy of *Food & Wine*. It was one of her favorite magazines, always filled with articles about new restaurants, great wines, up-and-coming chefs, and, of course, great recipes accompanied by glossy photos of finished dishes.

But tonight, try as she might, Suzanne couldn't quite get into it. Her thoughts kept returning to the file on Walter that had been stolen from Bobby's law office.

What could it have been about?

Suzanne racked her brain. She thought she pretty much knew everything there was to know about Walter and where he'd spent his time.

Wednesday mornings he'd always gone to the Olympic

Hills Country Club. He'd play a full eighteen holes and always refuse to use a cart or caddy.

Their spare time was spent together cooking, antiquing, or just reading in separate corners of the room.

Of course, there were weekends when Walter went away for medical conferences in other states, earning CE credits, and such. Suzanne rarely went along on these.

A few nights a month he'd attend one or another town meeting. And he'd spent one stint of volunteer work at a free clinic over in neighboring Sudsbury. Again, she hadn't bothered to ask about these things, and Walter hadn't volunteered much information.

Unexpected phone calls in the middle of the night had been a fairly common occurrence. He was a doctor, after all. Intrusions were part of the game. She'd never bothered to ask, "Who was that?" There'd never been a reason to question or doubt Walter.

At least she didn't think so.

That file preyed on her mind. What was in his file that was so important, so critical, that someone had broken into Bobby Waite's office in the middle of the night to steal it?

Had Walter, her Walter, with his big heart and almost naive sense of trust, been entangled in some sort of legal problem?

As sophisticated and intelligent as Walter had been, Suzanne always joked that he was "an easy touch."

He gave to almost every charity that asked. He purchased every candy bar or trinket sold by anyone who knocked on his front door. He'd buy at least two dozen boxes of Girl Scout cookies, especially the Thin Mints. In the middle of the night and alone on deserted roads, he'd stop to help anyone whose car had broken down.

Walter would give anyone the shirt off his back and extend credit to patients who didn't have money to pay.

Of course, Suzanne had heard disturbing stories from other doctors' wives. Sometimes about their own physician husbands and sometimes about other medical professionals.

There was a doctor in Jessup who, for an additional fee, was easily persuaded to write prescriptions. There were doctors who filed false Medicare claims or received false reimbursements. There were doctors whose licenses to practice had been created at FedEx Kinko's.

But she'd always pushed those rumors aside.

Just like she now pushed her magazine aside. She only wanted to sip her wine and think.

It had, after all, been a heck of a week thus far. Bobby's murder. Teddy's murder following right on the heels of that. Then Bobby's law office burglarized. It seemed like some of the pieces should fit together, but they didn't.

Was someone from Kindred to blame for all of this? Was one of their neighbors, someone right in their midst, wreaking all this havoc?

Suzanne took another sip of wine and willed herself to think harder, think about . . . possible suspects.

Okay, who? she asked herself.

Teddy had been at the top of Sheriff Doogie's suspect list, but then he'd gone and gotten himself killed. Had the same gun that killed Bobby been used on Teddy? She'd have to ask Sheriff Doogie about that. One more question to frost his ass.

What about Charlie Pepper, their egg man? He seemed like an angry, troubled man. Could he somehow be involved?

Okay, and what about Junior? His temper was volatile, and Toni had discovered, after their quickie Las Vegas wedding, that Junior had a record for assault when he was nineteen.

But was Junior smart enough to pull all this off? And, if so, what was his motive? Because the files that were stolen, if they were even connected to the two murders, didn't have anything to do with Junior.

The files concerned Walter and some woman named Lidia and the Neukommen Following.

Suzanne focused on a piece of artwork that hung on the

wall across from her. It was an Expressionist painting done in muted blues and greens that she'd picked up at the Darlington College Art Fair. She'd always thought of it as being soothing and tranquil. Tonight it looked tangled and impenetrable. She continued to stare, almost hypnotically. She felt her mind go blank, tension ease from her body. Almost as if she was meditating, she let her mind wander freely for a few minutes. Then slowly, ever so slowly, she circled back to thoughts of Bobby's funeral tomorrow.

She planned on going. And maybe, just maybe, his killer would show up as well.

CHAPTER 14

THE cash register *da-dinged* twice before its drawer opened automatically. Suzanne reached in and pulled out three dollars and forty cents in change and handed it to the waiting senior citizen.

"Here you go." She smiled warmly at him. He and his retired trucker buddy had just spent the last half hour at the Cackleberry Club, drinking cappuccinos and munching cinnamon apple scones. It tickled Suzanne that she'd gotten the older men in town to experiment with more than just "Coffee, black."

"You're all dressed up today. Got a date?" the man teased.

"Nah," she answered. "I like to look pretty in case a good-looking guy drops by." She winked and was surprised when the old gent actually blushed. She didn't think she was that dressed up. A black pencil skirt and white silk tank top. She had a jacket stashed in her car but doubted she'd wear it. Chances are, it was going to be warm inside the church.

"Last table," announced Toni. She picked up the dirty cups and plates, loaded them into a plastic tub.

Suzanne turned the sign on the door so it read Closed, then latched the front door. It was ten thirty and, with any luck at all, they'd be back by one o'clock. For the first time since the Cackleberry Club had opened, lunch had been cancelled.

"You think I look okay?" Toni asked. She pulled off her long black Parisian waiter's apron and revealed black slacks and a rose-colored blouse. Plucking at the collar, she added, "I never know what to wear to a funeral."

Petra strolled out of the back dressed in a navy blue shift and white pearl choker. "As long as you're not duded up in your jeans and Harley-Davidson T-shirt you should be fine."

"Actually," said Toni, "that's what I'd want folks to wear to my funeral. It'd be cool."

"And you'd probably want us to pass out those fake tattoos," laughed Petra.

"Fake tattoos," said Toni with a toss of her head. "Who needs a fake one?"

"Oh no . . ." said Petra. She really was the more conservative of the three.

"Marrying Junior wasn't the only crazy thing I did in Vegas," said Toni. She unbuttoned her top two buttons and pulled her matching pink bra down a couple of inches. "See?" Just above her right breast was a tiny tattooed set of dice.

"Dice?" said Suzanne. "Not even something feminine like a small rose or a heart? Toni, you don't even gamble, except for playing a little bingo."

"I gamble," laughed Toni. "I married Junior, didn't I?"

Petra picked up her purse, a quilted navy clutch. "What's the plan? We all going in the same car?"

"You two skedaddle on ahead," said Suzanne. "I have to make a quick stop."

"You sure you want us to go on?" asked Petra.

"She's sure," said Toni, almost pushing Petra out the door. "Gosh you look awfully conservative in that dress and pearls. Like a politician's wife or something."

"Thank you," said Petra. "I think."

SUZANNE waited as Toni's Mustang pulled away, belching oily smoke, then she climbed into her own car and bumped a half block down the dusty service road to the Journey's End Church.

The church itself was a 145-year-old wooden structure with a short wooden spire. White paint flaked off in places, and the stone stairway leading to the arched front door had a distinct list to it. But brightly colored pansies and snapdragons lined the walkway, and the parking lot was neatly kept.

Last year, the church's membership had petitioned to have the building registered as a historic landmark. They were afraid that, with its dwindling membership, the church might eventually be sold. If that happened, it could be turned into a gift store, antique shop, or some other tourist trap, or, worse yet, torn down entirely. The members of Journey's End were not huge fans of progress or change.

"Mrs. Deitz," said Reverend Yoder, lifting himself up from his desk as Suzanne gave a quick knock on the doorjamb, then walked into his small study at the back of the church. "Nice to see you. I must say, I was surprised to get your call earlier."

Reverend Yoder was as austere as his study. Tall, thin, gray eyes, gray hair. He had the look of an aesthete, but there was also a gentleness about him.

"Hello, Reverend," Suzanne said, extending a hand. And then, because time was limited, she got straight to the point. "Like I explained on the phone, I'm somewhat curious about Claes Elam and his Neukommen Following. And I was interested in possibly getting your take on the group."

"My opinion as a man of the cloth?" he asked. "Or as an interested observer?" There was a hint of mirth behind his gray eyes.

"Probably both," she admitted.

He held out a hand. "Sit down, please." The reverend sat behind his desk, and Suzanne settled onto a hard, wooden chair.

"You're not considering joining their community, are you?" Reverend Yoder asked.

Suzanne chuckled. "No, nothing like that. I'm just interested, that's all. Seems like my husband might have had some contact with them."

Reverend Yoder regarded her solemnly. "And I take it you have concerns?"

She knew she had to play it straight. "Yes, I do."

He leaned back in his chair. "I don't know too much about the Neukommen Following except that they fancy themselves to be like the Amish. In reality, they're nothing like them."

"How so?"

"The Amish, as you probably know, are an offshoot of the Mennonite religion. Amish people live a simple life and reject many modern conveniences such as cars and tractors. The Neukommen Following also professes to reject modern life. Except they really don't."

"What do you mean?" asked Suzanne.

"For one thing," said Reverend Yoder, "they own a couple of cars. And I happen to know they have electricity." He spread his hands. "Nothing wrong with that, of course, but it's contrary to what they profess and the face they present to the outside world."

"Here I thought they were this earth-loving, commune-type farming community," said Suzanne.

"Oh, they farm, all right," said Reverend Yoder as he swiveled in his chair then reached down to slide open a desk drawer. "But they're plugged into the progressive side of things, too." He shuffled in his drawer for a few moments and finally pulled out a flimsy paper tract. He laid it on his desk, facing Suzanne, and flipped the tract open.

Her eyes scanned the page. There were prayers, a paragraph about the group's daily prayer chain, and . . .

"A Web site?" exclaimed Suzanne. "They've got a Web site?" This didn't sound like a bunch of back-to-the-soil religious devotees to her.

Reverend Yoder simply nodded.

Suzanne continued to read the tract, which, when she really studied it, was more of an appeal for money. Send in fifty dollars and receive the book *Neukommen Truth* by Claes Elam, founder. Send in one hundred dollars and get the DVD. Send five hundred dollars and spend a weekend with the Neukommen Following. The interested faithful were directed to their Web site, www.Neukommen.com. And it was noted that Visa, MasterCard, and Discover Card were cheerfully accepted.

"Good Lord," breathed Suzanne.

"Well," said Reverend Yoder, "not quite."

Suzanne clenched her lips tightly. Could Walter have somehow gotten involved with these people? she wondered. And if he had, what had been going on? What was still going on?

She folded the tract. "May I keep this?" she asked.

Reverend Yoder nodded. "Of course."

"Thank you."

"Mrs. Deitz," said Reverend Yoder, peering across his desk at her, "you seem troubled."

"No, not really," said Suzanne. Then decided that lying to a man of the cloth probably wasn't the best thing. "Yes, I am," she told him, looking a little sheepish.

"You're worried that your husband was somehow involved with this group?" His words were straightforward, but there was kindness in his eyes.

"Yes," she breathed. "Possibly."

"Mr. Deitz, *Dr.* Deitz, was a good man. You shouldn't worry yourself unduly."

"Thank you," said Suzanne. "Your words are . . . a comfort." But her mind was still spinning.

"Here," said Reverend Yoder, reaching into his desk drawer again. "Let me give you one of these." He handed her a small copper-colored coin the size of a quarter.

Suzanne studied the coin. On one side were the words "Some people come into our lives . . . and quietly go." On the other side of the coin were the words "Some stay for a while and leave footprints in our hearts." Suzanne bit her lip. "Lovely," she whispered.

"Now I have another question for you," said Reverend Yoder. "Since I know you've been involved in two recent murders here in Kindred, do you think this Neukommen Following has some sort of connection?"

Suzanne was surprised he'd made such a suspicious leap. Then again, she had been asking leading questions.

"I don't know. Nothing seems to point to it, but . . . I don't know."

"Whoever the perpetrator," said Reverend Yoder, "I pray they're apprehended soon. These murders, of our own neighbors no less, have my entire congregation on edge. And undoubtedly the whole town. Kindred's always been a peaceful place. Suddenly it's becoming . . ." Reverend Yoder's lined face looked indelibly sad. ". . . Like the rest of the world."

"It is changing," agreed Suzanne as she shook the minister's hand to bid him good-bye. "But then, most things do change eventually."

"I'm calling a special prayer meeting tonight. We shall blend our voices as one and ask the Lord to bring the killer or killers to justice." He paused. "You're welcome to join us."

"Thank you," said Suzanne. "Perhaps another time."

"Then we shall pray for you, too. To help aid in your . . . investigation?"

"Thank you again," said Suzanne. "I can use all the help I can get."

CHAPTER 15

THE Good Shepherd Church was filled to capacity by the time Suzanne slipped in the front door. She wove her way through a throng of mourners and over to the guest book that rested on a podium at the back of the church. Scanning the names quickly, Suzanne saw that Sheriff Doogie had already signed it. Below his name were the names of the entire town council. Suzanne decided they must have all arrived together.

A printed card above the book requested that memorials be sent to the ACLU. Suzanne made a mental note to remember to send a donation from the Cackleberry Club and decided the memorial had to be Carmen Copeland's preference rather than Bobby's. He'd always been full of wacky jokes about lawyers, such as, "How do you save a drowning lawyer? Take your foot off his head." Or, "What do you call a smiling, sober, courteous person at a bar association convention? The caterer."

Gazing over the heads of the seated crowd, Suzanne saw Toni gesturing at her. She and Petra had managed to save an aisle seat for her, so she hurried to join them.

"We were afraid you'd be late," said Petra, fanning herself with a hankie. The church wasn't air-conditioned, and the heat seemed to be building in intensity.

"Where were you, anyway?" hissed Toni. She hunched forward, raised her penciled brows in a questioning manner.

But Suzanne was saved by the bell, or rather a cascade of organ music that swelled from the old pipe organ up in the choir loft.

"Mozart," murmured Suzanne, recognizing the attempt at a piano concerto. The selection had to be Carmen's. Bobby would surely have preferred something lighter such as Vivaldi or Handel.

As the music built to a crescendo, Carmen Copeland entered the church and walked slowly down the center aisle. Head held high, wearing a tight black sheath, Carmen clutched a small black bag and a sprig of purple violets.

Toni learned forward and whispered, "It's a friggin' funeral, not a wedding."

But Suzanne didn't respond. Her eyes were glued on Carmen Copeland's dramatic entrance and her over-the-top widow's garb. She'd always heard that the renowned author was a flamboyant and colorful character, but this was more than she'd bargained for.

Carmen's skintight dress managed to accentuate her ample yet perfect behind, as well as display a hefty amount of natural cleavage in front. Her thick, long, dark wavy hair fell across her shoulders; a double-layered veil covered her face.

Around Carmen's neck hung a richly hued gold necklace Suzanne assumed must be the real-deal twenty-four-karat kind. The large emerald pendant that dangled in its center was a minimum of four carats. Carmen's ring finger displayed a diamond that equaled the emerald in size. A diamond bracelet shimmered on her wrist.

Suzanne had read somewhere that most novelists

manage only a modest living, with just the top 1 or 2 percent jumping out of mid-list oblivion and becoming truly wealthy. It would appear Carmen was one of those lucky few.

If what a person wore spoke silently about who they were, Carmen's outfit spoke volumes. Her outfit did not scream "mourning widow." In fact, her ensemble seemed carefully calculated for show. And what a show it was turning into.

When Carmen reached the front pew, she reached into her black bag and pulled out a pristine white linen handkerchief. She didn't use it but clutched it in her hand with a dramatic flounce. Suzanne glanced at Toni, and Toni rolled her eyes. Neither one of them could quite believe this elaborate display.

The sound of clacking metal wheels caused everyone in the church to turn. Bobby's casket was being wheeled down the aisle. Six men, honorary pallbearers, most of whom she recognized, walked somberly alongside it.

Suzanne gave a short gasp as the reality of the situation hit her. Tears stung her eyes, then oozed down her cheeks. The last time she'd seen Bobby, he was slumped in the front seat of his car, covered with blood. Now here he was, being sent on his final journey, inside what looked like a slightly tinny bronze casket.

As the murder scene came back to her in a flash of sights and smells, so did the rush of horror she'd experienced that day. Suzanne breathed in again, trying to catch her breath and still her fast-beating heart.

As if sensing Suzanne's anguish and unease, Toni reached over and pulled Suzanne's hand into her lap, laced her fingers around it. Then Petra placed her own hand on top of Toni's and Suzanne's. Friends forever.

IF a funeral can ever be considered good, Bobby's turned out to be a seven on a possible scale of ten. The music got progressively better; the minister read a lovely prayer. And then the entire congregation was invited to raise their voices in song:

> *Amazing Grace, how sweet the sound,*
> *That saved a wretch like me . . .*

As always, Suzanne found the words and sentiment touching. She was a strong believer in song and prayer. Both could be a huge comfort.

As the notes slowly died, Vern Manchester stood up and walked to the podium. Although Vern was a member of the town council like Bobby, Suzanne hadn't realized that he and Bobby were friends. She'd never seen them together at any social function. Then again, she hadn't been to a lot of social functions lately. Maybe she'd have to remedy that, she decided. Get out and get going.

Vern pulled a sheet of paper from his suit pocket, adjusted his glasses, and looked around. He was a nice enough fellow, Suzanne decided. He and his wife, Lenore, had moved here a few years ago from Chicago. Although Vern claimed to have retired to what he called "the good life in Kindred," he'd built the Bridgeview town houses and, according to the *Bugle*, was considering another real estate project, low-income housing for seniors, in Kindred's downtown area.

"On behalf of Carmen and Bobby's many friends, thank you for coming today." Vern gave a halfhearted smile, then proceeded with his eulogy. "Bobby's short life of forty-six years was a rich and full life . . ."

Vern went on, sharing a few funny stories about Bobby along with poignant reminiscences. He spoke of Bobby's generous character and giving nature. He told of Bobby's golfing disasters and fly-fishing follies. The entire church laughed out loud when he told how Bobby once hooked the seat of his own waders instead of a rainbow trout.

Vern touched their hearts when he spoke of Bobby's

complete and perfect love for Carmen. And when he told of their honeymoon, most folks felt as if they were strolling with them on that romantic Caribbean beach.

At the conclusion of the eulogy, there wasn't a dry eye in the house. In fact, the eulogy was so perfect, so elegantly composed, Suzanne was convinced that Carmen Copeland, *New York Times* bestselling author and so-called "Queen of Romance," had written it herself. Especially the part about Carmen being the ideal spouse.

If Carmen was really such a wonderful, loving spouse, then why did she live in neighboring Jessup? For some reason, Suzanne wasn't buying into the old "she needs her space in order to write" mantra.

On the other hand, it really wasn't her or anyone else's business how Bobby and Carmen had lived their lives. Separately, together, or conveniently apart. Suzanne wasn't quite sure why she had let herself get so worked up about it.

Vern had a few more words to deliver.

"The funeral will now proceed to Kindred Memorial Cemetery where there will be a private burial for family members only."

"There's only one family member," whispered Toni.

Suzanne nodded back. It did seem a little strange.

They watched as Vern descended a few steps from the podium, then grasped Carmen's hand. That seemed to be the signal for the pallbearers to scramble to attention and position themselves around Bobby's coffin. The funeral director, Ozzie Driesden, helped them seesaw the coffin back and forth, then point it down the center aisle.

Walking slowly to the casket, Carmen placed a wreath of white lilies on top. Then, responding to Ozzie's nod, the pallbearers pushed the coffin down the aisle, with Carmen following and Ozzie resolutely bringing up the rear.

As Ozzie passed by, he nodded at Missy Langston, who was seated in the row directly behind Carmen.

The town council followed, then row after row emptied

out until most of the mourners were milling about outside on the manicured front lawn.

"IT was a nice service," Petra offered. "Very dignified."

"Vern didn't mention the cause of death," said Toni. "Or the circumstances."

"I'm not sure that would have been appropriate," said Suzanne.

Toni glanced around. "Do you think . . . ?" she began.

"What?" said Suzanne.

"That, you know, the killer's here?" asked Toni. She rolled her eyes expressively.

Suzanne stared at the hundred or so people who filled the yard as well as the ones who were ambling down the tree-lined street toward their cars. Most were people she recognized. They were the friends and neighbors who made up Kindred. "Maybe," she replied. It was the same thought she'd entertained last night.

"Back to the scene of the crime?" murmured Petra. She seemed distressed by Toni's remark.

"Except," said Toni, frowning, "the scene of the crime would be—"

"The Cackleberry Club," finished Suzanne.

"Creepy," said Toni, giving a little shiver.

"You got that right," agreed Suzanne. Unnerved by the notion, she glanced around and suddenly found herself staring into the dark eyes of Charlie Pepper. It would appear the egg man was still in town. Dressed in his Sunday worst, his hair tangled, his clothes slightly askew, Charlie looked like something the cat wouldn't drag in.

Suzanne eased her friends toward Toni's car. The last thing she wanted was some sort of nasty scene outside the Good Shepherd Church.

"See you back there?" asked Toni.

Suzanne nodded as Toni and Petra headed in the opposite direction from where she'd parked her car.

Sneaking glances at the crowd, wondering if the killer really had shown up, Suzanne fished for her car keys as she headed down the sidewalk. She'd looked around in church, hoping to notice a guilty face, but no one had stood out to her. Maybe Charlie Pepper, but he was just . . . weird.

The sun blazed down, a slight breeze riffled the trees overhead. Early morning had harbored a hint of rain, but now it had turned into a beautiful day. Suzanne wondered about the private service at the cemetery, figured it would be a beautiful day out there, too. Just very sad.

Suzanne was twenty feet from her car when she became aware of quickening footsteps behind her. She glanced over her shoulder, certain it was the egg man hurrying after her, come to lament the fact that he was under Sheriff Doogie's close scrutiny. Instead, she was surprised when she saw a complete stranger following her. Suzanne half turned, gave a sort of stutter step.

"I'm sorry," she laughed, apologizing to the stranger. "I don't usually startle so easily. It's just that—"

"Suzanne Deitz?" His voice was firm with no trace of emotion, his body language stiff and formal. With prematurely gray hair and ice blue eyes, he had a cool German shepherd look to him.

"Yes?" she answered.

The man reached into his suit jacket pocket. "I'm Tom Lyons, assistant state attorney general."

Suzanne softened her voice. "Were you a friend of Bobby's?"

He handed her a business card. "No. I'm here for you. The state attorney general's office is beginning a grand jury investigation regarding your husband's recent activities."

"What?" She stared at him. "But . . . my husband is deceased."

Lyons gave an acknowledging nod. "We understand your circumstances, Mrs. Deitz. However, Walter Deitz has been implicated in a four-million-dollar kickback regarding the state prison contract."

Suzanne stood her ground. "That's absurd!" she said.

Lyons stared impassively at her.

"What proof could you possibly have?" asked Suzanne. Her heart was beating like a frightened rabbit; she could feel her face getting flushed.

"Our office has been reviewing certain records, and the numbers are simply not making sense. When we contacted Claiborne Corrections, they pointed us in the direction of the contractors and subcontractors. That's when your husband's name came up."

Suzanne took a deep breath. "That *really* doesn't make any sense!"

"It's a mess right now," agreed Lyons, "but I promise you, we will get to the bottom of this. We're very adept at straightening out messes."

Suzanne put a hand to her cheek, feeling almost woozy.

"And finding the guilty party," Lyons added.

Suzanne tried to think, tried not to let her emotions get the best of her, fought to think rationally. Yes, they'd sort all this out. Of course they would. Walter was innocent, she had no doubt. "What do you want from me?" she asked in what she hoped was a cool, controlled voice.

"We're requesting you produce all of Walter's financial records and files for the past three years, including bank statements, investment records, trusts, real estate holdings, and any accounts he may have held offshore."

"Our only bank account was at First Community," said Suzanne. "We opened it to get a stupid toaster the first year we were married!" Her cool was oozing away, anger flooding in to take its place.

"We especially want to see any papers dealing with the Jasper Creek Prison." Lyons pointed to the card she still held between her fingers. "You have my number. Gather everything you can, then give my office a call. We'll make arrangements to pick up the documents—"

"What?" She was still stunned.

"And issue a receipt," finished Lyons.

"And if I don't comply?" asked Suzanne, even though she was pretty sure she knew the answer.

"You have until the end of next week," said Lyons. "Then we get a subpoena. And you have the pleasure of appearing before a grand jury."

Lyons left her standing there, feeling confused, scared, and more than a little angry.

Walter? Involved in some sort of kickback? No. Never happened.

Suzanne ran back toward the church, her heels slapping pavement, aware people were staring at her.

If only she could catch Vern. He'd been on the planning committee with Walter. Maybe he'd know something. Maybe he could help!

Looking around frantically, Suzanne finally spotted the top of Vern's bald head just as he bent low to speak to the driver of the funeral limousine. The limo's windows were carefully smoked, but Suzanne was pretty sure Carmen Copeland was inside that car.

No matter, she headed for it anyway.

"Vern!" she called out, waving at him. Now a few lingering mourners stared at her.

Vern had his hand on the rear door handle when he spotted her heading his way. He cocked his head slightly, like an inquisitive magpie, and waited as Suzanne trotted over.

"You just got a visit from Tom Lyons," were the first words out of his mouth.

Slightly stunned, Suzanne stared back at him. Vern didn't look at all happy. In fact, he looked downright miserable, and she didn't think it had anything to do with Bobby's funeral today.

"He talked to you, too?" asked Suzanne.

Vern gave her a hangdog look. "Right before the service. It was a miracle I could even get through it."

"Vern," said Suzanne, trying to keep her voice from shaking. "You were on the prison planning committee with Walter. You know he wouldn't do anything . . ." She searched for the right words. "Anything *improper.*"

Vern held up his hands, as if to deflect her anger. "Hey, Suzanne, you're preaching to the choir. I don't know what's going on, either. They're asking for *my* records, too!"

"What is going on?" asked Suzanne.

Vern shook his head. "No idea. But it's got people plenty scared. You don't fool around with the state attorney general's office!"

"You know Walter wouldn't abscond with any money," said Suzanne. "Walter only joined the planning committee because he cared about the impact on the community. He thought he could act as a watchdog. Make sure the trout streams didn't get filled in or the taxes get jacked up."

Vern shook his head. "I don't know what to tell you, Suzanne. Probably the best thing you can do is get a lawyer."

I had one, Suzanne thought to herself. *I just attended his funeral.*

CHAPTER 16

BECAUSE their breakfast offerings had been so limited this morning, really only coffee, caramel rolls, key lime scones, and cinnamon toast, Petra was going all out and serving several of their most popular egg dishes for lunch. There was the Fajita Scramble, of course. A spicy concoction of salsa, red peppers, strip steak, and eggs. And another dish Petra called her Bodacious Bacon Quiche.

Petra's real specialty, however, was an egg strata, her version being the Egg Strata-Various. Which meant, depending on her mood, various combinations of ingredients. Could be diced ham and green pepper or mushrooms and Swiss cheese. Today she'd gone for broke with goat cheese, green onions, and sautéed fresh-picked asparagus.

"You feeling any better, honey?" Petra asked Suzanne when she swung into the kitchen to grab two side orders of turkey sausage.

"Not really," said Suzanne. As soon as she'd arrived back at the Cackleberry Club, she'd quickly told Petra and

Toni about her encounter with the intractable Tom Lyons. Not really an encounter, either. More of an ambush.

They'd been outraged at the allegations against Walter and hastily assured Suzanne it must be some terrible mistake. And even though they'd seemed shaken, Petra and Toni were positive it would all get straightened out in the long run.

While their allegiance was heartening, Suzanne still wasn't sure what she was going to do in the short term.

"Suzanne!" called Toni. She stuck her head through the pass-through, looking frazzled. "We've got a six-car pileup in the Book Nook!"

"Can do," said Suzanne as she scooted out into the café, delivered her turkey sausage, and headed for their book section.

Easing herself behind the counter, she rang up two mysteries, a children's book, two gardening guides, four skeins of yarn, and a wheel of cheddar cheese. She answered a couple of questions, pointed one woman toward the mystery section, and jotted down a couple of special requests. Whew.

Even though Suzanne felt like she was running on vapors, she still loved nothing more than to be surrounded by books. Row upon row of shiny, new volumes that just beckoned for their spines to be cracked and eager readers to dive in. And when customers asked for recommendations, Suzanne was always pleased. There wasn't a better feeling than to recommend a book she loved.

Suzanne had just slipped a Mary Higgins Clark novel into a brown paper sack when she was aware of a large presence looming off to her left.

She glanced up. Sheriff Roy Doogie was shifting from one foot to the other. *Well, well.*

She pressed a handful of dollars into her customer's hand, thanked her profusely, then said to Doogie, "I didn't know you read books."

"I don't," said Doogie, hitching at his pants. "I read faces."

Suzanne lifted an eyebrow and stared at him. "Read mine," she said with a challenge.

Doogie stared impassively at her, his lined face studying her smooth one. Finally he said, "You're wearing makeup today. But you still look a little stressed."

"No kidding," said Suzanne.

"You had a visit from Tom Lyons," Doogie told her in an authoritative tone.

"Ambush," corrected Suzanne. She was liking that term more and more. Made her feel slightly righteous. "And how did *you* know about that?" she asked. *Probably because you were at the funeral,* she thought to herself.

Doogie tapped an index finger against the side of his head. "I know everything that goes on in Kindred. Not much escapes me."

"Except Bobby and Teddy's killer." Suzanne couldn't help herself. His line was such a perfect setup.

Anger blazed in Doogie's eyes. "Now that ain't fair! I'm workin' as hard as I can on that! Hell, I just got preliminary ballistics back on Teddy."

Suzanne gazed at him sharply. "Was it a forty-five?" Bobby had been shot with a forty-five.

"Yeah," said Doogie, reading her thoughts. "But we need a couple more tests to see if it was the same weapon."

"Huh," said Suzanne. "Okay, sorry. Apologies. I didn't mean to make you go bananas on me, okay?"

"You think I'm just some small-town sheriff who don't know nothin'," Doogie huffed. "Well, you're wrong."

"Really," said Suzanne, "I'm sorry. Wrong choice of words. If it's any consolation, I think you're running a fine investigation." Of course, Doogie still hadn't shared any thoughts with her on the missing file business. But why bring that up again and rile him any more than she already had?

"We're doing our best," muttered Doogie.

"Okay then," said Suzanne, as two more customers came up to the counter.

Doogie sidled away as she rang up the sales. Picking up a book titled *Country Quilts for City Girls,* he flipped through it nonchalantly. He looked like he wanted to say something more, but he didn't.

"About the attorney general thing," said Suzanne, when there was a break in the action. "You got any advice for me? I mean, legal-wise?"

Doogie snapped the book closed and stared at her, a crazed gleam lighting his eyes. "You have the right to remain silent," he told her. "Anything you say will be misquoted and used against you."

"Well, I know that!" growled Suzanne.

PETRA'S cake was a thing of sheer delight: a two-layer cake, with a square bottom layer and a taller, round, top layer. Wide stripes of white and lilac-tinted fondant decorated the sides of the bottom layer, while Petra had fashioned the top layer into a gift box with lilac, green, and white ribbons spilling from it. The very top of the gift box, set slightly askew, was a pure white disk with fondant beads circling the edge and a large fondant bow on top.

"Perfect," declared Toni. "When we have our cake show here at the Cackleberry Club, you're gonna win, gonna be our ringer!"

"Gorgeous," marveled Suzanne. "Almost too pretty to eat." But, of course, she knew the guests would ooh and coo but, ultimately, dive in. They always did.

Twenty minutes later Gregg and Brett came bustling in to decorate the Cackleberry Club. Gregg was tall, blond, a little ethereal, and slightly forgetful. Brett was short and dark, a dynamo with a long ponytail draped down his back.

"Honey," said Brett, thrusting spools of pink ribbon and

a huge bouquet of white carnations into Suzanne's hands, "get with the program and become the decorating goddess you've always aspired to be."

"You're telling me you need help?" laughed Suzanne.

"You got it," added Brett.

Suzanne and Toni both pitched in then, hauling in floral cushions and propping them against the backs of wooden chairs, helping Gregg and Brett arrange massive amounts of flowers in white crockery pots. White lace tablecloths were draped across the wooden tables, giving the place instant chic. They pulled out sets of Wedgwood china and Oneida flatware, placed sparkling wineglasses at each place setting. A few minutes later, the manicurist and masseuse arrived in a flurry to set up their respective stations. Flickering votive candles and rain forest sounds on the CD player completed the bucolic atmosphere.

When the twenty squealing guests arrived, they were right in sync. Most were dressed in summer halter dresses and fancier flip-flops. A few wore strapless French terry dresses, the better for the masseuse to knead those tired neck muscles! The bride-to-be wore a stunning strapless, black-and-white banana-leaf-print dress, gold toe ring, and frilly white veil.

With everyone enjoying Perrier, herbal teas, and white wine spritzers, Suzanne, Petra, and Toni proceeded to work their collective buns off.

They served a wonderful array of tea sandwiches: shredded carrot and cheddar cheese spread on triangles of whole wheat bread garnished with pimentos; cucumber, cream cheese, and sprigs of dill on thinly sliced French bread; and cranberry and thinly sliced turkey on dark bread with honey-yogurt mayonnaise. The salad was a luscious combination of strawberries, spinach, pine nuts, and honeydew melon.

"Everything on the menu is so healthy," remarked Suzanne, when the three of them finally took a breather in the kitchen.

"Yeah," chuckled Toni. "I feel like I should go out back and smoke a cigarette. Even things out."

SUZANNE and Toni topped off wineglasses as Gregg and Brett passed out goody bags to all the guests. He'd brought extras and surreptitiously slipped three bags to Suzanne, with the admonishment, "Hide these!"

She did.

But once tea sandwiches were eaten, cake was served, shower gifts opened, massages administered, and polish dried on happy toes, the party began to die down. And finally, when everyone had taken their leave, Suzanne and Toni dug eagerly into their bags.

"This is incredible," exclaimed Toni. "Coconut Shower Gel! Shea Butter Lotion! Veggie-Cucumber Calming Cream!"

"Is this your own line?" Suzanne asked.

Brett nodded happily. "We're thinking of calling it Country Goddess."

"Amazing," said Suzanne. "You guys are full-fledged entrepreneurs. You do everything."

"We like to keep busy," said Gregg.

"Hey," said Brett, edging toward Suzanne. "We were shocked to hear about all the trouble out this way."

"Yeah," said Suzanne, "it's been a real learning experience, getting sucked into two different murder investigations."

"Is the sheriff any closer to . . . you know?" asked Brett.

Toni answered for her. "Nope."

"We'll keep our ears and eyes open for you," said Gregg. "Promise."

"Yeah," said Brett. "Between tints and perms, we hear everything!"

* * *

"THE thing to do now," said Petra, "is sell the place." She surveyed the tables with their detritus of linens and dirty dishes, the candles that had burned down to glowing nubs, the ribbon and wrapping paper crumpled on the floor.

"I've got a better idea," said Toni, emerging from the kitchen with a tinkling glass pitcher.

"Oh, you are so right," exclaimed Petra. "Let's. Besides, Joey'll be here in a few minutes. We'll let him do the cleanup."

They moved into the Knitting Nest, eased themselves into comfy chairs, and enjoyed their wine spritzers in tall glasses garnished with rounds of fresh lime.

"I always thought folks who mixed club soda with wine were yuppie dilettantes," said Suzanne. "But this is tasty stuff."

"You're used to being a wine purist," Petra pointed out.

"Yeah," said Toni. "You're not a Budweiser gal like Petra and me."

"Speak for yourself," laughed Petra.

"So," said Toni, topping off her glass. "You want to tell us about your big, mysterious errand this morning?"

"Oh that," said Suzanne. For some reason, her visit with Reverend Yoder seemed like it had taken place days earlier, not just hours ago. So much had happened since. "I stopped by the Journey's End Church to ask Reverend Yoder if he knew anything about the Neukommen Following. Remember, I told you about the files that went missing from Bobby's office?"

Petra nodded.

"That reverend scares me a little," said Toni. "He always looks so strict and straitlaced. And his followers seem a little standoffish."

"They're just quiet people," said Petra. She inclined her head toward Suzanne. "What did the reverend say?"

Suzanne took a quick sip of wine, then told them what she'd learned about the Neukommen Following and their Web site.

"A Web site?" said Petra. "And DVDs? That seems awfully techie for a group that professes to renounce earthly ties."

"Yeah," snorted Toni. "Sounds like a real production line. In fact, I wouldn't be surprised if they're outsourcing their prayers to India!"

·CHAPTER 17·

"BAXTER," said Suzanne, as she opened the door to Walter's study, "it's time to snoop." It was Friday night, and Suzanne figured she'd conduct a little search of Walter's office, find those stupid papers that Tom Lyons thought held the clue to the missing money.

But after scrunching down in Walter's chair, pulling open all the desk drawers, and pawing through his files, she really hadn't found much of anything.

That's good, right?

So who had launched these bizarre charges? And why had Walter become the prime suspect? Because he was dead? Because he wasn't around to defend himself?

But I'm here. So I've got to defend him.

Still, there didn't seem to be anything that would help explain things or put him in the clear.

Maybe, Suzanne decided, something was stashed in their safe-deposit box.

Great idea. But where's the key to that puppy?

Good question. She pawed through the drawers again,

looked through an old wallet, and unzipped a plastic bank envelope and felt around. Nothing. She went through the two file drawers again. Nope.

Suzanne leaned back in the chair, Baxter at her side, and gazed about the office. It was a small room that Walter had turned into an office. Just enough room for a wooden desk, chair, and two-drawer file. The walls were covered in rich dark green vertically striped wallpaper; the floors were refinished oak. A collage of framed memorabilia hung on the wall. Wedding pictures, programs from a couple of plays they'd seen together in New York, a photo of Baxter as a puppy, an old engraving of Napoléon trying to rally his troops at the Battle of Waterloo, and an antique print of an orchard with the words, "To everything there is a season, / and a time to every purpose under heaven."

Suzanne stood up, stretched, glanced at the pens, cachepots, and knickknacks that sat on top of his desk, thought about that doggone safe-deposit key again. While she was standing there, dithering, the phone rang. Suzanne snatched it up on the first ring. "Hello?"

"Junior just called," came Toni's excited voice. "He got arrested in a bar fight and wants me to bail him out."

Suzanne couldn't help but groan. She wanted to tell Toni to let him rot in his cell but stopped herself. Why make more trouble for her friend? Instead, she asked, "What do you want to do?"

"Girl, I have no idea," was Toni's response.

"You want me to come over there?"

"Maybe," said Toni. "And then maybe you could drive me over to the law enforcement center?" This was accompanied by a slight sniffle.

"You sure about that?" asked Suzanne. "You sure you want to bail Junior out?"

"No," said Toni. "But, technically, we're still married. So—"

"Just for the record, Junior is technically still an asshole."

"I know that," said Toni. "Really I do. How soon do you think you can pick me up?"

"Ten minutes, honey."

"HAVE you ever posted a bail bond before?" Suzanne asked as she swerved into the parking lot. Sheriffs' cars, a highway patrol car, and a prison transport van sat in the parking lot. It looked like a darned law enforcement convention. Or maybe they'd all just come back from a doughnut run.

"No way," said Toni. "I don't have a clue what to do. I brought along about two hundred bucks in cash, but if the bail's more than that, I'll have to write a check." She paused. "And if it's more than five hundred bucks, I'll end up in jail alongside Junior for writing a bad check!"

"Maybe they take credit cards," suggested Suzanne.

"JC Penney's?" asked Toni.

"Probably not," said Suzanne. She wanted to say more but held her tongue. If there was one thing she knew about Toni, it was that she always took the side of the underdog. Even if it was her mutt of a husband.

"Hey," said Toni, pointing at her windshield. "You got a bullet hole in your windshield. That from the other night?"

"Yup," said Suzanne.

"You didn't get it fixed yet."

"Nope."

"How come you don't just call your insurance company?" asked Toni. "How come you left it there?"

"Inspiration."

Suzanne slid her car into a parking space, took care about opening her door. She didn't want to bang up somebody's car and have to tangle with them. Law enforcement officials were very protective of their vehicles. Even the fish and game fellows were known to get surly.

"I suppose we have to get this over with," said Toni as

she climbed slowly from Suzanne's car. She seemed to be running out of steam.

"Do we have to give Junior a ride home once we bail him out?" asked Suzanne. They walked up the steps into the large building, both looking a little tentative.

"No way!" said Toni.

Good answer, thought Suzanne. And once again, she was wise enough to keep her thoughts to herself.

Toni approached the front desk with her head held high and a brittle smile pasted on her face. "I'm here to post bail," she informed the officer on duty.

The officer, square-jawed with a military brush cut, glanced up slightly from his paperwork. He grabbed a form from a metal file holder and slid it across the desk. "Form ten fifty-six slash zero. Fill it out in triplicate, sign at the bottom."

Toni grabbed the form, then asked, in a syrupy-sweet voice, "By the way, how much is this gonna cost?"

The officer looked up and shrugged his shoulders. "Depends on who you're here for."

"Junior . . . I mean, his *nickname* is Junior. You see, his given name is Loren, but—"

The duty officer reached over and, with one swipe of his big hand, grabbed the form back from her. "No need to post bond, lady. That one's not going anywhere."

Toni fairly sputtered. "But . . . but . . . he just called me."

The officer interrupted Toni. "Maybe so, but his bail's been rescinded pending a ballistics report."

"Excuse me?" said Toni.

"Ballistics report?" said Suzanne. She'd remained silent this whole time; now she decided to get into the act. "What are you talking about? Are you telling us Junior *shot* someone?" The idea was too terrible to comprehend.

Toni clutched a hand to her heart. "Dear Lord, I always knew he was crazy as a loon."

The duty officer stared at Toni. "I take it you're the . . . uh . . . wife?"

"Good call," said Suzanne. "Yes, she is. So what—?"

"Here's the problem," said the officer, hunching forward. "Your boy didn't shoot anybody. Not that we know of, anyway. But he *was* arrested for drunk and disorderly conduct."

"Arrested where?" asked Toni.

"Hoobly's," said the officer. "That roadhouse out on County Road 18."

"That place is a *pit*," Suzanne pointed out. "Everybody out there is drunk and disorderly. Why single out Junior?"

"Because when he got patted down, he had a forty-five tucked in the waistband of his jeans."

Suzanne's heart thumped as she suddenly realized that a forty-five was the same caliber gun that had killed Bobby and Teddy.

"Oh," said Toni in a small voice.

Oh boy, worried Suzanne. *Could Junior really be the murderer?* The thought zoomed around in Suzanne's brain like a ball bearing in a pinball machine. On the one hand, Junior as the killer was horrific news. On the other hand, if he really was the prime suspect, and they could pin him to the murder using ballistics, then . . . well, then Bobby's and Teddy's murders were solved, weren't they? And life could get back to normal. Sort of normal, anyway.

Toni was still struggling with the facts of Junior's arrest, however. "How long are you gonna keep him?"

"Hard to say," replied the duty officer.

"And they're doing ballistics tests right now, even as we speak?" Toni asked.

The officer grimaced. "Well, no. See, it's Friday night. So the gun probably won't even get looked at by the state crime lab until Monday."

"So he's locked up till then?" asked Toni. "Or longer?"

Suzanne patted Toni's shoulder. "I'm sure he'll be fine."

Toni stared at the duty officer. "You're not going to shine bright lights in his eyes or poke him with electrical thingies, are you?"

The officer had trouble keeping a straight face. "No, ma'am."

"So Junior's really been booked," muttered Toni. She was still somewhat stunned.

"It's a done deal," said the officer. "They already did mug shots and fingerprints, then escorted him to lockup."

"So there's nothing more we can do here?" Suzanne asked.

The officer shook his head. Then, as an afterthought, added. "You could get him a lawyer."

Where have I heard that before? thought Suzanne.

Toni didn't say much on the drive home, and Suzanne's heart went out to her. She clearly had an internal struggle going on. Much as Toni made jokes and jabs at Junior's expense, she obviously still had feelings for him.

Suzanne pulled up in front of the white clapboard house where Toni rented an upstairs apartment. "You gonna be okay?"

Toni sighed. "I guess." She reached into her denim purse and grabbed her keys. A small, furry cat head with rhinestone eyes, a hybrid between Hello Kitty and Felix, dangled from her key chain. "Sorry to get you out at night like this. Kind of a bad start to the weekend, especially since tomorrow's your day off."

"Not a problem," said Suzanne. She did a little drumbeat on the steering wheel with her fingertips. "It's been a trip and a half."

Hesitating, Toni said, "You don't think Junior is the murderer, do you?"

"No idea," said Suzanne.

"When Garland fired him from the garage, Junior was pretty ticked off."

"What?" said Suzanne. "Junior *worked* for Garland?" This was a shock to her.

Toni nodded miserably. "What if Junior saw Garland's

truck the night Teddy was driving it. Maybe he thought it was Garland, and just went nuts!"

Suzanne thought for a few seconds. "But then some-body went down and finished Teddy off after the truck flipped," said Suzanne. "You think Junior is that cold-blooded? That crazy?"

"I don't know," was Toni's whispered answer.

"Try not to think about it," Suzanne advised her. "Just try to get a good night's sleep."

"You're a real friend," said Toni. She opened the car door, started to step out, then hesitated. Her face, illumi-nated by the dome light, looked incredibly sad. "What do you think Junior was fighting about? Out at that road-house?" Toni asked. "That they had to call the cops?"

"Hard to tell," said Suzanne. "But knowing Junior, I'm sure it wasn't anything of national importance."

"Bet it was a woman," Toni said in a hoarse whisper. And then she slipped silently away.

"DOGGONE that Junior," Suzanne muttered, as she walked into her house, still fuming about him. He was like the pro-verbial bad penny, always turning up at the most inopportune moment. She tossed her keys on the spindly little console table by the door, where they clattered, then skid-ded onto the floor. Hearing the noise, Baxter came creeping out, all doggy sleepy and slowly wagging his tail. "Rwwr?" he asked. He'd been keeping watch for her.

"Let's turn in, Bax," said Suzanne. "Call it a day." To-gether they climbed the stairs and padded into the bedroom. Suzanne pulled off her clothes and threw them on the floor, too tired to bother hanging them up. She put on an oversized T-shirt and went into the master bathroom to brush her teeth.

As the electric toothbrush did the work for her, Su-zanne's mind circled back to that safe-deposit box key. Where the heck was that thing?

She could ask the bank to drill out the lock, but she

didn't really want to. It was another inconvenience. Plus it would mean admitting to the bank that her husband hadn't confided in her. With this prison kickback investigation being launched, something that would ordinarily seem insignificant just might put Walter's integrity in question.

Turning off the toothbrush, Suzanne gargled for a full minute, then left the bathroom.

"Think hard, Suzie Q," she told herself as she slipped into bed.

Suzie Q. That's what Walter had called her the first night they'd made love. When she'd been substitute teaching and he was a new hire at the clinic and they didn't want anyone to know. They'd driven to a tacky trucker's motel outside of Pigeon Run and rented a room. Not so good, but not so bad, either. Suzanne could close her eyes and still remember the visceral passion, the hunger they had felt for each other, the sweetness of their coming together. And when Walter had come out of the bathroom, glistening wet from his shower, hair tousled, looking a little bit nervous, for this had been their first time together, he'd whistled and said, "Hey there, Suzie Q."

Suzanne closed her teeth over her lower lip and bit down hard. *Enough*, she told herself. *Save that for the mental scrapbook*. The scrapbook where they were still together, still bubbling over with plans.

She closed her eyes. *Okay, count sheep. Or at least skeins of yarn. One, two, three . . .*

Where was that key? Did he tell her and her brain just fogged it out?

Sheep, yarn, remember to count 'em. Four, five, six . . .

She imagined more sheep, little white puff balls scattered across a green meadow.

Suzanne's eyes flew open. Like emerging from a dark woods and stepping into bright sunlight, she felt a warm presence surrounding her.

Walter, is that you?

The notion brought a smile to her face.

She knew it was probably just the memory of him that was making her feel so warm and comfortable. Still . . .

Suzanne swung her legs out of bed. In his Lands' End dog bed, the plaid one with monogrammed initials that had cost way too much, Baxter let loose a wet snore.

This is crazy, she told herself.

Yeah, but . . .

Suzanne padded back downstairs, not bothering to turn on any lights. She knew the house like the back of her hand. Knew which step creaked, where the low, leather footstool was parked. Trusted her instincts.

That's it exactly. Got to trust my instincts.

Flipping on the light in Walter's study, Suzanne surveyed the room again.

The key was in here. She knew it. Walter was too methodical to put it anywhere else. A key for a bank box would be . . . where?

Suzanne's gaze bounced across the top of his desk. From the Tiffany pen set she'd given him, to his glass globe paperweight, to the small antique brass bank that sat atop his desk. Her eye stopped. The bank was a miniature of an old-fashioned bank. Probably from the thirties, kind of Cass Gilbert–looking, something they'd picked up on one of their antiquing forays.

Crossing the room in three quick steps, Suzanne snatched up the bank and gave it a quick shake. She heard a tinkling sound inside and knew it wasn't a coin.

Suzanne plopped down in Walter's chair, pawed through his desk drawers again, and finally located a lethal-looking letter opener. She wedged the tip into the lock on the bottom of the bank and gave it a half turn. The metal bottom dropped out, and a safe-deposit key spilled into her palm.

Grinning, Suzanne mouthed, *Thank you, Walter,* and headed back upstairs. Slept the sleep of the innocents.

CHAPTER 18

"RIGHT this way, Mrs. Deitz." The security guard in his baggy, gray rent-a-cop suit walked Suzanne down the narrow, oak-paneled stairway to the lower level of the First Community Bank. "Nice day, isn't it?"

Suzanne nodded, antsy to get inside the vault. She knew if she engaged in too much conversation, the chatter might go on for half an hour. He'd want to talk about the storm that was supposed to roll in tonight, the two murders, who was growing the plumpest tomatoes in town . . . everything would become a potential conversational hot potato. Besides, the guard's suit smelled like mothballs.

Suzanne herself was wearing her going-to-the-bank outfit. A navy blue linen dress with a short, matching jacket. In lieu of her usual funky turquoise jewelry, she wore a trio of gold bangles.

The guard clutched the handrail as he eased himself down the stairs. He had to be at least eighty years old. He had probably worked there when the bank was first founded. Shuffling slowly toward the large vault door of the safe-deposit room, he managed to produce a large brass key on a chain and ease it into the lock. To turn the key, and pull open the groaning, iron door seemed to sap all his strength.

Suzanne stepped briskly inside the vaulted room. "Thanks. Just give me a few minutes."

"Take your time," croaked the guard. He hobbled off, and she heard the door close behind her.

Now she was in a room lined with hundreds of boxes. *How many secrets are in here?* she wondered. *Death certificates, coroner's reports, last will and testaments, land deeds, packets of fifties with the bank band still wrapped tightly around them, naughty photos?*

Her eyes ran down the numbered boxes until she finally located 516. It was one of the medium-sized boxes, set in the middle of the wall of boxes. Suzanne stuck the key into the lock and turned it. There was a sharp click, and then the box slid out easily.

Suzanne carried the box to the oak table in the center of the room. The table was nicked and scarred, as though a thousand boxes had been quickly and carelessly hoisted onto it.

Lifting the lid, Suzanne gazed at the contents of the box. And was slightly disappointed. There wasn't as much here as she'd thought there'd be.

Slowly, she sifted through the papers that lay on top. Their marriage certificate. Okay, she'd wondered where that was. Deed and plat map for their two hundred acres of land. Check. And a long, narrow, dark blue cardboard box. Wondering about this, Suzanne pulled it out and opened the hinged top.

Gold coins shone at her from where they lay in black foam rubber nests. Five Krugerands, two Canadian gold maple leafs. Okay, that's nice. Last time she'd checked CNN, gold prices had been up. Or maybe it was silver. Probably, she decided, she should try to develop a working knowledge of that stuff.

Thumbing through the rest of the papers, Suzanne found

Walter's birth certificate—he'd been born in Wheeling, West Virginia—as well as two savings bonds and a short stack of stock certificates she already knew about. Small amounts of blue chip stuff they'd bought together.

And nothing else. No secret papers, stash of cash, or shady agreement that might indicate he'd committed grand larceny.

Closing the box, Suzanne carried it back to the wall and slid it into its slot. Then she put her index finger on the electronic button, and the door opened. The guard was still hovering outside.

EXITING the bank, Suzanne felt a pang of disappointment. If she didn't find anything to turn over to the assistant attorney general, what happened then? He'd get his subpoena and . . . what? Sneak his own peek in the safe-deposit box? Tear her house apart? Dig up her backyard? Huh. Baxter had already made a head start there.

Suzanne was lost in thought as she slipped out the bank's front doors, rounded a pillar sharply, and bumped into someone, almost knocking them down.

"Watch it!" shouted a hard, masculine voice. Hands suddenly gripped her arms, clamping them to her side.

She looked up, startled, into the lined, flushed face of Charlie Pepper, the egg man.

"Charlie." She shrugged her shoulders, trying to force him to release her. But Charlie continued to grip tight.

"What have you been telling the police?" he demanded.

She stared into red-rimmed eyes. "Nothing."

He relaxed his grip on her ever so slightly. "That sheriff still has a tail on me," he barked. "An unmarked car was parked outside my farm all night long."

"If it was unmarked, how did you—?"

Charlie Pepper glowered. "What are you saying? That I'm paranoid?"

This time she shrugged out of his grasp for good and

took a fast step backward. But Charlie's rant was far from finished.

"There's no reason to question me in Bobby's murder! None at all. Next thing you know, they'll try to pin Teddy's death on me, too!"

"Sheriff Doogie wouldn't do that," said Suzanne. She looked up and down the street, but there was no one in sight. *Gotta get out of here,* she thought. *This guy is bonkers.*

"You tell that good-for-nothing sheriff that he better take a long, hard look at Teddy's drunken son, Garland!" growled Pepper. "There's a man who just couldn't wait to inherit all that land!"

"Yeah, okay," Suzanne muttered. *What on earth?*

Pepper thrust his head forward, and now his anger was more than palpable. He shook a gnarled index finger at her and cried, "Just you watch out, Suzanne Deitz!" Then he turned and stomped off.

Breathing a sigh of relief, Suzanne watched him clomp down the street and climb into his van. And she began to wonder if she'd really seen an SUV that night. Or had it been Charlie Pepper's van?

THE Westvale Clinic was still open for business when Suzanne arrived. She waited at the door as a woman and a boy with a newly plastered cast on his arm made their exit, then she carefully eased through. She was carrying a large white pastry box filled with scones, muffins, and doughnuts that she'd gleaned from the Cackleberry Club yesterday. She'd kept everything all wrapped up nice and tight so the baked goods would still be fresh.

"Hello, there! I've missed you!" Suzanne chirped to Zelda Mae and Esther, the two women sitting behind the desk in the cheery waiting room. Zelda Mae was a nurse, Esther the office manager.

"Mrs. Deitz! How are you?" exclaimed Zelda Mae. She

came around the counter and gave Suzanne a big bear hug. "It's been too long."

Suzanne had to agree. Walter had been on staff here, but she hadn't been back to visit for a while.

"How you doing?" asked Esther.

"Doing just fine," she told them. "Working like crazy, of course."

"We hear the Cackleberry Club is going great guns," said Esther. "That you're even offering afternoon tea now."

"La-di-da," laughed Zelda Mae, but she meant it in fun.

Suzanne slid the box onto the desk. "Got something for you guys."

Esther lifted the lid, and both women sighed.

"No calories, right?" said Zelda Mae.

"Guaranteed fat-free," said Suzanne.

"From your oven to our hips," laughed Esther. She sobered slightly. "Heard about Bobby Waite. Teddy, too."

Suzanne waved a hand. "Sheriff Doogie assures me he's hot on the trail." She sincerely hoped he was, that somebody was, besides her.

"That's reassuring," said Zelda Mae.

"Say," said Suzanne, "I'm sorry I haven't gotten around to clearing out Walter's locker."

Esther stood up. "Don't you dare apologize. We figured you'd pop in when you had a chance."

"Okay if I run back there right now?" asked Suzanne. She kept her voice light.

"No problem," said Zelda Mae. "Not for you, anyway." She slid a drawer open, rifled around inside, pulled out a set of keys. "You need a master key, or have you got Walter's?"

Suzanne accepted the jingling set of keys. "Thanks. Knew I forgot something."

"Locker number seven," said Zelda Mae. "You remember where it is?"

"I remember," said Suzanne. Heading down the hallway toward the far recess of the clinic, Suzanne kept her fingers crossed that she wouldn't run into anyone. She didn't, until she got to the locker room and put her hand on the doorknob.

"Hey, pretty lady," came a man's voice. "Need some help there?"

Suzanne turned to find a tall man in hospital greens smiling at her. A good-looking man at that. Early to mid-forties, a tousle of brown hair, a crooked smile on his inquisitive face. The new doctor, she decided, then did a quick check of his name tag. Yep, Dr. Sam Hazelet.

"Just picking something up," she told him. She held up the keys and shook them to prove she was legit.

"You're on staff here?" he asked.

"No, my husband was. But he, um, passed away."

Sam Hazelet's brow furrowed. "Sorry to hear that." He put a hand to his cheek, then dropped it quickly, snapping his fingers. "You're Suzanne."

She nodded.

"Sam Hazelet." His look was suddenly one of concern. "You doing okay? I mean, you look like you are."

Suzanne gave him a quick smile. "Better than I thought I would," she told him.

"Well, good," Sam replied. He put a hand on the wall, leaned toward her a little. Suzanne caught a whiff of aftershave. Citrus with a hint of amber. Something sexy. Maybe from Calvin Klein or Tom Ford?

Suzanne stuck the key in the lock and popped it open.

"It's really nice to meet you," said Sam. "Seeing as how I'm the new kid on the block here." He took a step back. "See you around."

"See you," Suzanne told him as she slipped into the locker room.

Tall, narrow lockers painted a ghastly orange sat against the far wall, reminding her vaguely of high school. Good thing they didn't *smell* like high school.

She found locker number seven, stuck the key in the lock, and threw open the door.

She had to smile. There was her picture on the inside of the door, smiling back at her.

A pair of blue scrubs hung from a hook. On the top shelf were three books, on the lower shelf was a shaving kit, a Chicago Cubs mug, a small leather notebook, a Clif energy bar, and a small rat's nest of papers.

Suzanne swept everything into her oversized handbag. Better to go through this stuff at home, she decided. But first, she had another funeral to attend.

TEDDY Harlingen's funeral was being held in a small Methodist church near downtown. It was a pretty little church built of pink sandstone, with a small, tree-shaded cemetery just behind it. Many of the tombstones listed badly, and a few were rough, wooden crosses. Of course, only the earliest members of the church were buried there. Now everyone was pretty much buried at Memorial Cemetery out on Bailey Road. And the really progressive folks in Kindred were cremated.

Even though the church was located in a busy part of town, Suzanne was saddened when she saw the small turnout. So few family, so few friends.

There was Teddy's son, Garland, of course. And another son she had a nodding acquaintance with. Their wives were there, too, dressed in their best black dresses, with five children scattered among them.

Standing on either side of Teddy's casket, almost as if they were keeping guard, were two elderly men. They wore somber suits with World War II medals pinned to their jackets. Dark blue VFW caps sat jauntily on their heads. Teddy was receiving his military funeral after all.

Slipping into a back pew, Suzanne's eyes fell upon Sheriff Roy Doogie. He was sitting off to the side, his legs crossed, his head down. Probably snooping for suspects, she decided. Surprisingly, across the aisle and over from Doogie was Jack Mobley, the mayor of Kindred. Dressed in khaki slacks and a white golf shirt, Mobley looked like he couldn't wait to get out and whack a few balls down the fairways at Olympic Hills.

The funeral was solemn and brief. A couple of prayers, a single, simple eulogy. One of Teddy's young grandsons strummed out a song on his folk guitar. Suzanne thought it might be "Michael, Row Your Boat Ashore," but it was hard to tell, with all the clinkers he hit.

When the service was over, Suzanne waited at the back of the church. She wanted to extend her sympathies to Teddy's family, but Mayor Mobley got to her first.

He was a barrel-chested man with muscle that was slowly going to lard. His hair was thinning, and she could see pink scalp beneath his self-conscious comb-over.

"Suzanne," he said in a smarmy voice, as though they were old friends. They weren't. She'd met him only twice in passing. Both times he'd asked for her vote. "We need to clear up this little problem of yours."

She met his eyes with an even gaze. "I don't have a problem." She was aware that Sheriff Doogie was lingering some twenty feet away, feeding coins into the poor box maybe, or lighting vigil lights.

Mayor Mobley's face took on a pinched look. "I'm talking about the thing with Walter," he said through clenched teeth. "The *money*. The city can't have a serious allegation like this hanging over our collective heads. It's bad for a town like Kindred. Bad for economic development."

"Bad for the town," Suzanne repeated. The man was a clod and a sleazy politician at that.

"We've got two more companies talking about relocating to Kindred," said the mayor in a nattering tone. "We've been wining and dining the heck out of 'em, and they're about ready to jump, but we'd sure hate for them to get wind of any . . . shall we say . . . impropriety."

"Excuse me," said Suzanne. "I have an appointment." She turned to go, but Mobley reached out, quick as a snapping turtle, and grabbed her arm. She could feel his sweaty palm insinuating itself through her jacket sleeve.

"We've called a special town council meeting for 10:00 A.M. on Monday morning. Be there, Suzanne. And be prepared to offer a complete explanation!"

·CHAPTER 19·

SUZANNE kicked off her shoes and slung her black tote onto the sofa. She flipped through the mail, then let Baxter out the back door into the fenced yard.

What a wacky morning, she decided. Prowling through safe-deposit boxes and lockers, attending a sad little funeral, getting threatened by the big bad mayor.

Are we having fun yet? No? Well, heck, what are we gonna do about it? Go eat worms?

No, she thought. *But how about whipping up some nice chilled avocado soup?*

She padded into the kitchen, turned on the radio, danced around to "Get Off of My Cloud" by the Rolling Stones while she peeled an avocado, sliced an onion, and pulled cartons of buttermilk and sour cream from the refrigerator.

Everything whirred in the food processor for a couple of minutes, then she dumped the thick, green goodness into a large soup bowl. Setting the bowl on a wicker tray, she grabbed a soup spoon, salt and pepper, and a paper napkin and headed for the living room.

Suzanne sat on the couch and set the tray on the coffee

table, turned on the TV, flipped through the channels, and saw that *The Maltese Falcon* was on. Neat. She loved old black-and-white movies, loved the female film stars of the thirties and forties with their ripple-waved hair, thinly penciled brows, and carefully defined lips.

When she finished her soup, Suzanne pushed the tray aside, turned the volume down on the TV, and pulled her black leather tote bag closer.

Okay, what do we have here?

Books. Two medical books and one on investing. The investing book was one of those how-to books with a triple title: *Timing the Market. Stocks and Sector Funds. Practical Advice for the Newbie as well as Experienced Investor.*

Yeah, right.

Suzanne opened the shaving kit, found a few grooming basics, set it aside, shoved the mug and energy bar aside, too. Thought twice, peeled open the energy bar, chocolate peanut crisp, and took a bite.

The small nest of papers looked interesting, but they turned out to be old memos. Stuff about staff meetings, procedures for ordering supplies, something about a new copy machine. Like that.

Which left only Walter's leather notebook.

Nothing secret about that, however. She'd seen him jot lots of stuff on the unlined pages. Notes to himself, the occasional Japanese haiku, ideas for tying trout flies, even a few recipes.

She continued to turn pages, nibbling at the bar. More notations on the clinic, about companies that had caught his interest while watching *Squawk Box* on CNN in the morning, and a list of Things To Do, one of which included, "Fill in holes!!!"

Suzanne flipped through another dozen blank pages, was ready to snap the book shut, when she saw a scribbled note in Walter's neat, loopy script. The notation read, "Lidia/Neukommen."

There it was again. The Neukommen thing. Was the Neukommen Following somehow connected to the break-in at Bobby's office? And was that break-in connected to Bobby's murder? And what exactly was Walter's connection?

Suzanne walked to the back door, pulled it open, gazed out at a scraggly backyard that looked as though a troop of manic gophers had staged their own version of an underground Olympics. Except the various holes had been dug courtesy of Baxter, who was busy digging yet another hole right under the drooping cherry tree.

Maybe, Suzanne decided, she could just pop a plant into the various holes. Think of it as soil that had been lovingly prepped. Of course, if she did that with all the holes, there'd be plants scattered haphazardly all across the yard.

On the other hand, maybe she could show Baxter where to dig, try to channel his energy into something that was less random and more akin to actual landscaping.

Baxter looked up at her suddenly and wagged his tail, seemingly pleased that she'd taken an interest in his life's work. His muzzle was slathered with dirt, his front paws resembled a couple of mud balls.

"Baxter," Suzanne called to him. "Want to get cleaned up and go for a ride?"

"GOOD afternoon, Kinnnnnnnnnndred!" screeched the DJ. "Time for your daily hog report."

Not my hog report, Suzanne told herself as she clicked over to a CD. As far as she was concerned, she'd had enough run-ins with oinkers for the day. First there'd been that bizarre encounter with Charlie Pepper. And then Mayor Mobley, who really did have a slightly porcine nose, now that she thought about it.

As Melissa Etheridge rocked on the CD player and Baxter lazed in the backseat, Suzanne tried to figure out just where she was. She'd driven back and forth along this road in neighboring Deer County for the last twenty minutes, followed the sketchy directions given on the Neukommen Web site, and *still* hadn't found the turnoff she wanted. All she'd seen were a few farms, a small antique shop, woods and ravines, and an occasional burbling trout stream. Great if you were looking for a picnic spot or a place to set up an artist's easel, but not if you were specifically looking for the Neukommen Following's home base.

Making yet another U-turn, Suzanne headed back the way she came. As she passed a small farm, she noticed a short, pleasant-faced woman walking down her driveway, headed for her mailbox. Suzanne managed to pull her car alongside the woman just as she was about to reach in and gather her mail. But as the right side of her car lurched off the road and onto the dusty shoulder, dust flew everywhere, causing the woman to sneeze.

Pushing the power button for the passenger-side window, Suzanne called out, "I'm so sorry about the dust. I really didn't mean to do that."

The woman sniffled, waved a hand, and smiled as Baxter stuck his big head out the window. "I'm okay, don't worry about it. How can I help? Are you two lost?"

"I'm looking for the Neukommen Following," Suzanne told her, deciding then and there that the apple-cheeked woman was a dead ringer for Miss Marple.

The woman's smile disappeared.

"Oh," was all she said. But that was enough. The woman's one-syllable response subtly communicated her distrust as well as the important question: *Are you one of them?*

Suzanne quickly tried to put the woman at ease. "I'm Suzanne Deitz. I own the Cackleberry Club over near Kindred."

The smile popped back on. "Oh, I've heard about your place, especially the tea thing." She came closer to the car and gave Baxter a friendly scratch behind his ears. "I'm a big Agatha Christie fan and love watching old British movies, so I think I'd feel right at home at an English tea."

"Then you should drop by," urged Suzanne. "We serve a proper tea every afternoon and are probably going to have a costume tea next month." She hesitated. "Would you by any chance know how to find the Neukommen Following? I keep driving around in circles." Now Suzanne decided to twist the truth a little. "I'm trying to source fresh produce for the Cackleberry Club, and I understand they have an organic farm. If you could point me in the right direction, I'd really appreciate it."

The woman nodded without hesitation now. "Sure. Just turn around and head back down the road. Right at the bottom of the next hill, a small dirt road splits off on your right. It's pretty overgrown with weeds, but you should see some tire tracks. If you weren't looking for it, you'd for sure miss it," she added.

I did miss it, Suzanne thought. *Three or four times already.*

"Anyway," continued the woman, "just drive up that road for a mile or two until you see the village."

"Village?"

The woman gave a quirky grin. "My husband calls it the Village of the Damned, but he doesn't mean anything by it. He's just a fan of spooky old movies. Their place is really just five or six old buildings and a couple of barns. Nothing much."

"Thanks," said Suzanne. "And, please, drop by for tea."

"Oh, I will," responded the woman. "And don't be surprised if I show up as Miss Marple!"

Well, yeah, thought Suzanne as she drove away.

IT took Suzanne three minutes to find the turnoff. And then she was humping along the dirt road in dappled sunlight, tree branches slapping the sides of her car. The road twisted up through a pretty fern-lined gully and then leveled out on top of a woodsy hill. Another half mile through groves of bur oak and red maples, and the commune was laid out before her. Surprisingly, it wasn't as spotless and prosperous-looking as she'd imagined it would be.

Four dilapidated clapboard houses squatted alongside the road, another smaller building sat atop a ridge. Just beyond the main cluster of houses was an old-fashioned hip-roofed barn, its wood rustic and weathered and almost gone to silver. Backing up to the houses was a scattering of small outhouses. When Suzanne noticed a man emerging from one of them, she knew those outdoor facilities were still very much in use.

"This must be the place," she told Baxter. He hung his head over her shoulder, gazing solemnly forward.

Crunching slowly down the driveway, Suzanne pointed her car toward a large garden where a dozen or so workers hoed rows of tomatoes and picked beans and peas, stashing their produce in wicker baskets. They looked up to gaze at her car, then quickly turned back to their work. When Suzanne reached a rickety wooden fence that separated the road from the garden, she pulled over.

"You stand guard, Bax, while I check this out."

Glad she'd worn running shoes, Suzanne tiptoed out into the muddy field. With storm clouds building on the horizon and a scent of rain hanging in the air, she figured this garden was probably going to get a whole lot muddier.

"Hello," she called out, trying to sound friendly.

Not one of the workers paused to look up at her. They continued to pick their crops with single-minded intensity.

Approaching the woman who was closest to her, Suzanne said, "Hello there, is Lidia around?"

The woman stared at her with suspicious eyes. Her dishwater blond hair was pulled into a tight bun, a long apron covered a nondescript dress, and she wore work boots. Finally the woman just shook her head.

Okay, Suzanne decided. *Try, try again.*

She walked past the woman to a young man who was toiling away with a hoe. Despite the warmth of the day, he was wearing a wool jacket and a felt hat.

"I'm looking for Lidia," Suzanne said more forcefully this time.

The young man turned toward an older man with a bushy beard a few feet away, as if looking for approval. The man with the beard bent down and whispered something into the ear of a young boy who was nearby. The boy instantly dropped his basket and ran toward the largest house.

Five minutes later, although it felt like an eternity to Suzanne, a small, waiflike woman approached her cautiously.

"Lidia?" asked Suzanne. The woman had dark hair pulled into a lush ponytail, olive skin, and solemn brown eyes. She, too, wore a nondescript dress. In fact, it looked like a castoff from the Salvation Army store.

The woman nodded nervously. "I'm Lidia. Who are you?" She looked toward the other workers. "Did my parents send you?" she asked in a slightly louder tone. "They know we're not supposed to have any contact with our old family."

You can't see your family?

This was a cult, Suzanne decided. So what else couldn't they do? Make decisions for themselves? Leave the property?

Suzanne placed a hand on Lidia's arm and guided her away, out of hearing distance from the others. "Lidia, my name is Suzanne. I'm a friend of Bobby Waite."

The girl stared at her, her eyes suddenly big with hope. "Where is he? Is he here?" She peered toward Suzanne's car, but only Baxter's furry face stared back.

"You don't know?" Suzanne asked softly.

The girl shook her head.

Oh dear, thought Suzanne. "Then I have some bad news for you. Bobby's dead. He . . . he was murdered."

As if a chill wind had suddenly engulfed her body, Lidia began to shake. Then her breathing turned shallow and rapid. It was almost a minute before she could bring herself to ask, "Is it my fault?"

"Oh, honey. No," responded Suzanne. Lidia's question

shook her to the core. "Why would you ask that?" Studying the undernourished young woman who stood in front of her, Suzanne didn't think Lidia could save herself, much less destroy another human being.

"Bobby was going to help me," Lidia said, almost as though she were confessing. "Did Claes find out? He gets so angry sometimes. He . . ." She stopped, bowed her head. "I'm so sorry. Dear Lord, please forgive me. Claes is a true prophet. He wouldn't . . ." She suddenly broke down in sobs.

Putting her arms around Lidia, Suzanne pulled the girl toward her and cradled her gently. Lidia was so tiny and frail, almost like a bird. "There, there," said Suzanne, trying to comfort her.

"Now what am I going to do?" sobbed Lidia. "Bobby was going to help. Now we're lost."

"Maybe I can help you," offered Suzanne. Releasing Lidia, she offered a hopeful smile. Suzanne knew she had to do something. The depths of this poor girl's misery were heart-wrenching.

"Are you a lawyer, too?" asked Lidia, breathing in deep gulps of air and swiping at her eyes with the back of her hand.

"No, my name is Suzanne Deitz. But I'm pretty good at figuring things out. So are my friends."

Lidia stared at her. "Deitz?"

"Yes," said Suzanne. "If you're in some kind of trouble, maybe I could help you find another lawyer."

"I don't know," murmured Lidia.

Suzanne stared intently at her, knowing trust was a key issue here. She would have to win Lidia's trust in order to—

A loud shout broke into her thoughts.

Suzanne stared past Lidia to see a tall, thin man, dressed head to toe in black, striding purposefully toward her. The closer he came, the more she was aware of his anger.

"You there!" he shrieked in a strident voice. "You! Trespasser!"

Lidia's eyes went round, and she whirled toward the man. "Claes," was all she said. She turned back to Suzanne, her fear palpable. "You have to leave. Now!"

"Can we meet somewhere?" asked Suzanne. "I really do want to help you." She wasn't sure what she was offering, but knew her brand of concern was far better than anything the man bearing down on them had to offer.

Lidia was almost too frightened to answer. "We can't talk here, it's too dangerous."

"Then meet me somewhere," Suzanne whispered hurriedly.

"Where?" asked the girl.

Suzanne racked her brain. "Back down the main road there's a little antique shop. You know where that is?"

Lidia nodded.

"How about tonight," said Suzanne. "Nine o'clock?"

"Lidiaaaa!" bellowed Claes Elam. His shoulders were squared, his face was beet red, and a dark aura seemed to hang over him as he strode toward them.

Sensing an impending blowup, Suzanne thought fast and switched conversational gears. "So you'd be interested in selling to my store?" she asked Lidia, trying to make her voice sound light and breezy.

"Get away from her!" Elam screamed. "Get out of here! This is private property, and you are trespassing!" He shouted this last statement directly into Suzanne's face.

"You needn't be rude," Suzanne told him firmly. "I'm only here because I'm interested in sourcing homemade goods for my shop."

"Do you not hear me?" he bellowed. "Leave us now!" Elam threw back his head and, in an overly theatrical gesture, pointed at Suzanne's car. "Go!"

"Perhaps you've heard of us?" Suzanne continued in a normal tone of voice. "The Cackleberry Club? We sell a lovely assortment of home-baked pies and fresh produce."

"Enough!" shrilled Elam, and now spit seemed to fly from his mouth.

"Awright," said Suzanne, throwing up her hands, trying to act casual even though she was scared shitless by this maniac. "I get the message. You don't have to freak out." Suzanne turned to go, but not before she tried to catch Lidia's eye. But Lidia was staring firmly at the ground, her hands twitching, her face a mask of contriteness.

Suzanne had no idea if the woman would be brave enough to show up at the antique store tonight. She could only pray that Lidia would somehow dig into her inner reserve and find a dab of courage. Because if ever a girl seemed to dearly need help, it was this one.

CHAPTER 20

"WHAT are you doing here?" Toni looked up from one of the tables where she was stacking dirty dishes into a gray plastic tub.

"Checkin' on you guys," Suzanne told her.

"No, you're not," snorted Toni. "You know Petra and I have things way under control. You're just at loose ends. You did your laundry, grocery shopping, errands, whatever, and now you're itchin' for something to do."

"Could be," said Suzanne, as she slipped past Toni and pushed her way through the swinging door. Baking smells greeted her, wonderful aromas that signaled flour, eggs, butter, and cream had been mixed together by a talented kitchen alchemist. And, sure enough, there was Petra, bent over a cake, pastry bag in hand. The three-tiered cake she was working on was tall and elegant, covered in white frosting. Each layer featured a giant hot pink ruffled rose made from sugary fondant. Sprinkled around it were rose petals from the same fondant. "Wow, great cake," said Suzanne. "Who's it for?"

Petra squirted a final squiggle of gold frosting to finish

off the script across the bottom layer. "The Burmeister an-
niversary party tonight. Forty happy years."

Toni banged her way through the door, set down her
tub, and scrutinized Petra's cake. "I thought it was spelled
f-o-u-r-t-y."

"No way," said Suzanne.

"Sure it is." Toni thought for a minute. "You sure it's not
spelled f-o-u-r-t-y?" She gazed at Petra, who shook her
head no. "Well, it's a pretty cake, anyway, even if the sentiment or whatever you call it is misspelled." Toni put her
hands on her hips. "Yeah, I like that rose petal effect. Real
fancy."

"So . . . what?" Petra asked Suzanne. "You were just in
the neighborhood?" She added a final curled rose petal,
then stepped back, admiring her work.

"Something like that," responded Suzanne. "Anyway,
I'm not gonna bother you guys. I just want to duck in the
office and do a little Internet research."

"Sounds mysterious," said Toni.

"Not really," responded Suzanne. She was mulling over
in her mind if she should tell them about her little encounter with Claes Elam. If she did, they'd just worry. So for
now she decided to remain mum.

"You want a scone?" asked Toni. "I just put a bunch in
the cake saver out front. And brewed a fresh pot of tea. Assam. You always like Assam."

"Sold," said Suzanne. She followed Toni out to the
front, where two of the tables were occupied. The customers were having pie and coffee, although one of the women
was eating a scone.

"Petra made cream scones," said Toni, gently fishing
one of the large, golden scones from the pie saver, then
placing it on a plate that held a pristine white paper doily.
So maybe you want some lemon curd with it?"

Suzanne nodded. "Take a dollop."

"We were super busy earlier," said Toni. "Now things
have tapered off. Probably because it looks like it's really

gonna storm." She glanced up sharply just as the door flew open, and a woman stepped tentatively into the café. Clad in a nondescript brown dress, the newcomer's gray hair was flyaway, and her eyes seemed slightly unfocused.

"Help you?" asked Toni. She handed the scone to Suzanne and edged toward the woman.

"You're Suzanne?" the woman asked. Her voice had a nasal quality to it, although that could have been a result of crying. Her eyes did look red and swollen in a face that bore not a speck of makeup.

"I'm Suzanne," said Suzanne, taking a step forward.

"I'm Annie Pepper," the woman said. "Charlie's wife."

"Oh sure," said Suzanne, "sorry I didn't recognize you at first."

Annie Pepper waved a hand.

"Let's go somewhere where we can talk, shall we?" said Suzanne. Without waiting for an answer, she guided Annie Pepper toward the Book Nook. Toni watched them with a speculative look.

Parking Mrs. Pepper in one of the overstuffed chairs, Suzanne sat across from her in a swivel chair, a comfortable orange bucket design that looked like it had once been owned by the Jetsons. "What can I do for you?" she asked, noting that this was the second time today she'd offered assistance to a woman who seemed to be in some distress.

"Charlie quit delivering to you, right?" asked Annie.

"Uh, that's right," said Suzanne.

"He's gone a little crazy," Annie said in a hoarse whisper, her lower lip beginning to quiver. "Poor Charlie thinks he's under surveillance by the FBI or CIA or somethin'. And it's all because of"—she rolled her eyes—"the murders."

"I know Sheriff Doogie talked to Charlie," said Suzanne, "but that was just routine. Doogie pretty much interviewed everyone who'd been in and around here."

Annie leaned forward. "So you don't think Charlie's been singled out?"

Suzanne bit her lower lip. Lie? Fib? Fudge? Why not? "No, I don't think so," she told Annie. "And if Doogie's been a little overzealous in doing his job, it's probably because he's under a lot of pressure."

"Really?" asked Annie.

"Sure," said Suzanne.

Annie seemed to relax a bit. "Charlie's a good man; he really is."

Suzanne wasn't sure what to say. Charlie hadn't been particularly cordial to her this morning. In fact, he'd been downright menacing. "Uh, Annie," said Suzanne, "did Charlie ever resolve his thing with Bobby?"

"You mean that lawsuit with the Chemco company?" Annie asked.

"Yeah."

"I think Charlie was over it. He wasn't happy the way things worked out—or didn't work out, but Charlie doesn't hold much of a grudge."

This was news to Suzanne. "But Charlie does have a temper."

Annie's eyes slid away from her. "Sometimes," she admitted. "And the gambling can be a problem. Charlie gets awful upset when he loses."

Suzanne put her hands on her knees and leaned forward. "Annie, what do you want? Why exactly did you come here?"

Now Annie seemed embarrassed. "I came to see if you'd take Charlie back. His eggs, I mean. You know as well as I do they're fine eggs. Our hens are all free range. You won't find a cage anywhere on our farm."

"Charlie was the one who called it quits with us," Suzanne reminded her.

"But still," persisted Annie. "Would you take him back?"

Suzanne thought for a few moments. Did she really want Charlie Pepper careening through her back door while two murders remained unsolved? No, probably not.

"Tell you what," said Suzanne. "Once Sheriff Doogie wraps up these two cases, we'll for sure talk about it."

"WELL?" asked Toni, once Annie had left.

"So?" asked Petra, who stuck her head through the pass-through.

"She wants Charlie to be our egg man again," said Suzanne.

"What'd you tell her?" asked Petra.

Suzanne shrugged. "That we'll discuss his reinstatement after the murders are cleared up."

"You mean once Doogie gets off his fat ass and solves the crimes," said Toni.

"Why was she so upset?" asked Petra. "It's got to be more than just eggs."

"Annie says Charlie is paranoid," said Suzanne. "That he's waiting for the SWAT team guys in the black helicopters to drop down and grab him."

"Oh boy," said Petra.

"And," Suzanne continued, "he's apparently been gambling heavily and is upset by his losses."

"Sheesh," said Toni. "I hate losing at bingo, but I don't run around screaming at people."

Petra raised her eyebrows.

"Okay, so I got a little grouchy at Lotsa Luck Bingo when my dauber ran dry. So what!"

"At least you didn't bet the store," laughed Petra.

BACK in the office, Suzanne turned on the computer and watched as a new screen saver came on. Petra had been busy again. This time she'd scanned in some adorable, round-faced Botticelli angels and added the words, "When someone dies, an angel is there to meet them at the gates of heaven to let them know their life has just begun."

A comforting thought, Suzanne decided. Especially

since she was about to run a search on Claes Elam. And then venture back near his compound tonight. She could use a little angel power watching over her.

Suzanne hunched over the keyboard and Googled the word "Neukommen," then added "Claes Elam." She hit Search and waited to see if anything came up.

There were a few hits. Not as many as she thought there might be.

She found a short article from the *Bugle* that talked about the Neukommen group buying the old Sedelmeyer farm. And another local article about trends in organic farming that only mentioned Neukommen in passing.

Suzanne finally stumbled across one disturbing newspaper article from a small paper in Goshen, Indiana. A man by the name of Claes Elam had been brought up on charges of spousal abuse. But the charges against him had been dropped when the wife recanted her statement. The article further went on to report that the commune had packed up and moved out of the community shortly thereafter.

Was this the same Claes Elam? Suzanne wondered. Had to be. The impromptu flight had happened shortly before Neukommen had moved into the Kindred area.

Had the battered wife been Lidia? The article didn't say.

Suzanne did another quick search on cults. And found that cults and offbeat sects were definitely a big business.

Of course, the problem of a group built on twisted beliefs was hardly a twenty-first-century issue. Cults dated back to the beginning of time. Human beings, needful creatures that they were, always seemed to be looking for something. And there was always someone, often a demented leader with his own agenda, willing to help them find it. Especially if money, complete obedience, or sexual favors were part of the deal.

Interestingly, Suzanne found lots of information about deprogramming, too. Which prompted Suzanne to wonder, if Lidia wanted to leave Neukommen, and if Bobby had been trying to help her, would it be easy for her to give up the load of propaganda Claes Elam had probably been feeding her? Stop drinking the Kool-Aid, so to speak?

Searching through all this information on cults and cult leaders was making Suzanne nervous and edgy, so she turned her attention to researching Claiborne Corrections Corporation.

Turns out, private penal institutions were more common than she had thought. And Claiborne was a fast-growing company.

Who gave kickbacks? Or had contractors or subcontractors who did?

How many levels would she have to go down before she found some answers? Suzanne wasn't sure, but she knew one thing. She wasn't going to find Walter's name attached to any illegal deal. She knew that in her heart.

CHAPTER 21

LARGE drops of rain splotched down on Suzanne's wind-shield. The temperature had fallen a good twenty degrees but now seemed stalled at that awkward stage where air temperature collided with humidity, making it necessary to run the defroster nonstop. But even with the defroster sputtering away on high, Suzanne still had to swipe the insides of the windows with her hand.

A huge flash of lightning seared the night sky, illuminating the landscape, revealing rain pelting down even harder now, lighting up the little antique shop that was just ahead of her.

Crunching across the gravel parking lot, Suzanne pulled directly in front of Mona's Antiques and rolled to a stop. The place looked completely deserted. No lights burned inside. Good.

From the comfort of her car, Suzanne continued to gaze at the little shop. It was your basic whitewashed wooden building with a sharply pitched roof and small front porch. Up on the porch, a spinning wheel and butter churn sat next to an old-fashioned rocker. A row of dried corn cobs dangled from the edge of the porch's low roof. In the side yard, a collection of wooden wheels and farm wagons was scattered about. Behind that was a small graveyard, just a handful of cracked and tilting gravestones inside a rusting wrought-iron fence. Probably, Suzanne decided, this building had once been a farmhouse and the graveyard the family burial plot.

Suzanne eased open the car door, stepped out into an inch of standing water, then sprinted up onto the porch. She ran her fingers through her tousled hair, wiggled her shoulders like a duck shaking off water, then eased over to the rocking chair. She plopped herself down, happy to find a dry, comfortable place to wait.

Peeking at her watch, Suzanne saw it was just a few minutes before nine. Hopefully, she wouldn't have to wait too long, and Lidia would really show up. The girl had seemed so unhappy and nervous earlier today, as though she were itching to escape Claes and his merry band of . . . whatever they were.

Wind howled through the eaves above her, and water gurgled down metal drain spouts as Suzanne rocked slowly and thought about the Neukommen group as well as the kickback investigation that had seemingly popped up out of nowhere.

The research she'd done earlier had really opened her eyes about the business of private prisons. Penal institutions were not something Suzanne had paid much attention to before Walter had agreed to serve on the planning committee. In fact, she hadn't given it much thought afterward, either. She vaguely remembered that Claiborne Corrections had assured the folks of Kindred that privatization not only saved taxpayers money but also provided local jobs as well as county revenue at the same time.

The town council's vote to approve the prison's building outside of Kindred had been close, something like five to three. Suzanne figured that Mayor Mobley had voted yes,

Missy Langston had voted no. She didn't know about the others.

But scoring the prison had been a major coup for both Kindred and Claiborne Corrections. The business of imprisonment ran the gamut of food service to personnel to high-tech security. There was money to be made and, according to the research she'd done, the sky was the limit.

No wonder four million dollars had somehow disappeared. Probably greasing the skids somewhere. Just not Walter's skids.

Suzanne suddenly realized she'd been ruminating for a good ten minutes. Was Lidia going to show up or not? She hunched forward and looked around. Rain continued to pour down in giant sheets; the temperature felt like it had plummeted another ten degrees.

Wrapping her arms around herself, Suzanne decided she'd give it another ten minutes. She was tired and also feeling something akin to disappointment. Had Lidia changed her mind? Had Claes somehow interfered?

That idea unnerved Suzanne a bit, and the thought suddenly struck her that she was sitting in the middle of nowhere all by herself. She dug in her handbag for her cell phone. There, that made her feel better. If something happened, she could always fire off a call for help.

Ten minutes later, Suzanne stood up. Lidia hadn't shown up and probably wasn't going to. Maybe the rain had made it difficult; maybe something else had happened. Either way, there was nothing she could do about it tonight. Not every good deed turns out the way you want it to.

As Suzanne stood on the rickety porch, her hand touching the banister, a car suddenly approached from down the road. As it swept past Mona's Antiques, red taillights suddenly flared, and the car shuddered to a stop some hundred yards down the road.

Oh, shit. What is this?

Lidia? Somehow, Suzanne didn't think so.

Who then?

The rain was still pelting down, thunder rumbling all around her. With visibility severely curtailed, Suzanne could barely make out the parked car in the distance. She couldn't tell if someone was still sitting inside or if they'd stepped out.

Now what? Hunker back in the shadows of the porch? Or make a dash for her own car?

No, Suzanne told herself, calm down, call 911, and tell the operator where you are and that you think someone might be following you. *Is* following you. Be a blip on their radar, just in case.

She punched in the number and hit Send. The words on the tiny LED monitor flashed, "Call Failed."

Suzanne tried again. Nothing.

Oh great. So now what? Make a dash? Yeah, I'm gonna make a dash.

So, of course she needed keys. Suzanne pawed in her purse again, found her jangle of keys.

Go . . . now!

Lightning blazed just as Suzanne sprinted off the porch and headed for her car. And just as her fingers touched the car door, she was stunned to see a man standing alongside the mysterious parked car. With rain streaming in her eyes, he looked tall, thin, and dangerous.

Jerking her door open, feeling woozy and frantic, Suzanne hunched her shoulders forward, almost expecting to hear the crack of an automatic weapon.

Then she was hurling herself inside, locking the door behind her, jamming her key into the ignition. Suzanne gunned the engine, threw the transmission into reverse, and pushed the gas pedal to the floor. She sped backward a good fifty feet, never taking her eyes off the parked car ahead of her.

When she finally hit pavement, Suzanne spun her car in a tight 180-degree turn. It was a daring maneuver, similar to the techniques learned by students in those fancy evasive driving schools. While Suzanne wasn't trying to save the world or outwit terrorists, she did want to haul ass out of there.

Speeding back toward Kindred, Suzanne kept one eye glued on her rearview mirror to check if someone was following her.

Luckily for her, they weren't.

A massive bolt of lightning struck again, lighting up the bedroom and causing a groggy Suzanne to sit up straight in bed. Now a second lightning bolt flashed and sizzled like fireworks gone awry. Suzanne was positive one of the oak trees in her front yard had been zapped.

Wind continued to swirl around her house, and hard rain drilled her roof. Suzanne figured that the squirrels who lived in her attic, the ones she heard rolling acorns as if they were having a pro bowling tournament, were probably going bonkers. She sure was. It was doubtful she'd be able to fall back to sleep until this fierce storm finally moved out of the county.

Snuggling back down, Suzanne pulled a feather pillow over her head, trying to drown out the volume of noise. Of course, she wasn't the only one who disliked violent weather. Baxter was hunkered down next to her, rolling his eyes, whimpering in fear at every clap of thunder.

Lightning flickered again, and then . . .

Thunk!

Suzanne's eyes flew open. What was that? Tree branch hitting the roof? Neighbor's house tumbling away like Dorothy's farmhouse in *The Wizard of Oz*? Her oak tree really being hit?

As the storm seemed to build in intensity, Baxter pulled himself up and started to bark, his instinct to protect the home place overriding his aversion to rotten weather.

"Shush, be quiet, Baxter," Suzanne commanded.

"Rowrrr," he answered back.

She listened again, wondering if she was really hearing

pounding. She thought about calling 911 but couldn't decide what to tell the dispatcher. *Someone's knocking on my back door? A shutter came loose? The squirrels in the attic are staging a palace coup?*

Doogie already thought she was close to being a lunatic. She didn't want to add "paranoid, fraidy-cat female" to his arsenal of insults.

Suzanne blinked and stared at the combination CD player/alarm clock that sat on her nightstand. The reassuring pale green glow was gone, which meant the power was out.

Struggling into her terry cloth robe, Suzanne crept down the stairs in the dark. Baxter padded softly behind her. No way did he want to be left behind. After all, the dog ghoulies might grab him.

Suzanne fervently hoped it was just her fuse box on the blink and not some ax-wielding Jason-in-a-hockey-mask wannabe hacking away at the transformer box.

But when she hit the bottom landing, she could see into her front room and all the way through the picture window. Every streetlamp on her block was dark. In fact, the entire neighborhood was dark.

Knowing her neighbors were in the same boat came as a great relief.

Thunk.

Except there was that weird noise again, setting her teeth on edge. Not good. After all, Kindred hadn't exactly been a haven of safety these last few days.

Shuffling nervously into the kitchen, Suzanne put her hands out in front of her until she found the edge of the counter. Then she eased herself along until she came to her block of J. A. Henckels chef's knives. High carbon stainless steel, German engineered. Her fingertips danced lightly on the butts of the knives until she came to the largest butcher knife. Grasping the handle, she pulled it free, felt instantly more confident. She would have preferred a .38, but this is what she had.

Okay, now what?

Suzanne dug her free hand into her utility drawer, pawing around for a flashlight. When she found one, she flicked it on, aimed the beam directly at the back door. Checked the Schlage dead bolt lock set directly at eye level, ran the beam lower to the button on the doorknob.

And that's when things got weird.

Because just as the thin, wavering light hit the doorknob, it slowly started to turn.

Suzanne almost screamed! Yes, that door was solid oak and possessed a tried and true dead bolt, but still . . . someone was out there!

A scream rose in Suzanne's throat, then morphed into an angry growl as she fought to control the panic that rose up inside her.

No! she told herself fiercely. *Don't panic, don't run. Stand your ground and try to be . . . cool. Try to think.*

Easier said than done.

But she also had to figure out what she was up against! What was out there? Who was out there?

The window over the sink offered a view of the entire back porch and yard. Slowly, quietly, Suzanne pushed a kitchen chair over to the edge of the sink. She set her flashlight and knife down on the counter, then climbed onto the chair and put a knee on one side of the stainless steel sink. Balanced the other knee on the narrow divider. Awkwardly straddling the sink and pulling back the curtains, Suzanne peered out tentatively.

Darkness. Where were those spectacular lightning flashes that had woken her earlier? She sure could use some now.

As if on cue, lightning flared overhead. Her heart in her throat, Suzanne stared out into the backyard. She saw no movement, nothing out of place. As lightning flashed repeatedly, turning the sky into a veritable strobe light, she felt an odd déjà vu, like she was back in college, dancing under a strobe, writhing to the theme from *Flashdance* or Donna Summers's "She Works Hard for the Money."

She shook her head, trying to focus. Lightning had leached color from the trees, making everything look like a black-and-white negative. As Suzanne's eyes moved across the backyard again and over to the back stoop, she suddenly caught sight of something that looked like a pile of rags.

Huh? Wasn't there before.

Her mind didn't seem to be tracking as well as it should. Fear and nervousness hadn't heightened her senses at all. Instead, Suzanne felt sluggish, plodding.

Then the rags moved slightly, as if shivering in the cold.

Suzanne put a hand to her mouth. "Oh my God," she gasped.

Jumping down from the sink, she unlocked the door and rushed outside. Rain pelted her face as she switched on the flashlight and pointed it directly at the pile of rags. A small, white oval face peered up at her.

It was Lidia.

·CHAPTER 22·

SUZANNE's kitchen glowed like a shrine at Lourdes. Candles flickered everywhere. Votives, tapers, tea lights. Even the green frog candle she'd won at a library raffle had been enlisted.

Lidia sat huddled at the table as Suzanne filled a tea kettle with water and set it to heat on the gas stove, which thankfully still worked. Baxter sat a safe distance away from Lidia, reserving judgment.

Lidia's clothes were soaked and torn. Her breath was labored, and her eyes looked glazed over, as if she were on drugs or in shock. She hadn't spoken a word yet.

"Get something hot inside you, help you warm up," mumbled Suzanne. She was still trying to figure out how Lidia had made it to her house in the middle of a storm. How the girl had even known which house was hers.

As Lidia shivered yet again, Suzanne slipped off her terry cloth robe and draped it around Lidia's shoulders. "Maybe we should get you out of those wet clothes. What do you think?"

Still no answer.

Suzanne placed her fingers under the young woman's chin and lifted her face. And, for the first time, noticed blood caked around the edges of Lidia's mouth.

"What happened?" asked a startled Suzanne.

Lidia shook her head, and droplets of bright red seeped from her mouth and ran down her face in rivulets.

"You're bleeding!" Suzanne exclaimed. "Are you hurt? Did you fall down?"

Lidia shook her head, looking miserable.

"Please answer me." Suzanne was getting a funny, uneasy feeling deep in the pit of her stomach. "Do you know what happened? Do you know you're bleeding?"

Lidia wiped dirty hands across her mouth. "I'll be okay," she whispered in a sad, defeated tone.

Suzanne crouched down on the linoleum so they could be eye to eye. "You don't look okay. And you don't sound okay. Lidia, open your mouth. Let me see where you're cut."

Tears streaked Lidia's narrow face as she opened her mouth. Two of the girl's lower teeth were missing. Blood oozed from fresh wounds where her teeth should have been.

Suzanne reeled back in horror. "Dear Lord, what happened?"

"Punishment," whispered Lidia.

"Claes did this?" Suzanne didn't know whether to scream or cry.

Lidia nodded miserably.

"For . . . for talking to me this afternoon?"

"I suppose," was Lidia's soft answer.

Suzanne pushed herself up and snatched a clean towel. She ran it under warm water and then was back again, ministering to Lidia. "We have to stop this bleeding." She pushed the towel against Lidia's mouth. "Hold it tight against your mouth, honey. Let me think for a minute."

He did that to Lidia just for talking to me? Suzanne was suddenly flooded with guilt and remorse. And a trickle of pure fear. If she hadn't gone out there, he wouldn't have . . .

No, she told herself sternly. *This isn't about you right now; got to get help for Lidia.*

But where to go? What to do? Hospital? Sure, yeah, gotta get her to the hospital. The ER. They'll know what to do.

"Tilt your head back a little, Lidia," Suzanne instructed. She was feeling almost faint; she'd never seen such butchery. It was positively medieval. "I'm going to run upstairs and get you some dry clothes. Then we're going to take a quick ride to the hospital."

"No!" Lidia recoiled from her.

"You're hurt, honey. Hurt bad. You need to see a doctor."

"No hospital." Lidia was adamant.

Suzanne could be just as stubborn. "Yes, hospital. Then we have to get you out of here. And I don't mean just here, my place, I mean out of town. Out of the area if possible."

"No," said Lidia again. "Not without Trinity."

Suzanne frowned at her. Who on earth was Trinity? A female friend at the compound? Her cat?

"My daughter," said Lidia, as if reading Suzanne's mind.

Oh my God, thought Suzanne. Could this get any worse? "You have a child?"

"I do," whispered Lidia.

"And she's still with the Neukommen people?" Suzanne was stunned.

"Yes." Lidia's answer was almost painful.

"Okay, okay," said Suzanne, her brain spinning into overdrive. "We gotta think about this. But first we go to the hospital."

Lidia shook her head stubbornly. "No. Claes might come."

Suzanne knew she had to think fast. "A nurse then," she proposed. "Someone with medical training." She had no idea what kind of damage had been done inside Lidia's mouth, but she was afraid of bleeding, infection, complications, whatever.

Suzanne looked at Baxter, who stared back at her. He seemed to grasp the gravity of the situation. His tail thudded against the floor in a supportive gesture.

Suzanne spun on her heel and snatched the phone off the hook, praying that it was working. It was. From memory, she dialed the number for the Wellspring Hospice. With any luck, Angie Hathaway, the nurse who'd taken such good care of Walter, would be there tonight.

LUCK was with them.

"My Lord, girl, what did they do to you?" Angie Hathaway shook her head and stared at Lidia. Angie was a no-nonsense woman with a plain, kindly face who wore her glasses on a chain around her neck. With her snow white hair, white uniform, and white Nikes, she looked like an aging angel, albeit an angel with a nursing degree.

They were crowded into a small medical supply room. White laminate shelves were stacked with gauze, syringes, bandages, and gowns. A collapsible wheelchair was jammed into one corner. There was also a sink and counter with a drug cabinet above it. A key, Angie's key, dangled from the lock.

Tears streamed down Lidia's face as she made little mewling sounds, like a homeless kitten.

"Hush, just open your mouth a little," prompted Angie.

Lidia finally complied, allowing Angie to survey the damage.

Angie shook her head. "She needs stitches."

"Can you do it?" asked Suzanne. She knew Angie was a very capable woman who probably knew as much as most doctors.

"Heavens no," said Angie, "this girl should probably see an oral surgeon." She gently inserted a wooden tongue depressor in the side of Lidia's mouth, taking care not to touch the affected area. "She's pretty much been butch-ered."

Lidia shook her head resolutely. "No. No doctor, no hospital." Her hand crept out and grasped Angie's hand. "You do it. Please?"

"I'm not qualified," protested Angie. She was sympa-thetic but knew this was beyond her skills.

"Can't you do something?" asked Suzanne. "A stopgap until I get her to change her mind?"

Angie thought for a moment, then spoke directly to Lidia. "I can rinse your wounds with saline and pack them, but you're still probably gonna need stitches."

Lidia nodded. "Okay." Then she turned her pleading eyes on Suzanne. "But first we get Trinity? Like you prom-ised?"

Suzanne had to agree. "Okay, okay. We'll get Trinity. Tomorrow we'll go get Trinity."

CHAPTER 23

"I hope you realize you're late," Petra called out as Suzanne stepped through the back door and into the kitchen. She was facing the gas range and cracking brown-speckled eggs into a large yellow bowl, two at a time. "The Quatro Cheese Quiches are already in the oven, and so are the poppy seed buns. Which means I really had to hustle *my* buns, since Sundays are always so busy."

"Last night was a bit of a *Twilight Zone* episode," Suzanne told her.

"Lost your power?" Petra asked, whirling around, wire whisk in hand. She gazed quizzically at Suzanne, then her eyes fell on Lidia, who cowered two steps behind her. "Looks like you brought a friend," Petra said in a gentler voice.

"This is Lidia," said Suzanne. "And do we ever have a story to tell."

Suzanne quickly filled Petra in about her visit to Neukommen, meeting Lidia, getting chased off by Claes Elam, then Lidia showing up in the middle of last night's storm. Petra's eyes got bigger and bigger as each chapter unfolded. And when Suzanne finally got to the part about the pulled teeth, Petra let out a horrified gasp and clapped a hand over her mouth.

"Sounds like something out of a horror film," said Petra, when Suzanne had finally finished. Her gaze shifted to Lidia. "Are you in pain?"

Lidia's thin shoulders rose in a shrug. How could she not be hurting?

"Suzanne's right, you know," Petra told the girl, but with sympathy in her voice. "You've got to see a doctor. And Suzanne, you've got to call Sheriff Doogie immediately."

"Can't," said Suzanne. "There's more to it."

"More?" said a startled Petra.

"Trinity," said Lidia. Although this time it came out *Twinity,* because of swelling in her mouth and gums.

Petra looked genuinely confused. "Who on earth is Trinity?"

So, of course, Suzanne had to finish the story.

Petra was appalled and outraged. "Her child is still out there? Good Lord, that's awful. Who knows what could happen!" Then, seeing the stricken look on Lidia's face, Petra softened her statement by adding, "Hopefully, one of the other women will look out for your little girl."

Lidia nodded, but there were tears in her eyes.

"That's why I don't want to call Doogie," said Suzanne. "My plan is to go back out there tonight and get Lidia's daughter."

Petra raised her eyebrows. "Just sneak in there? Stage some kind of commando attack?"

"Well, sort of," said Suzanne. She hadn't formulated a detailed plan yet, but that was the gist of it. "And then I'll spirit Lidia and Trinity over to that women's shelter in Jessup where they'll hopefully be safe. And where the law will protect them."

"Harmony House," murmured Petra.

"That's the place," said Suzanne. "The director, a woman by the name of Sookie Sands, is a real firecracker. She started the place on a shoestring, then hustled up all sorts of grants and donations to keep it going."

"Uh-huh," said Petra, nodding. "And you're adamant about not calling Doogie?"

"He doesn't have any jurisdiction over the Neukommen group," said Suzanne. "They're the next county over."

"I see," said Petra. But by the look on her face, it was obvious she really didn't.

"So Lidia's going to spend the day upstairs in our loft, while I figure things out," Suzanne said with far more heartiness than she felt. The Cackleberry Club had a half-floor loft above the Book Nook. Most of the time it was used for book storage, but it was clean and cozy and had a nice futon. In fact, Toni had slept up there for a week or so after she'd left Junior and before she'd moved into her apartment.

"Better get her upstairs then," said Petra. "We've got Emily coming in to help today, and you know how she likes to talk." Emily was a student in culinary arts at Darlington College. She was terrific in the kitchen but no great shakes as a waitress, which was what they really needed today.

SUZANNE took five minutes to get Lidia settled, then hustled back downstairs. Emily came charging in, ready to help, and Sheriff Doogie was close on her heels. Suzanne figured this thing with Lidia was going to come back to haunt her; she just didn't think it would happen this fast.

Doogie settled his bulk at the counter and immediately corralled Suzanne.

"I got a call this morning. From a fellow by the name of Claes Elam."

"Really," said Suzanne. Her hand remained steady as she poured coffee into a ceramic mug for Doogie.

"Elam says you were at his place yesterday, stirring up trouble with his people. Trespassing. He was pretty hot under the collar about it."

Suzanne slid the coffee across the counter with a smile. She had her story worked out and was gonna ride that horse forever. "I did stop by there," Suzanne told him, "hoping they might sell me some of their organic peas and carrots and zucchini. We're thinking of adding an organic vegetable quiche to our repertoire."

"Vegetables?" said Doogie. He suddenly looked confused.

"Yes," said Suzanne. "You know, those pesky crunchy things that the Department of Agriculture recommends you eat three to five servings of each day? Don't you know your food pyramid, Sheriff?"

Doogie ignored her question. "This Elam fella says you were chitchatting with his wife. Then he starts screaming about how she disappeared last night. Run off somewhere."

"Disappeared?" said Suzanne. Surprise showed on her face. First she'd heard, right?

Doogie peered at her sharply. "Listen to me, Suzanne, we're not playing twenty questions. This is serious stuff."

"Maybe she ran off with another guy," suggested Suzanne. She was aware of Petra hovering on the other side of the pass-through. "Women are like that, you know. Fickle in their ways." She threw in a knowing eye roll.

"Did you kidnap or otherwise entice Lidia Elam away from the Neukommen farm?" Doogie had his serious face on.

"Kidnap or entice?" said Suzanne. "No. I most certainly did not." *I offered to help, and that was it.*

"But you were there."

"I just told you I was." Suzanne stared at Doogie. "But I have to say, it struck me as a strange, somewhat sinister place. Lots of inhospitable vibes and women possibly being held against their will. So I can see why someone might try to get out of Dodge."

Doogie blew on his coffee, then took a quick sip. He grimaced, as if it was still too hot. But he also seemed satisfied with Suzanne's answers. "For a man of the cloth, that Claes Elam sure knows a few choice words."

"You think he's really a man of the cloth?" asked Suzanne. She'd pretty much come to the conclusion that Elam was a fake, a poser.

Doogie hunched his shoulders. "That's not the point. He's worried a crime might have been committed."

"Last I heard, people could come and go whenever they wanted in the good old U.S. of A. Besides," Suzanne pointed out, "Claes Elam doesn't even live in your jurisdiction. The Neukommen farm's located in Deer County."

"It's only a corncob's throw away," said Doogie. "And for some reason he thinks his wife might've come *here*. Which makes it my business."

"Sheriff," said Petra, pushing her way through the swinging door, smiling sweetly, balancing a large tray of sweet rolls, muffins, and scones. "Can I interest you in some fresh baked goods?"

As Sheriff Doogie shifted his attention to her tray, his eyes practically popped out of his head. "Is that a caramel roll?" he asked.

"A *chocolate* caramel roll," said Petra. "With candied pecans." She set the tray down, grabbed a pair of silver tongs, and placed one of the sticky rolls on a plate for Doogie. "And I have strawberry rhubarb breakfast rolls, too. And pineapple scones."

"Oh boy," said Doogie. He looked like he was going to pass out from ecstasy.

"Suzanne, get a couple pats of butter for the sheriff, will you?" asked Petra.

Suzanne got the butter and brought it back to Doogie. By that time, he'd already wolfed down half of his caramel roll.

"Man, this is good," purred Doogie. He was definitely enjoying his carb fix and had blessedly dropped his line of questioning. Now Suzanne figured she could ask a few questions of her own.

"What's going on with Junior?" Suzanne inquired. She did a quick check on Emily, who seemed to be holding her own.

Doogie scooped up an entire pat of butter, slathered it on the rest of his roll. "Not much," he answered, his mouth full. He glanced around. "Where's Toni?"

"She's off today," Suzanne told him. "So you can go ahead and talk freely. If you want."

Doogie grunted. "Just waitin' for the ballistics report."

"Do you think it was Junior's gun that killed Bobby and Teddy?"

"What you're really asking," said Doogie, "is, did Junior do it?"

"I guess I am," said Suzanne.

"Well, I don't know that yet," said Doogie. "Junior's got a prickly temper, that's for sure. Plus I made a few phone calls and found out the boy genuinely likes his guns."

"So Junior owns more than one weapon?" asked Suzanne.

"Let me put it this way," said Doogie, "he's been working on his collection."

"But if Junior's weapon comes back clean, if the ballistics don't match, then he's off the hook?" asked Suzanne.

"Maybe," said Doogie. "It doesn't mean Junior didn't pick up a spare weapon at a gun show or through a private sale, though."

Suzanne gazed across the top of Doogie's hat, wondering about motive. Bobby had drawn up divorce papers for Toni, which had really ticked Junior off. And, of course, Junior had been fired by Garland, Teddy's son. Maybe Junior had seen Garland's truck roar by, driven by Teddy, and then suddenly gone crazy, just like Toni had speculated. Junior might have just lost it. He did have one hell of a temper.

"I'M not sure what the soup du jour is," said Emily, fumbling with her order pad, giving an embarrassed apology to her customer. "Let me ask."

She ran back to the counter where Suzanne was refreshing a customer's coffee. "I am *so* sorry, Suzanne. Please tell me again what the soup of the day is."

"No problem," said Suzanne. "It's curried sweet potato soup. But it's listed on the blackboard." She tapped at the sign with a fingertip.

"Oh," said Emily, glancing up, seeing the day's special spelled out in pink and orange chalk. "You must think I'm a big goof, huh?"

"Not at all. You've just discovered that working the front of the house is a lot different than being in the kitchen."

"That's for sure," said Emily.

"It takes experience to become a good waitperson. And if it's any consolation, Petra tells me you're already a terrific pastry chef."

"That's my dream," said Emily. "To graduate as a pastry chef. To be as good as Petra."

"She's a pistol," admitted Suzanne.

"She told me you guys were even going to host a cake show this fall. With classes and contests and all that good stuff. I'd love to be part of it. Maybe even enter the cake-decorating contest myself."

"Stick around then," said Suzanne. "We'll need all the help we can get."

WHEN there was a lull, when Emily seemed to be humming along at a faster, more confident pace, Suzanne slipped into the Book Nook. Three boxes of books had been delivered yesterday, and they were still unopened. The week's crisis had taken a toll on the Cackleberry Club's usually efficient operation.

Grabbing a box cutter, Suzanne sat down on a stool and began to slice open cartons. When she was finished, forty-eight books in shiny new dust jackets littered the counter and floor. Now all she had to do was sort, assign inventory numbers, and find spaces for each book on the already crowded shelves. Suzanne was the one who pretty much decided which books to order, and she'd soon discovered that books were as addictive as her favorite chocolate mousse truffles. She couldn't order just one.

She was sliding the latest John Sandford book into its alphabetical slot when she became aware of footfalls behind her. Then she was suddenly enveloped in a cloud of floral perfume. Tuberose with top notes of ylang-ylang. Something expensive. And romantic. Suzanne pushed the book into place and turned around, ready to assist her well-heeled customer.

Carmen Copeland was standing barely five feet from her.

·CHAPTER 24·

"CAN I help you?" Suzanne stammered. She knew this wasn't the brightest conversation starter. Then again, she didn't know what else to say to Bobby's widow. She wasn't sure if she should offer condolences or greetings, since Carmen had already discarded her widow-in-mourning garb.

In fact, Carmen looked like she'd just returned from a month on the French Riviera. Her skin was lustrous with a light summer tan, her dark hair long and loose, and in her fuchsia sheath dress she looked poised, polished, and slightly lethal. Carmen's strappy sandals had to be Manolos or Jimmy Choos, and the leather hobo bag slung casually over her shoulder looked just like the "it" bags celebrities like Paris, Nicole, and Lindsay carried. Buttersoft leather. Not the imitation spread.

Carmen extended her hand. "I'm Carmen Copeland. You know, Bobby's wife."

Suzanne took her hand. "Suzanne Deitz. Yes, I know who you are. And welcome to the Cackleberry Club. But first let me say, I'm so sorry about Bobby. I thought of him as a friend."

Carmen offered a thin smile. "You're very kind." She gestured at a large overstuffed chair. "Do you have a moment? Can we sit down?"

"Of course," said Suzanne. She watched as Carmen glided toward the chair with ease. Instead of plopping down gracelessly like most customers did, like she did, Carmen seated herself like a lady.

"First time you've been here, isn't it?" asked Suzanne. She smiled at Carmen and, for the first time, the elegant author looked nervous.

"Yes. I probably don't get out as often as I should. Don't do a lot of book signings."

You tore yourself away from work to have dinner with Lester Drummond, Suzanne thought to herself.

"A strange thing," said Suzanne. "We sold out of most of your books this past week. We had a huge inventory of backlist, and now we're down to just a handful."

"I'd be happy to sign whatever's left," offered Carmen.

"Our customers would be thrilled," said Suzanne. "But I know you didn't come here just for that." She was rabidly curious as to why Carmen was sitting across from her.

"You're asking why I chose this time to drop by?" asked Carmen.

Suzanne nodded. Carmen's impromptu visit did seem slightly out of character.

"I wanted to thank you," said Carmen, lowering her voice. "I know you've been . . . well . . . nosing around about Bobby's murder. And that other one, too."

"Who told you I was looking into them?" asked Suzanne. Is that really what she was doing? Well, yes. Sort of.

"Let's just say I have it on good authority," said Carmen.

"You have your sources."

"A writer always has sources," said Carmen, again

favoring Suzanne with a thin smile. "Anyway, long story short, I wanted to tell you that I approve of your, shall we say, *parallel* investigation."

"I wouldn't exactly characterize my amateur sleuthing as an investigation," Suzanne said slowly. She felt like she might be on shaky turf here. She wasn't sure if she should be flattered by Carmen's praise or nervous about being questioned by someone who could be a possible suspect. Time, once again, to try to stay cool. To reserve judgment.

"I'm not particularly overwhelmed by Sheriff Doogie's investigating skills," said Carmen. And now a little of her haughtiness came through.

"Don't underestimate Doogie," Suzanne told her. "He's actually quite diligent. I realize he sometimes comes off like a good old boy, but he's very clever at concealing his true skills."

"I should say he is," said Carmen. "Which is one of the reasons I've been considering hiring a private investigator."

"Interesting idea," said Suzanne.

"And probably quite necessary," said Carmen, "since nothing seems to be happening at the moment." She narrowed her eyes and cocked her head to one side. "Or is there? Perhaps you're privy to some new development?"

"Afraid not," said Suzanne. If she was, she certainly wasn't going to tell Carmen. She barely knew the woman. Besides, Carmen had obviously come here to pry. So what now? Pry back? Why not?

"Carmen," said Suzanne. "Perhaps *you* have an idea who might have killed Bobby."

Carmen looked startled but recovered quickly. "Not really," she murmured. "Of course, Bobby had the occasional disgruntled client. Or winning round in court that might possibly make an enemy out of the opposition. But I can't think of anyone who seriously wanted him *dead*." She paused, put a hand to her chest, as though she was deeply distressed. "Obviously, I was wrong."

"Bobby never mentioned any of the grudge holders by name?"

"He'd chatter on about things while we were fixing dinner, but I never listened very hard." Carmen looked sorrowful. "Probably my mistake. Now it's too late."

"Not too late to solve his murder, though," put in Suzanne.

Carmen wiped at her eyes. "Bobby was so wonderful and charming. Shy in his own way, then positively garrulous over a glass of wine." Carmen smiled sadly, remembering. "Every Friday night we'd open a new bottle of wine. You know, to expand our repertoire of taste."

These last revelations puzzled Suzanne. From the way Carmen was speaking about Bobby and their life together, she made it sound picture postcard perfect. Yet Carmen and Bobby had lived in separate houses, in separate towns.

Suzanne wasn't quite sure how to bring up the fact that most happy marriages didn't involve separate housing. It was love, honor, cherish, and take out the garbage, please. And grab those newspapers while you're at it, hon.

She decided the best way to pull more information from Carmen was to flatter her.

"You realize," said Suzanne, "I'm totally in awe of you. To sit down, focus your energy, diligently gather research, then write an entire book seems amazing to me. A feat of heroic proportions. Which is why I can understand why an artist of your caliber might really need their own space."

Carmen held up a hand. "I know where you're going with this. It was one of the first things Sheriff Doogie brought up when he questioned me. In fact, a lot of people found it unusual that we lived apart. But we were both extremely private people. Good together, good apart." Carmen smiled as if she'd given a fine explanation. She really hadn't. "And I did have my house up for sale. Our situation was . . . uh . . . changing."

"Of course you have your other house," said Suzanne, using a matter-of-fact tone but taking a wild guess.

Carmen stared at her. "You mean the one on Long Island? Outside of Montauk?"

"Right," said Suzanne.

"You knew about that?" Carmen seemed unsettled.

Suzanne waved a hand airily and ignored the question. "You're a best-selling author; you need a change of scenery once in a while. And an ocean view is always stimulating." *Had Carmen been planning to leave town?* Suzanne wondered. *Was she still planning to leave?*

"I do like a change of pace," Carmen murmured.

"Carmen," said Suzanne, completely switching gears, "what do you know about the files that were stolen from Bobby's office?"

Carmen sat up straighter. "Nothing. I never got involved in Bobby's business."

"Do you think the theft might be related to Bobby's murder?"

Carmen gave a slight shudder. "No idea. Sheriff Doogie thought it might be, but Sheriff Doogie is"—she searched for the precise words—"bogged down. Obviously ill-equipped to solve these awful crimes."

"Seems like more than just a coincidence," Suzanne pressed. "Bobby murdered, his files stolen the next night."

"Sheriff Doogie has been unable to find a connection so far."

"Actually, there are a couple of connections," said Suzanne. "Though they're a bit tenuous."

"What are you talking about?" asked Carmen. A small frown insinuated itself between her perfectly arched brows. She didn't like being put on the hot seat.

"One of the files had to do with the Neukommen Following," said Suzanne. Another had to do with Walter."

"Walter," said Suzanne.

"My husband. Who passed away."

"Oh," said Carmen. "My condolences. I didn't realize . . ." She stopped. "How do you know which files were stolen?"

"I just know," said Suzanne.

"Missy Langston," snapped Carmen. "Being indiscreet again. I'll have to deal with her—"

"Carmen," said Suzanne. "Were you somehow involved with the Neukommen group?"

Carmen reared back. "No! Why would you even suggest that?"

"How about Claiborne Corrections?"

She shook her head. "Not at all."

Suzanne dug in her heels. "But I happen to know you had dinner with Lester Drummond, the prison warden, just last week."

The frost line, which Suzanne was pretty certain began somewhere near the Arctic Circle, now ran smack-dab through the middle of the Book Nook. The look on Carmen's face went from moderately cordial to ice cold in a matter of seconds.

"How would you know about that?" demanded Carmen. "Who told you? Or were you spying on me? Or spying on Bobby?"

"I wasn't spying," said Suzanne. "But this—"

"This is quite enough," said Carmen, standing up quickly. "I'm afraid I must be going."

"Carmen," Suzanne said to her back. "Help me out. These strange goings-on might all be connected in some weird way. They might—"

But Carmen was already slipping through the door.

Suzanne watched from her window as Carmen strutted across the parking lot, climbed into a dark green Mercedes SUV, and zoomed away.

Now it was Suzanne's turn to frown.

"GET your books put away?" asked Emily, when Suzanne rejoined her in the café.

"Uh, not quite," said Suzanne. "How are you doin'?"

"Great," chirped Emily as she measured Irish breakfast

tea into a blue and white ceramic teapot. "But we're starting to get really busy."

Suzanne glanced around. Three people sat at the counter, two tables were occupied. "Believe me, it's going to get a lot busier."

"When that church down the road lets out, I bet they all head over here, huh?"

"Not really," said Suzanne. For some reason, the Cackleberry Club counted very few members of the Journey's End Church as customers. She wasn't sure why. Maybe the parishioners preferred to stick to themselves, or maybe they were literally poor as church mice and simply couldn't afford breakfast out.

Whatever the reason, it didn't matter, because ten minutes later the Cackleberry Club got slammed. Customers streamed in like crazy. More customers arrived on the front porch, peered in the windows, then milled about, waiting expectantly for tables.

"Help!" Petra yelped from the kitchen. Her voice sounded especially plaintive.

"Go back and give Petra a hand," Suzanne instructed Emily. "Whip up some of those cheesy omelets of yours."

"Really?" Emily was thrilled by the reprieve and delighted to show off her skills on the grill.

"I'll get Joey to help me out here." Suzanne whirled on the slow-moving Joey, who was bip-bopping along to his iPod, clearing tables at a glacial pace. Pulling the buds from his ears, she heard a sharp burst of music, then got right in his face. "Joey, you gotta help me."

"Huh?" He was still wondering where his music had gone.

"We're busy, and I need you to pinch-hit as a waiter."

"Okay."

Pulling him quickly into the kitchen, Suzanne whipped off Joey's short white apron, draped a long black Parisian waiter's apron around his neck, and tied it in back. Then she wrapped a black-and-white bandana around his head.

Joey stared into a small, cracked mirror that hung beside the back door. "Hey, I look cool. Kinda like a gangbanger."

Petra tapped him on the shoulder with a giant metal spatula. "No longer are you Joey, lowly squire of dirty dishes. Today I dub you Sir Joseph, master of the waitstaff."

"What do I gotta do?" he asked, his grin a mile wide.

"Just follow instructions," said Suzanne. She grabbed an omelet and a stack of French toast that Petra had plated and handed them to Joey. "Take these to table two, that's the one closest to the door. Set them down gently, and smile. If they need more coffee, refill their cups. If they need salsa or syrup, deliver it. In other words, make it happen."

"I can do that," said Joey, galloping out with the orders.

"Then come back for another pickup," Suzanne yelled after him.

"Is this gonna work?" laughed Petra. She and Emily were shoulder to shoulder at the grill, flipping corn and red pepper pancakes, scrambling eggs, turning strips of bacon.

"Search me," laughed Suzanne, "but it's a heck of a lot of fun, isn't it?"

"Beats working a cash register at Save Mart," giggled Petra.

EMBOLDENED by their promotions, caught up in the frenzy of the lunchtime rush, both Emily and Joey performed masterfully well. Customers beamed at the stacks of buckwheat pancakes dripping with maple syrup and the fluffy, cheesy omelets that were set in front of them. They dug into their food, slurped coffee, happily loosened their belts, burped surreptitiously into gingham napkins, and gossiped leisurely with neighbors. They wandered into the Book

Nook, bought books, more books, copies of the *New York Times*, and (no surprise here) the last remaining copies of Carmen Copeland's romance books.

The women eased their way into the Knitting Nest and marveled at the wondrous array of richly hued yarns, elegant needles, and colorful threads. A few of them tried to buy the shawls, afghans, and needlepoint pillows Petra used for display purposes.

It would appear that Sunday at the Cackleberry Club was another huge success.

When the lunch rush finally tapered off, Suzanne went upstairs to check on Lidia. The young woman was curled up, sleeping, but woke when she heard floor boards creaking as Suzanne tiptoed toward her.

"Hi," Lidia said in a small, sleepy voice.

"You feeling better?" asked Suzanne.

Lidia nodded. "Lots." She pushed a patchwork comforter off her. Suzanne recognized squares from one of Petra's old dresses as well as an electric blue cowboy shirt Toni had once worn.

"Time to take your antibiotic." Suzanne moved closer. "Here, sit up a little." Lidia complied, and Suzanne handed her a yellow capsule and a glass of water. "Hey, the swelling's gone down. Looks like the ice pack helped."

Lidia nodded, swallowed, said, "Thanks." Then she stared, big-eyed, at Suzanne. "We're still going tonight, aren't we? We're going to get Trinity?"

The look of longing on Lidia's face only increased Suzanne's resolve. "Count on it," she said.

By four o'clock it was pretty much over. The kitchen was cleaned, tables were set for Monday morning's customers, and dirty dishes were running through the wash cycle in their industrial dishwasher. Suzanne split the tips between Emily and Joey and sent them on their merry way.

Feeling tired but in a good way, an accomplished way, Suzanne worked in the Book Nook for an hour or so, finally getting the new stock recorded and shelved. Then she sat down in front of the computer.

When Petra put a hand on her shoulder, she was startled. For some reason, she thought Petra had taken off, had gone home for the night.

"What are you looking at now?" asked Petra. She studied the screen, then answered her own question. "Oh. Messianic leaders. How charming."

"I just want to know what I'm in for," said Suzanne. "Hey, did you know that most cults are authoritarian in their power structure? That the leader is regarded as the supreme authority?"

"Mmm," said Petra. "The Jim Jones syndrome."

"And look at this," said Suzanne. "Cult leaders tend to be domineering and charismatic. They persuade their followers to forsake their families, jobs, and friends to follow them." She tapped her fingers on the keyboard. "Sounds a lot like Claes Elam. And look at this part; cult leaders dictate specifically what members wear, how they think, when they eat and sleep." She shook her head. "This is crazy stuff."

"You realize you're not going out there alone tonight," said Petra. Her hand, still resting on Suzanne's shoulder, tightened its grip slightly.

"Oh, Lidia's going along. She says she knows a back way in."

"That's not what I meant," said Petra.

Suzanne spun around in her chair. "What? You want to come along?" She was shocked. Pleased, but shocked.

"Of course I do," said Petra. "Especially after what that horrible man Elam did to that poor young woman upstairs. I can't just stand by and let him get away with that shit. Puts the women's movement back into the dark ages."

"You *really* don't have to get involved," protested Suzanne. *Who knew what would happen tonight? How dangerous things could get?*

"I'm already involved," said Petra. "Besides, that's what friends are for. To pull your fat from the fire from time to time."

"Let's just hope it doesn't get that hot," said Suzanne.

"What you want to do," suggested Petra, "is go to Google Earth. Zoom in on the Neukommen place, and print out a topographical map. That way we'll know where we're going. We won't get confused by different roads or tripped up by streams and gullies."

"Smart," breathed Suzanne. "How'd you get so smart?"

"Silly girl," said Petra. "I used to be a schoolteacher, too."

TWENTY minutes later, Suzanne had her maps and she had Lidia. They tromped down to the kitchen, where Petra was paging through a book on advanced cake decorating.

Petra looked up. "Everybody ready?" They'd all changed into dark clothing and looked like a trio of female commandos. All they needed was camo face paint.

"As ready as we're ever gonna be," said Suzanne. Now that the moment had arrived, she felt jittery and on edge. Going back there still seemed like a gamble. Humping down a deserted road through forests and fields, lights out, hoping to find the exact building where Lidia's child was housed. Lotsa luck.

"Then let's do it," said Petra, giving Lidia a hopeful smile.

The last one out the door, Suzanne hesitated, glancing back at their array of kitchen knives.

Take along a weapon or not? Suzanne wondered.

Is a knife classified as a deadly weapon, like a gun? Maybe.

Suzanne decided that strapping a butcher knife to her hip did seem awfully drastic. Maybe a little too Special Forces. But she ought to have something, just in case.

Petra's rolling pin lay atop the freestanding butcher

block table. It was practically an antique, fifty years old, constructed of heavy oak.

Suzanne ran over, grabbed it, hefted it. And grinned.

Oh yeah.

CHAPTER 25

DARKNESS enveloped them like a shroud as Suzanne cut her lights. Low-hanging clouds pressed down, the forest closed in.

Driving blind now, slowing to a crawl, Suzanne eased her car along bumpy ruts. They'd come in on a small county road, one she'd never been on before, then turned off onto an even narrower gravel road. Now, cutting cross-country, they were hopefully circling around behind the Neukommen property.

"This is very creepy," murmured Petra, who sat hunched in the passenger seat, squinting, trying to read the lay of the land. Brambles reached out to tickle windows, making little click-tick sounds, while Lidia fretted in back. "Like venturing through a haunted forest, waiting for ghouls to grab us," Petra added.

"But we're getting closer," said Suzanne. "I think."

"Whoa!" cried Petra. "What's that up ahead?"

Suzanne hit the brakes, then rolled down her window and stuck her head out. A lazy black ribbon cut through the land ahead and, when she listened carefully, she heard a telltale gurgling. "A stream." Switching on her Maglite, Suzanne consulted the computer printout that lay crumpled on the seat beside her. "Yeah, we're right on target. But this is as far as we go with the car."

"So now we hotfoot it through the woods?" asked Petra.

Suzanne nodded. She looked back at Lidia, who was squirming nervously. "This is right?" she asked. "We cross this stream and then . . . ?"

"Up the hill," said Lidia. "At the big bur oak, you take the left-hand path."

"Follow it past the orchard and right to the nursery," said Suzanne. They'd gone over this before, but she felt the need to rehash it again.

"A long, low building," added Lidia.

"With one or two women inside minding the kids, maybe a guard outside." Suzanne looked grim.

"There's a guard?" asked Petra.

Suzanne hefted the rolling pin. "Not to worry."

"I didn't think you were gonna bake a cherry pie," said Petra.

"Okay, gang," said Suzanne, trying to sound determined. "This is where the rubber meets the road. Petra and I go in and grab Trinity. You wait here."

"No," said Lidia. "I'm coming with you."

"We talked about this," said Suzanne. "What if we run into Claes? What if he *recognizes* you?"

And what if you decide to stay? was Suzanne's unspoken worry. *What if this all goes to shit?*

"I have to come," Lidia insisted. "Otherwise Trinity won't go with you. She'll be too afraid."

Suzanne glanced at Petra, who gave a reluctant nod. Lidia was probably right.

"Okay," said Suzanne, relenting. "But I want you at the back of the pack."

"I love it when you talk Delta Force," Petra murmured. "So macho."

Quietly, carefully, they picked their way across the bab-
bling stream, hopping from rock to rock. When they got to
the other side, they held hands and pulled each other up the
embankment as mud sucked at their feet.

Off in the distance, an owl gave a low hoot. There was a
rustle of bushes off to their right. Probably a foraging rac-
coon or woodchuck. Hopefully not one of Claes's guards.
Hopefully there were no guards at all tonight.

Moving silently, Suzanne continued to lead the trio. They
clambered up a grassy hill, breathing heavily, finally making it to the tall bur oak Lidia had described.

Suzanne leaned against the tree and felt the roughness
of the bark beneath her fingers. What was she doing here?
What were any of them doing here? Then she looked back,
saw the naked longing on Lidia's face, and knew they had
to keep moving.

"There's the path," whispered Petra.

Suzanne nodded. From here on, it was going to be tricky.
They had to stay quiet, keep low, and strike fast.

Luckily, the apple trees were full and laden with fruit,
giving them excellent cover. They moved closer. Suzanne
could just make out the long, low building Lidia had described. Two kerosene lamps burned inside; a figure moved
against the windows. She could also see the shadow of
someone seated outside.

Crap. Now what?

Moving slowly, silently, Suzanne reached back and removed Lidia's head scarf. Then she knelt down and filled it
with apples. Tucking the rolling pin under her left arm, she
motioned for Petra and Lidia to stay put. Then she headed
for the bunkhouse, trying to appear as nonchalant as possible, humming a little tune.

She was twenty feet from the house before the guard
heard her coming. He was sitting in his chair, whittling a
piece of wood.

"Hey!" he called out. She'd startled him. He stood up,
uncertain what to do.

Suzanne bent forward and gave a slight giggle.

The guard peered expectantly through the dark. "Alicia?" he called, his voice tentative.

"Hey there," purred Suzanne, strolling a little closer, staying in the shadows. She knew that if he was young, he could be teased. "Look what I picked for you," she murmured softly. She held up the apples. She knew he couldn't quite see them in the dark, but he'd be able to read her gesture.

"What're you doin' over here?" he asked. The young guard had dropped his worried tone.

Suzanne picked that moment to affect a little stumble. She cried, "Oh," caught herself, but let the apples spill from her kerchief and tumble onto the ground every which way.

The guard scrambled to help her, bending forward. As soon as his head was within two feet of her, Suzanne brought the rolling pin crashing down on the back of his head. She tried to hit the part of his head that would stun him like a fish, not damage the cortex of his brain and turn him into a lifelong vegetable.

Stepping back quickly, Suzanne watched as the young man hung suspended in midair for a few seconds. Then, in almost slow motion, he crumpled to the ground.

"Night, night," she whispered. Then motioned for Petra and Lidia. They scurried toward her, their footfalls whispering in the long grass.

"Is he dead?" Lidia asked, looking down at the guard.

"Sleeping it off," murmured Petra.

"Listen, guys," began Suzanne, "we don't have much time." She peered at Lidia. "You ready for this?"

Lidia nodded vigorously.

"Do they have a phone to call for backup?"

"I don't think so," said Lidia.

"Good," said Suzanne, her adrenaline pulsing. "You and I will rush in to the bunkhouse, grab your daughter, and whip back here as fast as possible. Petra, can you stand guard?"

"Give me that rolling pin, and I will."

"Atta girl," said Suzanne. She grabbed Lidia's hand, and pulled her toward the children's dorm.

BUNK beds lined the side walls; at the far end of the room a woman sat at a small wooden desk, her back to the door. Two kerosene lanterns burned on either side of her. Small snores and gentle sighs punctuated the darkness.

Suzanne nudged Lidia with her shoulder. "Call to her. Let her know we're here."

"Rachael?" Lidia's voice was low, tentative.

The woman's back stiffened, then she spun around in surprise. "Lidia?" Rachael rose unsteadily to her feet. "You're back?"

Suzanne moved stealthily across the room. The last thing she wanted to do was wake the children. "Sit down," she told Rachael in a determined voice. "And stay quiet. We don't want any trouble. Lidia just came to get her daughter."

Rachael remained standing, her face bunched in anger. She was a chunky girl with small, dark, sunken eyes. "That's not possible."

"Anything's possible, cookie," said Suzanne. She turned to Lidia, "Go on, get Trinity."

"Gladly," breathed Lidia.

"No!" screeched Rachael. She cartwheeled both arms out wildly in an attempt to block Lidia.

Suzanne, who was a head taller than Rachael, pressed the flat of her hand against the girl's chest and shoved her back down into her chair. Rachael sat down hard, emitting a loud oomph.

Lidia tiptoed quietly among the sleeping children, lifting coverlets, searching for Trinity.

Thirty seconds passed, then a minute.

"What's wrong?" Suzanne called in a hoarse whisper.

Lidia's voice rose in panic. "I can't find her!"

Suzanne stared at Rachael. "Where is she?"

"I don't know." There was triumph in Rachael's voice.

"What's going on?" Now Petra stood in the doorway.

"I can't find Trinity!" cried Lidia, fighting back her rising tide of panic.

Petra strode forward, grabbed one of the lanterns, and held it up. "She's got to be here somewhere," she said in her no-nonsense tone. Her eyes cast about the room, taking in the dozen or so sleeping children who were stirring restlessly now. A few were even sitting up in bed. "I can't believe this," she said. "All these children are part of this . . . this *cult?*" She spat out the word *cult* like she was referring to dog poop.

"They are blessed," came Rachael's singsong voice.

"They need their mothers," shot back Petra.

Suzanne's eyes fell on a door just to the left of Rachael's desk. "What's back there?"

"Nothing," said Rachael.

Suzanne leaned over, rattled the doorknob. It was locked. But the rusted metal doorknob hung down loosely, a piece of junk. Turning sideways, Suzanne focused every ounce of bundled energy she had, tried to recall every kung fu and jujitsu move she'd ever witnessed on late-night TV. Drawing her left knee up high, she spun sideways a half turn, and kicked the door with lighting speed. It flew open.

"Check it out!" Petra cried, as Lidia rushed into the darkened room.

Suzanne kept watch on Rachael, who was rocking from side to side and shooting daggers with her eyes. "Is she in there?" Suzanne called out. No answer from her two co-conspirators. "Did you find her?" she called again.

"Oh dear Lord." It was Petra, sounding deeply stunned.

CHAPTER 26

"WHAT'S wrong?" asked Suzanne. Keeping a watchful eye on Rachael, she backed through the doorway and into the room. Then snuck a quick look.

Petra and Lidia were kneeling on the floor, peering into a small wire cage. The kind of cage you'd keep a medium-size pet in.

Except there was no pet inside. There was a little girl.

"Claes, you *monster!*" Suzanne seethed through clenched teeth. Then she couldn't help staring.

Trinity was tiny. Barely two feet tall with a small, elfin head. Lidia unlatched the door, reached in, and lifted her out. Cradled her gently to her breast. The child wound her tiny hands into Lidia's hair, then turned and stared at the women.

Petra stared at Trinity, awestruck. "How old are you, honey?"

The little girl with the elfin features gazed back at her. "Eleven," she said with a lisp.

"That can't be!" Petra said in a harsh whisper. "She's the size of a doll."

"She's a dwarf," whispered Suzanne.

"A primordial dwarf," murmured Lidia. "And I love her more than anything."

THEN they were running back toward the car, moving fast. Buckthorn tore at their clothes, damp leaves whipped their faces. Just as they hit the creek, a bell clanged out dully a half mile behind them.

"They know!" cried Lidia.

"Hurry up!" urged Suzanne.

Not wasting precious time to pick their way across the stepping-stones, they splashed wildly through the fast-moving creek as water chilled their ankles.

Lidia scrambled into the backseat with Trinity, Petra and Suzanne clambered into the front seat.

Cranking the ignition, Suzanne revved the engine, hit reverse, and tore up a good twenty feet of pastureland. Then she spun her car around, and they were jostling back over rutted roads and finally onto the relative smoothness of a county road.

"Gotta call that shelter," said Petra. She was twitching and shaking with excitement, too. She could barely dial her cell phone.

Suzanne glanced in the rearview mirror at Lidia. "How did you know what she was?"

A smile flickered on Lidia's face. "Your husband."

"Walter?" Suzanne was shocked.

"From the free clinic," Lidia added.

Suzanne fixed her eyes on the ribbon of road ahead. Mileposts flew by as she pushed the needle up to eighty. Her better sense told her to slow down, so she eased off on her speed. But her brain kept leaping ahead in hyper-drive.

The free clinic. Walter had volunteered at a free clinic over in Sudsbury a little over a year ago. It was mostly garden-variety ear infections, influenza, and broken bones for folks who couldn't afford health insurance, but they dealt with other stuff, too.

"That's where you met Walter? Dr. Deitz?" Suzanne asked. "That's how you knew where I lived?"

Lidia nodded. "He told me lots of things about Trinity. Why she's the way she is. About her medical condition. He told me Bobby Waite could help me get legal custody of her and get her in a school and find government programs to help pay her medical costs."

Oh, jeez, thought Suzanne. *Is that why those files were stolen? Is that why Bobby was killed? Is Claes Elam a murderer? Could that be right?*

Somehow, a larger part, the linchpin to the whole murder mystery saga, still seemed to be missing. But Suzanne didn't know what it was.

Petra switched off her cell phone. "Sookie's expecting us. She says just drive around to the back and pull into the garage."

"Terrific," said Suzanne. She was still jazzed on adrenaline, and her teeth were chattering, even though the car heater was cranking out a steady stream of heat. Slaloming down the road, she glanced quickly in the rearview mirror at Lidia and Trinity. If she'd had a baby carrier in her backseat, Trinity would have easily fit into it.

"Where are we going?" asked Lidia, clutching her child closely.

"Harmony House," said Petra. "That women's shelter we told you about." She reached over and put a hand on Suzanne's knee, patted it gently. "Slow down, honey. Take it easy. Don't kill us now."

"I know, I know," said Suzanne. She sucked in a deep gulp of air, blew it out slowly.

"You did good," said Petra. "I particularly liked your kung fu kick. You've still got great moves for an old broad."

"I made it up," said Suzanne.

"Still," said Petra. "I woulda broken a hip."

* * *

SOOKIE Sands looked just like her name. Wavy blond hair, kindly open face, long paisley earth mother dress. She was in her mid-forties but dressed like she'd come of age in the sixties: strands of beads, silver rings, sandals. Suzanne almost expected to see a mood ring on her finger and find saffron incense burning in the ashtray.

Sookie and her cohorts bustled Lidia and Trinity into Harmony House, and then Sookie took over from there. Mother and daughter were spirited upstairs, while Suzanne and Petra were shown to a large living room with moody lighting and comfortable low couches. A young woman with long, dark hair served them Japanese green tea in small ceramic cups without handles.

They waited, aware of the hum of serious activity going on around them.

"This is a great old house," said Petra, gazing around. "Look, stained glass windows, lots of woodwork, a working fireplace."

"Probably a dozen bedrooms upstairs," said Suzanne.

"All nice and safe," added Petra.

SOOKIE appeared some fifteen minutes later. "I think they're settling in nicely," she told the women. Her voice was low and throaty. A woman you could trust.

"What if Claes Elam decides to show up?" asked Suzanne. That was her one colossal fear. That Claes would figure out where Lidia and Trinity had taken refuge.

Sookie waved a hand, and her rings glinted in the low light. "We have very good security here. Heavy wooden doors, wrought-iron security bars, a number of closed-circuit cameras. And, I might add, a hotline to local law enforcement."

Petra leaned forward and asked the question that had been buzzing around Suzanne's brain. "Do you think Claes is the girl's father?"

Sookie settled back into a beanbag chair and crossed her legs. "That's the sixty-four-thousand-dollar question, isn't it? Because of the child's obvious condition, I asked Lidia, and she said no. Says she's been with the group for three years. So . . . I have to believe her."

"But Claes could have adopted the girl," said Suzanne. "Which would make him her legal father or guardian or whatever."

"Which could complicate things enormously," said Sookie. "Except for the fact that Claes Elam physically assaulted Lidia. That's a felony right there, a chargeable offense that probably carries a prison term. But that's for our attorneys to deal with. Here we just minister to bodies and souls and leave the legal wrangling to someone else."

"You must have good attorneys," said Petra.

Sookie smiled. "We've been blessed. We have a very dedicated group who do pro bono work for us."

"Bobby," said Suzanne.

Sookie nodded sadly. "Yes, he was one."

"Which might explain why he had a file on Lidia," said Suzanne. *But it still doesn't explain why he had a file on Walter.* "Listen," said Suzanne, "it's possible Claes Elam could have murdered Bobby."

Sookie frowned. "Are you serious?"

"She is," said Petra. "Suzanne's been looking into things like crazy."

"Well, bless you," said Sookie. "But knowing Claes Elam is a possible killer puts us all at risk." She hesitated. "We're going to have to be extra cautious until we can move Lidia and Trinity out of the area."

"Call the police," urged Suzanne. "Get them to put someone outside tonight."

"I'm going to do exactly that," said Sookie.

CHAPTER 27

IN an airless room that smelled of Pine-Sol and burned coffee, the town council meeting started out ugly and got even uglier.

"No one in their right mind would believe what you're saying," Suzanne told them, her voice dripping with ice. She'd shown up at 9 A.M. this Monday morning, prepared to do battle. And missiles were definitely being lobbed in both directions.

The eight people seated at the large oval table in the council chamber squirmed uncomfortably in their hard chairs. Suzanne knew she'd just insulted Kindred's entire town council, but she didn't really care.

Mayor Mobley turned his beady eyes on Suzanne, who was seated, odd man out, at the head of the table. The hot seat. "Don't get uppity with us, Suzanne," he said in his best condescending tone. "Accepting kickback money is a serious crime. You know that. You already had a visit from Tom Lyons."

Suzanne stood her ground. "If there was any sort of

impropriety, wouldn't the prison be at fault? Claiborne Corrections?"

Mayor Mobley twitched an eye at her. "We're already dealing with them—quietly. But you have to realize, the money was kicked back from contractors."

"And subcontractors," Vern Manchester added not so helpfully.

Suzanne's eyes scanned the table. Down at the end, Vern Manchester seemed to be studying his knuckles with great intensity. Sitting next to him, Missy Langston looked nervous and downright embarrassed to be part of this kangaroo court.

"You have no proof," Suzanne told the group.

The mayor inclined his head slightly, nodding to the woman seated next to him, Frances Shandler. Fanny. A woman whose husband ran a plumbing supply place. Meanspirited and filled with gossip, Fanny had once accosted Toni at the Pixy Quick and pretty much accused her of being the town tramp.

Fanny Shandler opened a manila folder and removed a stack of documents. She tipped the papers sideways, tapped them on the table so they were all nice and neat, then slid them over to Suzanne. She seemed to take a perverse pleasure in doing so.

With all eyes on her, Suzanne sifted through the top three papers. Her experience with handling invoices from publishers and restaurant supply houses served her well. She was a quick study.

"These are invoices and receipts for construction material," she said. "What do they have to do with Walter?"

Mayor Mobley's eyes shone with intensity; a sheen of sweat slicked his chubby face. She'd just given him the opening he craved.

"The receipts are phony," he told her. "Those materials were never ordered. Obviously, invoices were dummied up for the accounting firm to cover up the missing money." He exchanged a knowing glance with Fanny. "If you add everything up, you'll find it totals exactly four million dollars."

"You can add," said Suzanne. "Bully for you. This still doesn't link Walter to any sort of crime or wrongdoing."

"Keep going," he told her, indicating the stack that sat in front of her.

Suzanne flipped through a few more pages. Now there were copies of cashier's checks made out to Counselor Corporation. "This is supposed to mean something to me?"

"Look at the next page," urged the mayor.

Suzanne flipped to the next page, to what was apparently the back of the check. On the endorsement line was the signature Walter Deitz.

You could've heard a pin drop in the room. Suzanne felt like her heart was in a vise, and she was going to be sick. She fought to steady herself and draw in slow, cleansing breaths.

When she finally had herself under control, Suzanne said, "I don't believe it."

"Walter must have set up a shell corporation," hissed Mobley.

Fanny Shandler pursed her lips. "The proof's right there in black and white."

"But these are Xerox copies," protested Suzanne. "Walter's name was probably forged." She thought for a few seconds, frowned, then said, "Where did you get these?"

"A packet was sent anonymously to city hall," the mayor told her.

"That's very convenient, isn't it?" said Suzanne.

"We think one of the contractors involved in the kickback had a change of heart," said Fanny Shandler. "Was feeling guilty."

"Suzanne," said Mayor Mobley, in his smarmy tone, "Realize, please, no one in this room is accusing *you* of misappropriation of funds. But we are going to want this money repaid."

Suzanne's heart skipped another couple of beats.

The mayor quickly went on to explain. "I've been in

close contact with Warden Drummond over at Jasper Creek. Though the prison is not technically liable for the missing money, Claiborne Corrections has agreed to a two-million-dollar repayment over the next two years."

Suzanne was stunned. "Why would they do that?"

"For one thing," said the mayor, "they will now turn this matter over to their in-house attorneys and proceed with their own investigation. I'm sure they're expecting to recover all funds in full." The mayor held up his index finger. "We've chosen to deal with the prison in this somewhat laissez-faire manner because we don't want to alienate them. The prison is an excellent tax base for this community and has brought many new jobs to Kindred. In other words, the prison is good for economic development, and nobody here wants to upset that applecart."

"But when we find the one or two bad apples," said Fanny Shandler, picking up on the mayor's metaphor, "they will be routed out."

"Two million dollars," said Suzanne. "But you said four million was missing."

"Which brings us to you," said the mayor, smiling, but looking more like a toothy barracuda anticipating lunch. "Two million dollars. We'll give you the same deal we gave the prison. Two million over two years."

She felt like she'd been slapped. "You're not serious."

The table stared back at her.

"We *are* serious," said Mayor Mobley. He laid his hands flat on the table, studied his fingernails for a few seconds, then looked up. "Did you bring Walter's records as we requested?"

Suzanne's heart skipped another beat. "There weren't any."

Everyone seemed to ease back in their chairs then, and Suzanne realized it didn't look good for her. It didn't look particularly good for Walter, either. On the other hand, she was 99.9 percent sure that the documents had been forged. She just didn't know who'd done it. Or why.

"Let me . . ." She paused. "Let me get my attorney working on this."

SUZANNE was steamed as she stormed from the meeting. She was also more than a little unnerved. She knew she could hire an attorney and fight this, but then the whole county was going to know. A seed of doubt would be planted. And everyone would treat her—and Walter's memory—with a niggling suspicion. That's just how small towns were.

She rounded a corner in the hallway a little too closely, slammed into it with her shoulder. *Oh, crap*, she thought, her upper arm suddenly going numb, tears stinging her eyes. She glanced around, suddenly feeling helpless and stupid, and ducked into the ladies' room.

Missy Langston caught up with Suzanne a few minutes later as she was splashing cool water on her face.

"Suzanne," cried Missy, "I'm so sorry." She held her hands out to her side, palms up. "In fact I'm *mortified.*"

Suzanne sniffled and stared at the girl. "Missy, they're coming after me on this."

Missy bit her lower lip. "I know."

"I gotta get a lawyer."

Missy was more than sympathetic. "I can help you on that. Let me go back to the office and round up a few names. Friends of Bobby's that you can trust."

"That'd be good, Missy. They've really got me backed into a corner."

Missy nodded in agreement. "The mayor is"—she shook her head—"positively *rabid* over this."

Suzanne suddenly felt like her head was about to blow off. Pain gripped the back of her neck and galloped toward her frontal lobes. She had to do something . . . figure this whole thing out.

"Missy, Bobby mentioned there had been an offer on my land. Can you find out who it was?"

Missy looked stunned. "Sure, I could try to track down the buyer." She hesitated. "You're . . . you're gonna try to sell some land?"

"It would be a last resort," said Suzanne, "but maybe."

"Then I'm on it," Missy assured her. "I'm heading back to the office right now."

"Thanks," said Suzanne as she watched Missy ease out the door, looking determined and a little guilty, too.

Suzanne dug in her handbag, found an orange Tylenol tablet way in the bottom. She dusted it off as best she could and swallowed it dry. Then she turned, stared at herself in the wavering mirror, and squared her shoulders.

She understood that if she was going to hire a nice, nasty, go-for-the-jugular lawyer, it was going to cost her. She'd have to lay out serious cash just for the initial down-stroke.

If she didn't protect herself, and the town council came after her, well, she could eventually lose her house and even the Cackleberry Club. Her livelihood. Petra's and Toni's livelihood.

Something else lurked in the dark recess of Suzanne's mind. If things went really, really badly, if Walter turned out to be guilty, and the shit seriously hit the fan, then selling her land, certainly not for two million dollars, but maybe two or three hundred grand, might also give her some negotiating power with the city.

SUZANNE was halfway down the courthouse steps when she spun on her heel and marched back in, straight to the office of the county registrar. She'd resolved to dig deeper on her own, and this was as good as any place to start.

A woman in a pea green muumuu stood behind the counter, munching a Baby Ruth bar. She gave Suzanne a warm smile as she approached.

"Hello," said Suzanne, "I'd like to get copies of all the documents filed here that relate to Claiborne Corrections."

The woman popped the last of her candy bar into her mouth and chewed slowly. "Um, I think that's confidential information."

"Did you ever hear of the Freedom of Information Act?" Suzanne asked. She didn't know if that particular law applied here, but it was worth a try.

The secretary gaped at her. "Huh?"

"It's a recently enacted law that gives citizens the right to peruse all legal documents except those that deal with national security. And since this is basically a city issue, or at the very most a county issue, I don't see any reason for you not to give me access." She smiled at the woman. "Do you?"

The woman shifted from one leg to the other while she digested Suzanne's words as well as her candy bar. Within a few seconds she made up her mind and decided she'd comply with Suzanne's request.

"You want everything? Land permits, zoning, tax records, building permits?"

"Let's look at everything concerned with actual construction."

Ten minutes later, the woman brought Suzanne a stack of documents. "This is pretty much it."

Suzanne skimmed them quickly, then asked, "May I use your copier?"

The woman nodded. "Sure, but paper and toner aren't free. County says I gotta charge you. How many copies you want to make?"

"Mm . . . I'd say about twenty."

"Ten cents each," said the woman.

Suzanne whipped two one-dollar bills from her purse and slapped them down on the counter. "Warm that baby up."

CHAPTER 28

"HAVE I got a news flash for you," said Petra.

Suzanne looped her handbag over a hook on the back wall, inhaled the smell of fried potatoes and sizzling bacon, and knew instantly that Petra was whipping up her famous Spuds and Bacon Frittata. "What happened now?"

"Our friend Sookie just called. The Child Welfare Board staged a raid on that Neukommen group this morning!"

"What!" yelped Suzanne. This was good news, great news, in fact. For every action, a reaction. Or, as Suzanne preferred to view it, sweet karmic justice.

"Yeah," said Petra, wiping her hands and beaming with excitement. "Apparently Sookie pulled a few strings. Talked to a girlfriend who knew a gal at the Welfare Board. Don't you love it?"

"Thank goodness for the old chick-feminist best-friend-forever network," laughed Suzanne.

Petra bubbled on. "They took every one of the children away, then separated the women from the men and asked the women if any of them wanted to leave. Three of them did, bless their little hearts!"

Toni came crashing through the swinging doors into the kitchen. "Petra just told ya?"

Suzanne nodded.

"I wish you guys woulda called me last night. I would have loved to go along. Sounds like you had one heck of an adventure! Finding that little kid and all." Toni sounded almost wistful.

"Social justice," crowed Petra, raising a clenched fist.

"Don't start the revolution until I get two more orders of Eggs Benedict," said Toni.

"What about Claes Elam?" Suzanne asked. "Any word on him?" She doubted if he'd taken this morning's raid lightly. In fact, Claes had probably gone ballistic. If he'd had a shit fit just because she showed up at his farm, how would he react to the Child Welfare Board swarming his property? Especially when they were accompanied by law enforcement officers who might have charged him with felony assault against Lidia? She hoped Claes hadn't barricaded himself in a barn with stolen grenade launchers and tried to start World War III.

Petra turned back to her grill. "Haven't heard a word about that dingbat yet."

"What can he do?" asked Toni. "Now that the law's involved." She grabbed a tea towel, spun it over her head like a lariat, glanced at Suzanne, and suddenly sobered. "How'd your meeting go?"

"Oh jeez," said Petra. She glanced around. "Suzanne?"

"It pretty much sucked," said Suzanne. She took one of the long, black aprons, folded it in half, then tied it at her waist. "The mayor is still pointing his fat little finger at Walter."

"Honey, I'm so sorry," said Toni. She put a hand in the middle of Suzanne's back, rubbed in a circular motion.

Suzanne waved a hand. She didn't want to worry them too much. That might come later.

"That guy Mobley is a turd," said Toni.

Petra grabbed two eggs, cracked them one-handed into a bowl. "He's up for reelection."

"Won't make dogcatcher," Toni said confidentially.

"You never know . . ." said Suzanne, and her voice trailed off. She knew that if Mobley trumped up this scandal, then showed the town how well he handled it, he might score major brownie points.

Ducking into the office, clutching the stack of copies she'd just liberated from the county registrar's office, Suzanne paged through the phone book; dialed the number for Bremmer Construction. They were the company that had done excavation for the prison. Alfred Bremmer's name was on the invoice.

"Hello, this is Suzanne Deitz," she told a perky receptionist, "may I please speak with Alfred Bremmer?" She waited more than a few minutes on hold, and when the perky receptionist came back on the line, her manner was considerably less perky.

"He's in a meeting," the girl said flatly.

"Okay," said Suzanne. "How about your controller or chief financial officer?"

"Um, they're in meetings, too."

"I see," said Suzanne. "Everybody's in a meeting today. Okay. Thank you."

She drummed her fingers on the desk, dialed another company. Ceramide Cement. When she asked the same question, she received pretty much the same answer.

Crap, she thought. Word was out, and nobody, but nobody, was going to talk to her. There was one idea she could probably bag. So, now what? Suzanne frowned. She was searching under her stack of papers for that stupid stress ball when the phone rang.

True to her word, Missy had called back.

"It's Dodd Development," she told Suzanne. "The people who were interested in your land."

"Never heard of 'em," said Suzanne. She scanned her

papers. Nope, not there. Must not have worked on the prison.

"I think they're the group who did that shopping center over near Cornucopia. The Skylark Mall."

"Okay," said Suzanne. Whatever. "Say, did you ever check Bobby's appointment calendar to see where he was headed that morning?"

"I double-checked, but I still couldn't find anything. Sorry."

Suzanne dropped the phone to her chest and gazed out the door and into the café. Toni was flirting with a trucker at the counter; the rest of the customers were eating breakfast and looking relatively content. From every outward appearance, the Cackleberry Club appeared warm and copacetic. But, of course, it really wasn't. A nasty undercurrent was at work that could destroy everything she'd worked so hard for.

"Suzanne," said Missy. "You still there?"

"Uh-huh," said Suzanne. She spoke urgently into the phone. "I'm in big trouble, Missy. And I think it's because of Bobby."

"Excuse me?"

"Not that Bobby got me in trouble, but it's all connected somehow. The kickback, the files, the murders."

"Oh . . ." said Missy, letting her voice trail off.

"What would you say if I wanted to come take a look in Bobby's office?"

There were a few seconds of silence, and then Missy said, "Sure. I guess so."

"Thanks, honey, see you in a bit."

JUST as Suzanne was leaving, Lenore Manchester, Vern's wife, came in. She was a chubby woman who fancied herself quite the fashion plate. Lenore favored colorful, artsy clothes, spiked and gelled white blond hair, and way too much makeup. Especially in the eye shadow department.

Today Lenore was wearing cobalt green eye shadow that looked like bright green caterpillars sprawled across her lids.

"Suzanne," Lenore said, her brows raised in twin arcs. "May I have a word, please."

Suzanne ushered Lenore into the Book Nook. It occurred to her that barely a week ago Vern had dropped by to pick up a cookbook for Lenore. "Was the cookbook . . . ?" she began. But Lenore cut her off.

"Suzanne," Lenore said in her trademark anxious bray, "I need to talk to you."

"Sure, Lenore." Probably, Suzanne decided, Lenore was going to ask for a book donation. The library had a fund-raiser coming up, and Lenore headed that committee. The Cackleberry Club had donated books before and would continue to. After all, it was for a good cause.

"We want you to resign from the library committee," said Lenore, staring at her with a flat-eyed gaze.

"Are you serious?" said Suzanne. She was flabbergasted. She and Lenore had always been relatively friendly; now Lenore was coming on like gangbusters.

Lenore pursed her lips. "You've been making way too many waves around town."

"*I* have?" Suzanne said, her tone chilly now. "I think Mayor Mobley is the one who's overstepped his bounds." *And let his mouth run a little too much,* she thought to herself.

Lenore ignored her words. She had come to speak her piece, and now she tried to ride roughshod over Suzanne. "The kickback allegations are a huge problem, Suzanne. And your involvement in these two murders is equally troubling. That said—"

Suzanne held up both hands. "Enough. I hereby resign. Consider me off the library committee." She didn't need this crap. Didn't need Lenore haranguing her.

Lenore looked stunned. Her mouth kept working as if she still had a few more choice words she wanted to let fly.

Suzanne held up an index finger. "But when this is resolved, Lenore Manchester, and it *will* be, I'm going to expect an apology."

Lenore's eyes narrowed as she dug into her handbag. "I seriously doubt an apology will *ever* be in order." She pulled out the cookbook Vern had picked up for her and set it down on the counter. "And I'm returning this cookbook. I expect to receive full credit in the mail." Then Lenore turned tail and stormed out.

"Well, shit," Suzanne muttered. She and Lenore hadn't been buddy-buddies, but they hadn't been sworn enemies, either. Now she guessed the gauntlet had been thrown down. Sighing heavily, Suzanne picked up the book, used her fingernail to scratch a tiny piece of dried food from the dust jacket, then tossed it on the 40 percent off table. So much for happy customers. And the library committee? Well, she could only tackle one thing at a time. She'd straighten out that little problem once she'd dealt with the bigger ones in her life.

"What was that all about?" asked Toni, suddenly appearing. "Lenore flew out of here like the Wicked Witch of the West putting the pedal to the metal on her magic broom."

"I just got kicked off the library committee," said Suzanne.

Toni looked surprised. "And Lenore delivered the happy news?"

Suzanne nodded.

"Well, shit," said Toni in a kind of drawl. "What does she know, anyway? Lenore thinks she's such hot stuff, when I happen to know she's still got a pair of parachute pants from 1982."

SUZANNE found a parking spot just down the street from Bobby's law office. As she headed down the sidewalk, wondering just how many folks in Kindred knew about this morning's town council meeting, she caught sight of a friendly face and a beckoning wave.

Turning into Root 66 Hair Salon, Suzanne grinned as Gregg and Brett rushed to greet her.

"Girl, it's about time you showed up!" called Gregg. "I can see your roots a mile away."

"They're not that bad," said Brett, leaping to Suzanne's defense. He reached out, lifted up strands of hair, then gasped, "Oops, you're right. With your silver blond hair and those dark roots, you're looking a trifle skunky, m'dear."

"You sure know how to make a girl feel wonderful," laughed Suzanne.

"That's what we're here for," said Gregg. "To dispense a whole lotta wonderful."

"What can we offer you today?" asked Brett. "Cut and color? Tint and foil?" He peered speculatively at her eyebrows. "Maybe a brow waxing?"

Gregg shook his head. "No, no, no. What Suzanne really needs are lash extensions."

"The hottest new trend," cooed Brett. "All the ladies want lashes out to here." He curled a hand out theatrically then peered at her. "Seriously, hon, how you holding up?"

"We heard about the hullabaloo at the town council meeting this morning," Gregg told her in a conspiratorial tone.

"What? How did you guys—?" began Suzanne.

Before she could continue, Brett shrugged his shoulders and said, "Small town, lots of busy little mouths."

"So the mayor expects you to cough up millions?" asked Gregg.

"The last thing Suzanne needs to worry about is the mayor," laughed Brett. "*He's* the one who needs help."

"With that bad comb-over," shrieked Gregg. "If I could only get my hands on him."

"We're talking beaucoup *makeover*," said Brett in a giddy tone.

"Better than that," said Suzanne, "would be for him to lose the election."

"I hear you, girl," agreed Gregg.

"Missy?" called Suzanne. She pushed open the office door, an old-fashioned, walnut door with a window of frosted green glass. Black letters etched in sans serif type spelled out Waite & Pearson, Attorneys at Law. Pearson was a sort of partner who was mostly retired and had a condo in Florida on Sanibel Island. Suzanne wondered if that's who Missy had in mind to defend her.

Missy popped out of the back utility room, a stack of freshly made copies in hand. "Hey, you made it."

"This is really nice of you," said Suzanne. "I don't know what I expect to find, but . . . well, like I said, it's really nice of you."

"As long as none of the clients actually *see* you rummaging through files," said Missy, looking a little nervous. "So what I'm gonna do is lock you in, then take a quick lunch down at Kowalski's Diner, where everybody and his brother-in-law can see me. You know, just in case?"

Suzanne nodded. She understood. "You've been busy?"

Missy shrugged. "The sheriff just dropped by again, asking his usual questions. And I've been mostly trying to figure things out and keep my head above water. I just got done forwarding all of Bobby's e-mails to Carmen. She'll probably send 'em on down to Mr. Pearson."

"Tough being here alone," said Suzanne.

"Yeah, it's like Bobby's ghost is still here." Aiming a thumb over her shoulder, Missy said, "Bobby's office is . . . well, you know where it is. I left a list of possible attorneys for you on his desk. So take your time and then pull the door shut when you leave."

"Thanks again," said Suzanne.

"Hey," said Missy, scurrying out the door. "As far as I'm concerned, you were never here."

SUZANNE listened as Missy's footsteps died away. Good, she decided. This is probably the best. Quiet. Covert.

But . . . where to start?

Suzanne looked around, feeling a little lost, then wandered into Bobby's office. It was a large, comfortable suite with two enormous windows reminiscent of cathedral windows, frosted glass that ended in a peak. Low, wide windowsills held a tangle of potted pink geraniums that had obviously seen better days. Two walls of Bobby's office were a natural red brick and hung with wildlife art, a citation from the Kindred Chamber of Commerce, two framed ticket stubs from an Aerosmith concert, and a photo of Bobby posed with another guy in front of a floatplane. They were each holding good-sized lake trout and looking pleased with themselves.

Sitting down in Bobby's squishy leather chair, Suzanne felt a little strange. Like a trespasser. Except, she reminded herself, she was also trying to figure out who killed him.

She pulled open the top desk drawer and was confronted by a jumble of pens, pencils, message pads, keys, a cell phone charger, a pocket knife, rubber bands, computer disks, and books of matches.

Suzanne picked up one of the books of matches and studied it. KC Tavern. Never heard of it.

She opened the rest of Bobby's desk drawers, found notepads, a file filled with brochures from Canadian fishing lodges, an old Sony Walkman, a few jazz CDs, and more junk.

Now she turned to the credenza that sat against one wall. It was a large piece of furniture with two horizontal file drawers that slid out. Suzanne pulled up a chair and proceeded to browse her way through the client folders. She didn't find much of anything.

The bottom drawer was devoted to Carmen's files, which Suzanne found interesting. There were dozens of thick contracts, countless royalty statements, foreign rights contracts, and even a couple of line-edited manuscripts.

Much as Suzanne wanted to peek at the dollar amount on the royalty statements, she didn't.

That left Bobby's computer. She jiggled the mouse to get rid of the screen saver, then tracked back through his browser to see what he'd been looking at recently.

Nothing earth-shattering. Amazon.com, Salon.com, something on eBay, the E*TRADE Web site.

Not exactly hot clues.

Suzanne leaned back in the chair and steepled her fingers in front of her. She stared at Bobby's printer, a big old Xerox DocuPrint, and a scanner that was unplugged with its cord wrapped around it. She was missing something . . . but what? Bobby had been involved with either the Neukommen group, Claiborne Corrections, or something with Walter. Still, nothing was jumping out at her. She fingered the list of attorneys Missy had drawn up for her, folded it, and put it in her pocket.

So what now? Back to square one?

Well, back to the Cackleberry Club anyway. And then . . . well, she was going to figure out this mess if it was the last thing she did.

·CHAPTER 29·

SUZANNE was just about to back her car out when Doogie's maroon cruiser screeched to a halt behind her. Red and blue lights twirled wildly as he cut his engine, successfully blocking her in.

Then Doogie leapt from his cruiser and was standing at her window, bellowing at the top of his lungs, hopping up and down like a maniac.

"You lied to me!"

Suzanne jumped from her car and squared off against him. "What are you talking about?"

"You said you didn't know anything about Claes Elam's wife disappearing, and you were the one who took her!"

"Lidia walked away from Elam of her own volition," Suzanne explained. "After he ripped out two of her front teeth! When she showed up on my doorstep in the middle of the night, what was I supposed to do? Turn her away? Drive her back out there so that maniac could mutilate her some more?" Suzanne matched his intensity.

Doogie didn't want to hear any of it. "Then," he sputtered, "then you have the nerve to go back out there *again* and kidnap her child." His face was as red as a tomato as raw emotion belched forth.

"Lidia went back for her *own* child," said Suzanne. "I just sort of helped with the transportation." She knew it sounded weak, even a little dishonest, but she didn't care.

"Here I've been keepin' you in the loop on these two murders all along! And you go and cut me out completely. I thought you *trusted* me! I thought we trusted each other," he wheezed painfully.

He had her there.

Suzanne decided there was only one way to mollify him and save him from having a heart attack right there on Main Street. "Sheriff, I apologize. I was wrong."

"You're darn tootin' you were wrong." He was over-the-top indignant. "You shoulda *tòld* me!"

"Seems to me you were the one who brought up the fact that the Neukommen Following wasn't even in your county," said Suzanne.

The sheriff waggled a finger in her face accusingly. "No, *you* brought that up."

Suzanne decided to try another angle. "You realize," she said, "some of those women and children were literally being held prisoner."

Now Doogie was on the defensive. "Hey, you'll get no argument from me on that subject. But until somebody files a written complaint, either with me or Sheriff Burney over in Deer County, nobody can do nothin'. Our hands are tied."

"You should have known something was wrong," said Suzanne. "Sheriff Burney should have known."

"Don't mess with me, Suzanne. I'm not the grand poobah savior of all mankind. I'm just the duly elected county sheriff."

"Who's up for reelection."

"Yup. And I expect to get it."

"Well . . ." Suzanne was running out of steam. They both were. "I still think it's a good thing the Child Welfare Board went in this morning."

"Course it is," said Doogie. "Those kids shouldn't be with that crazy man. They need to be with folks who'll love 'em and take care of 'em. They need to attend a proper school and a bona fide church."

"Amen," said Suzanne.

"Okay then," said Doogie. He dropped his head, peered out from under the brim of his hat at Suzanne.

"I'm sorry," she said again. "I was wrong."

Doogie waved a hand. "Your heart was in the right place. You just maybe went about it all wrong."

"I'd do it all over again," Suzanne told him.

"I expect you would. Even with your own problems hanging over your head."

Suzanne's upper teeth worried her lower lip for a few moments. Then she said, "Sheriff, I don't know how much you really know, but I am in serious trouble."

Doogie's eyes closed slowly, reminding Suzanne of a reptile that was slumbering on a nice warm rock but still very much on the alert. "I thought it was Walter's reputation that was in trouble."

"Same thing," said Suzanne. "You got any ideas?"

Doogie adjusted his gun belt as he thought for a while. "No. But I can nose around some."

Suzanne squinted at Doogie. "If I give you some papers and things that have to do with construction of the prison, could you run a check on some of the contractors?"

Doogie shrugged. "S'pose so."

Suzanne had the photocopied documents in her bag; now she grabbed them and passed them to Doogie. "I guess you heard about the town council meeting this morning?"

He snickered. "Heard you been forging new friends."

"More like frenemies," said Suzanne.

"It doesn't help that you're mixed up in Bobby and Teddy's murders," said Doogie. "Folks are still scared about that." He shook his head ruefully. "Specially since they're still unsolved."

"You've got major problems, too," acknowledged Su-

zanne. Those two unsolved murders were hanging painfully over his head. Over his career.

"Big time," muttered Doogie. "Gotta shake somethin'
loose."

"I was just upstairs looking through Bobby's office,"
Suzanne admitted.

Doogie looked sideways at her. "You find anything?"

She shook her head. "No. Did you?" She knew he'd
dropped by earlier.

"Nothing concrete," he told her. "Nothing that points
squarely to Bobby's killer. Or Teddy's." He rubbed his
cheek with the back of his hand. "I've decided to take another look at Carmen Copeland."

"Carmen? Why?"

Doogie chuckled, but he didn't sound amused. "Funny
thing about that. She just bought a gun this morning."

Suzanne was stunned. "Are you serious?"

"Got a call from Dale Swan. You know, the fella who
owns Trails & Tails Gun Shop? Ever since the murders,
I've been havin' all the local gun dealers report in to me on
sales."

"Smart," said Suzanne. "And Carmen bought . . . ?"

"A .38," finished Doogie. "Anyway, I know Carmen's
gonna get all high and mighty on me and claim it's for
protection, but . . ." His voice trailed off.

"But what?" pressed Suzanne.

Doggie slid his Smokey Bear hat off and scratched his
sparse gray top hairs with his big hand. "I'd sure hate to
see *another* murder around here."

SUZANNE was happy to get back for afternoon tea service,
that respite in the day when the Cackleberry Club was
redolent with the rich scent of Assam, black currant, and
rose hips tea. Then, of course, there were the scones. Today Petra had whipped up batches of buttermilk scones as
well as maraschino cherry scones.

"Let's use those cool Chinese teapots today," suggested Toni. She and Suzanne were behind the counter, getting ready to brew tea.

"Okay," said Suzanne. She reached over her head to grab the blue and white pots, heard the front door whack open and boot heels clunk sharply across her floor.

"You!" screamed a shrill male voice.

Suzanne turned and was shocked to find Claes Elam standing there, pointing a bony finger at her and wearing his trademark black suit jacket and pants. She noticed for the first time how tattered they were. Probably not selling enough of those DVDs.

"You come like a thief in the night to steal my children!" he rasped.

The customers in the Cackleberry Club set down their cups and turned to stare at Claes, who looked like some sort of raggedy scarecrow.

Toni was the first to react. "Get out of here, you dumb cootie," she shouted. She grabbed a cast-iron frying pan and brandished it above her head. The pan was blackened from nearly constant use and heavy as a son of a gun. "Don't you dare come in here and threaten us!"

Claes Elam lifted his chin and, with fire in his dark, limpid eyes, pointed his finger at Toni. "Infidel," he thundered. "Devil woman."

"I been called worse than that, asshole," snarled Toni, who was always game for a good fight.

"Don't provoke him," warned Suzanne, edging closer to a rack of knives.

"You shrew," Claes growled at her. "You abducted my wife and kidnapped my baby child!"

The shutters of the pass-through slammed open, and Petra stuck her head out. "What is the *problem* out there?"

"Another devil woman!" yelled Elam, catching sight of Petra.

Petra glowered at him. "Is that who I *think* it is? Is that the peckerwood poser who puts little children in *cages*?"

Her head disappeared, and then she suddenly reappeared, sweeping through the swinging door, apron flying, hair in a Medusa swirl, clutching her biggest, baddest meat cleaver. "Get out of here," Petra thundered at Claes Elam. "Tangle with us, and I'll split open that empty, muddled head of yours and serve you en brochette."

There were oohs and ahs from the customers. One man applauded.

"Woman, know thy place!" Elam shouted at her.

"That's it!" screamed Petra. "You are gonna be one sliced and diced male chauvinist pig."

"Oink, oink!" taunted Toni as Petra rushed him. "You're stinking up our restaurant!"

"Petra, don't!" screamed Suzanne. They last thing they needed was a knock-down, drag-out fight in front of customers! But Petra was not to be deterred. She slashed at Elam with her meat cleaver while Toni aimed her pointed cowboy boot at his butt and landed a nasty kick.

The struggle took on the dimension of a human tornado, spinning its way across the café, scattering customers in its path. Somewhere in the fray, Elam managed to grab Petra's arm and struggle to gain control of the meat cleaver.

"Get him!" yelled Petra, who was being forced to her knees.

"I'm trying!" Toni screamed back. She leapt at Elam and grasped his belt. Jerking hard, trying to pull him off Petra, she revealed a good two inches of dirty underwear.

Suzanne searched in vain for some sort of weapon, ended up grabbing an antique set of Dutch boy and girl salt and pepper shakers. Salt bounced off Elam's head, pepper managed to smack him directly in the nose and evoke a thunderous sneeze.

At that exact moment, the front door of the Cackleberry Club whapped open like a gunshot, and a body clad in tight blue jeans and a black T-shirt came hurtling through the air, like a circus performer shot from a cannon.

The man hit Claes Elam like a lineman trying to hamstring a quarterback, and dropped him to the floor like a sack of canned goods.

The meat cleaver clattered on the linoleum as Petra jumped away and grabbed Toni.

Not quite believing her eyes, Suzanne crept forward to try to identify their savior. As the man sat astride Claes Elam, riding him like a bucking bronco, he turned and flashed a grin at her.

It was a face Suzanne recognized instantly. "Junior!"

"Junior?" yelped a startled Toni. She broke her embrace with Petra and took a step forward. "Sweet mother of pearl, is that really you?"

CHAPTER 30

BUT Claes Elam was no slacker in the fisticuffs department. Scrabbling his arms and legs, blood gushing from his nose, he managed to dislodge Junior, partially regain his footing, and head-butt Junior in the chest. Claes, maniac that he was, wanted the fight to continue. He shook his head angrily, as though a swarm of killer bees was attacking him, then put up his fists, ready to box.

This time Junior didn't fool around. He balled his fist, then cocked his right arm and thrust it forward at lightning speed, effectively sucker punching Elam in the gut.

"Oof!" Elam's eyes crossed, and he doubled over like he was racked with the fiercest cramps of his life. His breath hissed ominously, like a balloon's dying gasp. When Claes Elam dropped to the floor this time, he stayed down.

"He's done it!" yelled Toni.

"I believe he has," said Petra.

The men at the counter, lined up like a peanut gallery, broke into wild applause. The customers who'd fled from the tables now sauntered back and joined in.

Junior, sensing a pivotal moment in regaining his

popularity, perhaps even hoping for a comeback with Toni, quickly grabbed Elam by the scruff of his neck. Dragging him squirming and moaning across the floor, Junior kicked open the front door. Claes Elam's boot heels clunked once as they crossed the doorjamb, and then he was gone. He'd just been given the biggest bum's rush of his life.

Junior reappeared in the doorway, made a big production of dusting off his hands, then took a bow to yet another round of applause. There were also shout-outs of "Good job!" and "Well done!"

Toni quickly pulled Junior aside. "What are you doing here? Where did you come from?"

"We thought you were in jail," said Suzanne.

"You didn't do something stupid like break out, did you?" asked Toni.

Junior continued to look pleased with himself. "Just got released," he crowed. "The ballistics test came back, and I'm completely cleared." He thumped a hand against his own chest. "I'm an innocent man. Better yet, a free man."

"No kidding," said Suzanne. Her suspects were dropping like flies.

"Only thing hanging over me now," said Junior with a goofy grin, "is Sheriff Doogie told me not to leave town."

Suzanne glanced at Petra, who mumbled, "Gee, we were kind of hoping you *would* leave town."

But Junior stuck around, clearly reveling in his role as defender of the Cackleberry Club. Toni sat him down at the counter and fussed over him unnecessarily, bringing him tea sandwiches of curried chicken salad and cream cheese with pimento. Then finally a plate of scones that Junior tucked into with great enthusiasm.

"Sure beats jail food," said Junior, his mouth jammed with pastry.

"Oh, really?" said Suzanne. "And here I was under the impression they'd hired a new executive chef."

"Bologna sandwich on stale bread and some crummy

orange drink is all you get," said Junior. "And the drink ain't even carbonated."

"Sounds awful," said Toni. She was still buzzing around Junior, even fawning over him a little.

Junior shrugged his forelock off his forehead and shook his head. "Nobody ever said life in the slammer was easy."

Suzanne raised an eyebrow. "Well, thank you, Plato, for that philosophical observation."

"You don't have to be so sarcastic," said Junior. "Especially seeing as how I risked life and limb today."

"You sucker punched him," laughed Suzanne.

"Still . . ." said Junior. "I *did* get rid of the guy. Kind of like . . ."

"Pest control," Toni offered.

Junior grinned. "Yeah, like that there. Pest control." He tried the words out for himself. "Maybe I can rent myself out for pest control. Pest removal."

"You could start by removing yourself," mumbled Petra. But only Suzanne heard her clearly.

SUZANNE comped more than a few lunches that afternoon and gave substantial discounts to the guys at the counter. Nobody seemed all that ruffled, however, and she decided there probably wasn't one person present who hadn't witnessed some sort of wacky scuffle in their lifetime. Of course, usually those disagreements took place in rough bars or at county fairs, not cafés trying to hold a civilized tea. A first time for everything, Suzanne mused. Along with Mad Hatter Teas, Mystery Teas, and Victorian Teas, they could add Rough 'n' Tumble Teas to their afternoon repertoire.

Even after most of the customers had left, Junior continued to hang around, seemingly stuck in place at the counter. Suzanne hoped Junior didn't plan on becoming a permanent fixture.

"Hey, Suzanne," called Junior, as she reached up to grab a silver tin of ginger-peach tea. "How you doin' with your investigation? Now that I'm no longer a suspect," he added with a smirk and an annoying chuckle.

"Still working on it," she told him, keeping her voice neutral.

"You oughta take a closer look at that asshole kid of Teddy's," Junior suggested.

Suzanne balanced the tea tin in one hand and turned to face him. "Who are you talking about?"

"Garland," said Junior. "Who else?"

Suzanne pressed closer to Junior. "Explain, please."

Junior shrugged and threw her a bug-eyed look. "All he ever talked about was Teddy's farm. And every time I seen Garland at Schmitt's Bar, he'd get drunk and brag about the inheritance he was gonna get."

"Every time?" Suzanne asked him. "Is that more than five times, less than twenty?"

Junior's eyes drifted away from her. He was starting to lose interest. "I dunno. I heard him say it once, I guess."

"Interesting," said Suzanne. Garland's drunken words might have been small-town braggadocio, but the notion chilled her. Because Charlie Pepper had pretty much said the same thing a few days ago. That Teddy's drunken son, Garland, couldn't wait to inherit his father's land.

"OKAY," said Petra, "are we gonna do this thing or not?" She put her hands on her hips and gazed at Suzanne and Toni. The café was closed; Junior had finally straggled off into the great beyond.

"I'm still up for it," said Toni. "How about you, Suzanne?"

"Sure," said Suzanne. They'd put a note on the calendar some three weeks ago about sitting down to plan their upcoming cake show. That circled date had finally arrived.

"Excellent," said Petra. "I was planning to whip up some

fettuccine Alfredo and a garden salad. And, if you've a mind, I have a nice bottle of Chardonnay in the cooler."

"Believe me," said Toni, "that's something I can wrap my mind around."

Thirty minutes later they were seated at the large round table, twirling pasta, munching salad, breaking off pieces of crusty French bread, and clinking glasses.

"This wine is fabulous," announced Toni, reaching for the bottle. "Don't mind if I do freshen my drink."

"I think we could all use another splash," said Petra. She laughed, blew a few strands of hair out of her face. "Crazy day, huh?"

"Crazy week," said Suzanne.

"Looks like we can drop Junior from the list of suspects," said Toni.

Petra peered speculatively at Toni. "I hope you're not going to get all gushy over him again. You're not, are you?"

"Course not," said Toni, but she was hesitant about meeting Petra's gaze.

"If he strolls in here wearing that black mesh tank top," Petra warned her, "you're putty in his hands."

"I know," said Toni in a small voice.

"OUR cake show," said Suzanne, tapping her pen against a blank page of lined paper, "needs a name."

"How about Take the Cake," suggested Toni. "The first annual Cackleberry Club Take the Cake Show."

"It's a mouthful," said Petra.

"Isn't it supposed to be?" Toni asked playfully. "Okay, how about this, The Cackleberry Club Cake and Bake Show."

"Take the Cake sounds better," said Petra. "More playful."

Suzanne wrote down Take the Cake in her notebook. "And," she prompted, "we're all agreed that the big draw will be our cake-decorating contest?"

The women nodded.

"So we need divisions," suggested Petra. She took another sip of wine and said, "Wedding cakes, for sure. And maybe a special techniques division."

"Excellent," said Suzanne. "What else?"

"A junior division might be fun," said Toni. "Get the kids involved."

"And a nontiered division," said Petra. "Gotta have that for all the sheet cake bakers and decorators. And maybe something like best use of flowers."

"How about a weird cake recipe contest," suggested Toni. "You know, like cake tempura or potato cake?"

"Gack," said Petra.

"We probably have enough already," Suzanne added tactfully. "Okay, Petra, besides the cake-decorating part, you mentioned something about a cake auction and a cake social?"

"Ooh, what about a cake social?" said Toni.

Petra leaned forward. "We'd serve a variety of cakes, only cut in tiny, tiny pieces, almost like petit fours, so guests could sample three or four different kinds."

"Or five or six," said Toni. "Yeah, I'm lovin' that idea. And we could maybe serve homemade ice cream or gelato?"

"Why not?" said Suzanne. "If we're going to do this, let's do it right."

"We'll probably have to set up a tent outside," said Petra. "Because I can't tell you how many people have expressed *tremendous* interest in a cake show."

"People are so into cakes right now," said Suzanne. "Which means we'll want to have demos, too."

"Probably tap some of the culinary people from Darlington College," said Petra. "And get Jenny Probst from the bakery. Between those guys and the three of us, we could orchestrate demos on sugar paste, frostings and fillings, and maybe even a demo on chocolate."

"Yum," said Toni. She took a piece of bread, dabbed it

in her Alfredo sauce. With the bite halfway to her mouth, she paused and cocked her head.

"What?" asked Petra.

Then they all heard it. Someone running at top speed across hard-packed soil. Beating a hasty path right for their door.

Suzanne half rose in her seat, fearing Claes Elam had decided to make a return visit. But it was a wild-eyed man she didn't recognize who burst through their door, drew a shaky, rattly breath, then screamed, "Fire!" at the top of his lungs.

"Where?" Petra asked, a hand to her heart.

Suzanne dashed for the phone, leaving a clatter of chairs in her wake, and began to punch in 911.

"The ch-church!" yelled the terrified man.

"Not the Journey's End Church!" said Toni, knocking her wineglass over. "The one just down from us?"

The man nodded miserably.

"Oh my God!" said Suzanne. Then began shouting into the phone.

CHAPTER 31

A church on fire is a dreadful thing to behold. Black smoke billowed from the roof in ugly gouts. Windows exploded as flames danced and hissed. A tower of swirling flame, like an incandescent tornado, twisted and danced around the church spire. Sparks tore from the flaming cross.

Toni ran toward the burning church, then stopped abruptly as she suddenly hit a wall of hot air. Suzanne and Petra, following close on her heels, were also halted then driven back by waves of intense heat.

Reverend Yoder and another man frantically wielded a garden hose, their faces bright red and streaked with soot. But the paltry stream of water aimed at the raging fire did little good.

Sirens blatted, engines roared as Kindred's fire department arrived in a mad flurry. Men in black rubber coats and boots hurled themselves off the shiny red trucks, uncoiling reels of hose, coupling it to nearby hydrants.

An ambulance arrived. The two EMTs jumped out and watched nervously as the firemen aimed huge jets of water directly into the flames.

Petra groped for Suzanne's hand. "This is awful! Poor Reverend Yoder, the poor congregation."

The heat grew so intense, the women were forced to move back another thirty feet. Flames danced higher, the atmosphere got hotter and drier. Sparks and cinders spackled the darkening sky overhead.

Another wail of fire engines signaled the arrival of the Jessup Fire Department.

"I guess it's a two-alarm fire now," said Toni, nodding at the newly arrived trucks.

A dozen more firemen uncoiled hoses and joined the fray. And the whole time, cars continued to pull into the Cackleberry Club's parking lot. Word had spread all over town that the Journey's End Church was on fire, and folks had come to witness that terrible spectacle.

"Here comes Doogie," said Petra.

Suzanne watched as Doogie's tricked-out cruiser, followed by a second sheriff's car, careened through the bottleneck of traffic, proceeded along the berm, then ground to a halt right beside them.

Doogie jumped out, looking official and more spry than Suzanne had seen him in years. He had a large roll of yellow tape in his hands, and he and two deputies proceeded to unfurl it and string up a Sheriff's Department—Do Not Cross perimeter.

When Doogie finished with that, he dashed forward for a word with the fire chief, who was directing the operation.

"What do you think's goin' on?" asked Toni.

"Don't know," said Petra. "But here comes Doogie. Let's ask him." She nudged Suzanne's arm. "Suzanne? You're the sheriff's big buddy these days."

Suzanne saw the look of grim determination on Doogie's face and knew it wasn't good. "Sheriff," she asked, "can they even save it?"

Doogie grimaced, and Suzanne saw that his eyes were

red from smoke, and tiny cinders had burned little holes in the front of his sweat-stained khaki shirt.

"Probably not," said Doogie. "Fire's pretty much under control now, but there's not gonna be anything left to save." He lifted an arm and wiped his brow. "The place was old and built entirely of wood. Wood floor, wood ceiling, wood pews. And, of course, it was dry as a tinder-box."

"This is so awful," said Toni as a gust of wind caused the flames to curl upward and scatter a cloud of cinders and ash.

"Ouch!" said Petra. A tiny cinder had grazed her cheek.

"Get back!" yelled Doogie, and the crowd that had pressed around them suddenly heeded his warning. "This flying stuff is dangerous, and the wind ain't helping things!"

They all backpedaled across brown grass to Suzanne's parking lot.

"There are cinders falling on the Cackleberry Club's roof!" Suzanne pointed out in alarm. That was all they needed: another fire!

Doogie sprang forward and within minutes two firemen were aiming a jet of water at Suzanne's roof.

"Thank goodness," said Petra. "It's one thing to burn something on the stove, it's another thing to burn the entire kitchen!"

Suzanne watched as, one after the other, the firemen began to retreat from the burning church. The flames had been beaten back; now they faced only smoldering ash. The firefighters looked hot, tired, and defeated. The only thing to do now was let everything cool down. Then bring in the fire investigators.

"C'mon," Suzanne told Petra and Toni. "Let's make a jug of lemonade and gather up all our leftover scones and muffins. Those firemen are gonna need a lift."

"To say nothing of the church's congregation," said Petra. She'd recognized quite a few members from the church. Most simply looked shell-shocked, but a few were leaning on each other, sobbing.

The three women scurried inside and worked like crazy. Toni and Suzanne carried two tables outside and stacked them with paper cups and paper napkins. Back inside, they whipped up several gallons of lemonade, dumped in a couple trays of ice cubes, stirred everything together.

"Good," said Suzanne. "Petra, how are you coming with the baked goods?"

"We had about three dozen scones and muffins left over, and I grabbed another two dozen from the freezer and heated them in the microwave. So, to answer your question, I think we're good to go."

They carried everything outside and set it up. Almost immediately, people began filtering over to their table. Then half the firemen stumbled over, mostly to get a drink.

"This is real nice of you," a young fireman told Suzanne.

She poured another glass of lemonade for him, then said, "Send the rest of your guys over, too."

He bobbed his head and replied, "I'll do that."

A half hour later, it was pretty much over.

"Are you going to bring in a fire investigator?" Suzanne asked Doogie.

He took a sip of lemonade and squinted at the blackened, smoldering ruins. "Depends on what the chief thinks." He crumpled the paper cup in his fist, then strode off to talk to him.

Suzanne, Petra, and Toni watched as Doogie held a hurried conference with the fire chief.

"That church has historical significance, you know," Petra remarked.

"Not anymore it doesn't," replied Toni. "It no longer exists."

"Maybe they can rebuild," said Suzanne, still the optimist.

"Maybe," said Petra. "But something tells me that church isn't exactly rolling in bucks."

"They'd have to hold a bake sale or something," muttered Toni.

"It's gonna take more than a bake sale," said Suzanne. "They're going to need a miracle."

THEY were cleaning up in the kitchen when Doogie rapped on the outside door, then stumped across the café floor.

Suzanne ducked her head and peered out the pass-through. "We're in here."

"I better not come back there," Doogie called. "I'm awful dirty."

The three women trooped out front, and Suzanne handed Doogie a tea towel so he could wipe his grimy face.

"I'm gonna ruin this thing," he warned her.

She shrugged. "Don't worry about it." Then she stared at him. "What's wrong?"

Doogie shook his head. "It doesn't look good."

"Oh, no," breathed Petra. "You think it was arson?"

Claes Elam? wondered Suzanne. *Did he do this as some sort of retaliation? Had he somehow gleaned that Reverend Yoder suspected him of being an impostor?*

Doogie pulled out a wooden chair and sat down heavily. "Fire chief thinks arson is a real possibility. From what he can piece together so far—the sudden explosion, rolling flames, localized warping, and all that other fire mumbo jumbo—he thinks some kind of accelerant might have been used."

"What do you mean by accelerant?" asked Petra.

"Oh, there's lots of kinds," said Doogie. "You could use

plain old gasoline or turpentine or get fancy and use something like acetone."

"Acetone," said Toni. "What's that used for?"

"It's a solvent," said Doogie. "Auto body shops use it a lot."

"So anybody who works around cars would have access to it," said Petra.

"Yup," said Doogie, looking exhausted.

Like Junior, thought Suzanne. *It would appear he's not off the suspect list quite yet.*

"IT'S a good thing you didn't come to work today," Suzanne told Baxter as she held up a Milk Bone. "There was a fire. A terrible fire over at the church."

Baxter stared at her, and the reddish brown dots over his eyes—the dots that looked like eyebrows—raised in sudden concern. A neighbor, Julie Burgoyne, had let him out and fed him earlier.

"I don't know *what's* going on around here," Suzanne continued as she handed him the treat. "Two murders, a crazy man who holds people against their will, this crap with the town council, and now the church burning down." She stared at him. "What do you think? Random acts of strangeness? Or all related?"

"Rwrrrrr," said Baxter, chewing and swallowing quickly, then fixing her with his most serious look.

"Yeah," said Suzanne. "That's kinda what I think, too. But I just don't know where to look next. In fact, I have no idea."

She pulled open the refrigerator, grabbed an already-opened bottle of Shiraz, and pulled out the wine stopper.

"Run out of ideas," she murmured again.

Baxter sat up, neck arched, gazing straight at her.

"Oh," she said. "You have an idea?"

"Crrrrrr," he told her.

"Carmen," she said, handing him a second dog treat. "Not bad, Bax. I might have to give her a jingle. She does seem to flit around on the periphery of some of these things. And she did just buy a gun."

"Rrrrrr."

"I know, I know. I'll be careful."

CHAPTER 32

MORNING at the Cackleberry Club turned out to be crazy busy. Instead of Eggs in Purgatory, their usual Tuesday special, Suzanne switched it to Toad in the Hole, then also added Jumpin' Jack Spuds, a molten concoction of potatoes, chorizo sausage, and pepper jack cheese, along with a goat cheese and sautéed zucchini omelet.

Those three dishes seemed to draw people like crazy. And, of course, there was the matter of the ruined church. Sitting barely a block from the Cackleberry Club, that sad mass of charred embers was pulling in shocked gawkers by the carload. So, once again, the Cackleberry Club had become a meeting point, a flash point so to speak.

"I need a Scramble Deluxe and a Jumpin' Jack," said Toni, ticking off her orders. "And please tell me those banana–chocolate chip muffins are ready."

Suzanne came into the kitchen on Toni's heels. "What about scones? I need scones."

"Then slip your little piggies into that oven mitt and pull the pans out of the oven," said Petra. "Should all be ready."

Suzanne cracked open the oven and was hit with a wave of heat, an uncomfortable reminder of last night's fire. "The blueberry scones could go another couple minutes; the muffins are ready now," she told Petra.

"Go ahead and slide that chocolaty goodness right out of the oven," said Petra.

Now Joey stuck his head in the kitchen, spiky hair and all.

"What's this?" laughed Petra. "Grand Central Station?"

"There's about a million people in the Book Nook," said Joey. "Just thought you guys oughta know."

"Go on," Toni told Suzanne. "I'm on these orders like Jarlsberg on toast."

Suzanne wove her way through the tables, past a small, round table they'd set up with pints of fresh raspberries and blueberries, and into the bookstore.

There really weren't a million people waiting. In fact, there were five customers browsing. Not exactly the dire emergency Joey had made it out to be.

"Got any more of those Carmen Copeland romances?" a woman asked. She had curly brown hair; a friendly, crooked grin; and wore a neatly fitted denim shirt and khaki slacks.

"We're sold out," Suzanne told her. "But I called my distributor, and we should have more by the end of the week."

"I'll be back," promised the woman.

Another woman approached the counter. A younger woman Suzanne had seen around town. "Did I hear you say you were getting some of those romance books back in?"

"Absolutely," said Suzanne. "In fact, I just ordered *Midnight Love,* the newest one, as well as Carmen Copeland's entire backlist."

"Great," said the woman. She paused, as if wanting to chat, then stuck out her hand. "I'm Toby Baines. I work at the phone company."

"Oh sure," said Suzanne. "I'm Suzanne Deitz. Nice to meet you."

"I've been curious about those romance books for a while. Always promised myself I was going to read one."

"Carmen's books are very popular," said Suzanne.

"My husband, Dennis, was on the Prison Planning Committee," said Toby. "Anyway, once when I dropped him off for a meeting at the school, I kind of ran into Carmen. I guess she was going with her husband to the meeting or something."

"Really," said Suzanne.

"She didn't say who she was or anything," said Toby, "but she just looked famous. Kind of dazzling. You know what I mean?"

Suzanne nodded. It wasn't the first time she'd heard Carmen described in those terms.

Glancing over toward the café, where the pace had slowed considerably, where she probably wasn't needed at the moment, Suzanne continued to fritter about the Book Nook. She unpacked some colorful cardboard posters a publisher had mailed her and arranged them on the top shelf. She decided it might be time to do a new book display.

She rattled around in the office, dug out a toy train, two stuffed teddy bears, and some alphabet blocks. Then she arranged the train and teddies with a hand-picked selection of a dozen children's books, spelled out Kids Books with the alphabet blocks. Fun. Next time, she decided, she'd do a tea display. Feature some of their colorful ceramic teapots and tins of tea with some of the books on tea poetry, tea parties, and maybe a couple of tea shop mysteries.

She was just setting out the new magazines when the phone rang.

It was Sheriff Doogie.

Suzanne thought about pitching the idea of Claes Elam as arsonist to him and decided, *Why not?* "Sheriff," said

Suzanne. "We had a nasty scene with Claes Elam a few hours before that fire started."

"That a fact," said Doogie.

"Anyway," said Suzanne, "I wondered if he might not be considered a suspect in the church fire."

"You think he had something against that church?"

"Well, no. Probably not," said Suzanne.

"Then why do you think he's a suspect?"

"Because he's a crackpot?"

"Lots of people are cracked, but that don't make 'em arsonists. Anyway, Elam's already in custody."

"He's been arrested?" Suzanne couldn't have been more delighted. "The assault charge on his wife? On Lidia?"

"She's not his wife," said Doogie. "Elam staged some kind of phony, multiple marriage ceremony. Oh, by the way, *he's* a phony, too. Turns out he never went to divinity school like he claimed. Got his degree over the Internet."

"Whoa," said Suzanne.

"Happy now?" asked Doogie.

"I'm happy those people are no longer under his spell."

"Yeah," said Doogie, sounding disgruntled. "But that still doesn't solve the murders. Or the arson at the church."

"I thought about that accelerant you mentioned," said Suzanne.

"The acetone," said Doogie.

"Yeah," said Suzanne. "I know Junior's working at Shelby's Body Shop. So he might have access to something like that."

"You think Junior had something against the church?"

"Not really," said Suzanne. "I just thought . . ." Her voice trailed off. She didn't know what she thought.

"We ain't gonna go through the whole town roster, are we?" asked Doogie.

"Boy, you're snippy today," said Suzanne.

The sheriff let loose a yawn. "Lack of sleep."

"So why did you call?" asked Suzanne. "Why aren't

you stretched out in one of your own jail cells, catching a few z's?"

"I wanted to ask if you noticed anybody hanging around your place or the church today."

"Sure," said Suzanne. "Lots of people."

"I meant somebody strange," said Doogie.

"You mean like an arsonist?" asked Suzanne. "A fire-bug?"

"It's not uncommon for pyromaniac types to return to the scene of the fire."

"I'll keep a lookout," Suzanne promised him.

"Do that," said Doogie.

Suzanne had just dropped the phone back on the hook when it shrilled again.

"Doogie?"

"No," came a small voice. And then, "Suzanne?"

"Lidia? Is that you?"

"It's me."

"How are you?" asked Suzanne. "How's Trinity?"

"We are so good," said Lidia. "Good and safe and happy. I can't thank you enough for all your help."

"No problem," said Suzanne. "Just knowing you two are out of that awful Neukommen place is all the thanks I need." *Nice to have a happy ending for once,* Suzanne decided.

"Sookie told me Claes was arrested," said Lidia. She sounded surprised. "Charged with assault and maybe even kidnapping!"

"Are you okay with that?" Suzanne asked. What she really wanted to say was, *You're not having second thoughts, are you?*

"No, no, don't worry," said Lidia. "I see now that Claes was an evil man. He deserves whatever punishment is meted out."

"Glad to hear you say that," said Suzanne.

"Guess you were worried I was going to have a change of heart or something," said Lidia.

"The thought did cross my mind," said Suzanne. "But you're a sensible woman; I knew your intellect would win out."

"Thank you," said Lidia. "Hey, I really called to tell you I'm moving. We're moving. In about an hour."

"Where you going, honey?"

"Sookie found a place for us up in Minneapolis. "It's a special shelter for moms with kids. And they're gonna take me to a doctor, a specialist. Trinity, too."

"Sounds good. Let me know when you get settled, okay?" Suzanne wiped a tear from the corner of her eye. She decided it was awfully nice when things finally worked out. Now, if only a few other things could be settled as well.

"LUNCH is gonna be fairly simple today," Petra told them. "I'm doing muffuletta sandwiches, shrimp salad, and Suzanne's egg drop soup."

"That's it?" asked Toni.

"That's plenty," said Petra. "Unless you want to jump in here and make with the magic."

"Not me," said Toni. "I can barely boil water. I can screw up a peanut butter and jelly sandwich."

"No, you can't," laughed Suzanne.

"Seriously," said Toni, "I can."

"Mind if I bug out after lunch?" Suzanne asked the women.

"No problem," said Petra. "I know you've still got lots of stuff to untangle."

Suzanne nodded. Her plan was to drop in on Carmen Copeland unannounced. Meet the woman on her own turf so she couldn't run away, then grill her about Bobby and her possible involvement with the prison.

"Hope it works out," Toni told her.

* * *

THE Victorian mansion Carmen called home was one of the few architectural styles Suzanne could actually recognize and put a name to. Although she'd never thought of herself as being particularly romantic, she'd always fancied the idea of living in a large, rambling home much like this. One complete with tower rooms, cupolas, gingerbread trim, and overgrown flower gardens. Probably, if you were a romance writer, this was the kind of home that served as superb inspiration.

Still, it was with trepidation that Suzanne approached Carmen's massive front double door. Grabbing the bronze ram's head door knocker, she slammed it against the brass plate. Nothing. She waited another sixty seconds. The curtains didn't part, no tentative footsteps sounded from within, no one peered down from the widow's walk above.

Suzanne banged the knocker again and waited, a little more impatiently this time, thinking about how Carmen would really have a fit if she knew she'd searched through Bobby's office.

Finally, the doors swung open, and Carmen Copeland stared out at her. Carmen wore a sea foam green strapless dress and silver sandals with the Prada logo. A large silver cuff circled one wrist, and her hair hung loosely.

"Can I help you?" Carmen asked coolly.

"Carmen," said Suzanne, "I'm sorry to bother you, but I was in the neighborhood . . ." Kind of a white lie, but what the heck.

Carmen's eyes looked slightly glazed.

"Remember me?" said Suzanne. "Suzanne Deitz? From the Cackleberry Club?"

"Yes," said Carmen finally. She pursed her lips and wrinkled her nose. "Unfortunately, Suzanne, I'm right in the middle of writing a critical chapter, so I'm unable—"

"Carmen," said Suzanne. "I really need to talk to you. Just . . . two minutes. Okay?"

Looking disgruntled, Carmen replied rather ungraciously, "I suppose." This was followed by a long, resentful sigh.

Following Carmen down a long, central hallway, Suzanne glanced quickly about. The home was utterly magnificent. The walls in the entryway were covered with a spectacular Chinese red fabric and accented with crystal wall sconces and beveled glass mirrors. Speeding past the living room, Suzanne spotted damask couches, a Chinese lacquer screen, an elegant gaming table that might have been Chippendale, and a spectacular white marble fireplace.

Carmen turned suddenly, and Suzanne followed into a smaller room, a parlor, really, that Carmen had obviously turned into her writing studio.

"This is lovely," said Suzanne, as Carmen indicated a wing chair covered in rose pink fabric. She sat down, looked about the room, wondering if she could pick up any clues about this strange, somewhat exotic woman. She also wondered where Carmen had stashed her newly acquired gun.

Another fireplace, this one smaller with an ornate, carved mantelpiece, was across from her. To Suzanne's left was a lovely tall secretary, probably mahogany, with bookshelves above a cluttered writing surface and three drawers below. There was also an enormous desk that held two iMac computers, a color printer, and a scanner. The wood-paneled walls were hung with dozens of paintings.

"My office," said Carmen, settling into a high-backed chair. "Such as it is."

"It's great," said Suzanne. Then her eyes were drawn back to the paintings, which seemed to clash with the rest of the decor.

"Ah," said Carmen. "You've noticed my paintings."

Suzanne stared at a grouping of rather strange paintings. They seemed to be a combination of illustration, graphics, and wild paint strokes. One depicted a bizarre, cartoonish red dog with a building in its mouth. One was a conglomeration of canvas, newspaper ads, and cardboard, splashed with purple and orange paint. What a gallery would probably call multimedia.

"I collect outsider art," Carmen explained.

"I've heard the term," said Suzanne, "but don't really know what it is."

"Outsider art is anything outside the mainstream," explained Carmen. "The whole phenomenon actually began with insane asylum art, but now encompasses naive, self-taught, and eccentric art."

"Wow," said Suzanne.

"It's very hot right now," continued Carmen. "Some of it, a lot of it, is appreciating like crazy."

"Once an outsider artist becomes mainstream," said Suzanne, "are they still considered an outsider?"

"You sound like my accountant," said Carmen in a droll tone. "Anyway, this is all temporary." She waved her hands in an all-inclusive gesture. "Some of it's going to be sold, some is going to be rearranged. I've taken this house off the market and plan to stay here after all. So I'll be doing some serious redecorating and repurposing. This place has too much of a mausoleum feel right now to suit my sensibilities."

"What about the house in Kindred?" Suzanne asked. "The house where Bobby . . . uh . . . lived."

"That will be sold," Carmen told her.

"I see," said Suzanne, fumbling for words. "Well, your staying here is great news, especially for the community. I suppose you'll still teach creative writing at Darlington College?"

"Perhaps," said Carmen. And now a mischievous smile played at her lips. "But my new sideline project will be a clothing boutique."

"Seriously?" said Suzanne. "You're going to open a shop here?"

"Actually," said Carmen, "I'm going to open it in *your* hometown. Bring a little touch of New York, Paris, and Milan to Kindred."

Suzanne thought about her own practical wardrobe of denim, colorful T-shirts, and easy shifts; of the green muu-muu worn by the woman at the courthouse. Was there really a market for high fashion in Kindred?

On the other hand, women in Kindred loved fashion as much as the next person. Maybe, she decided, they just hadn't had a source for the hot, trendy items you saw on celebrities who were featured on *Entertainment Tonight* or in *Life & Style* magazine. Maybe Carmen was right on the pulse of things by launching her own version of a hot store similar to L.A.'s Kitson or Lisa Kline. Maybe the women of Kindred and Jessup would all suddenly blossom as fashionistas. Maybe the Cackleberry Club would have to start serving mojitos and calamari.

"That's just great," said Suzanne, trying to work up some real enthusiasm.

"I've been in discussions with Missy," said Carmen, "and she's agreed to manage my shop."

"Missy?" exclaimed Suzanne.

"Well, the law office is closing," said Carmen. "Obviously. So she has to do *something*. Besides, Missy's a good manager. Smart, honest, and a fairly decent self-starter. And she's young and attractive," Carmen added. "That's a real plus."

Carmen's mention of Bobby's law firm brought her back to the here and now. The real reason she'd dropped by to talk to Carmen.

"Carmen," said Suzanne, "you don't know anything about a kickback, do you? On the Jasper Creek deal?"

Carmen gave her an even stare. Repeated the word, "Kickback?" in a flat monotone.

"The thing is," said Suzanne, the town council is pressuring me because a lot of money has somehow disappeared. Money that had been earmarked for construction."

"And you are asking me this . . . *telling* me this . . . why?" said Carmen.

Suzanne fumbled for a reasonable explanation. "Because

Bobby was on the planning committee. Because maybe he knew of some impropriety with contracts and things . . ." She hesitated. "And because maybe Bobby was killed because of it."

Carmen stood up abruptly. "I think it's time you left."

CHAPTER 33

SINCE she was only a few blocks from Harmony House, Suzanne decided to swing by and say hello to Sookie Sands. Thank her for stirring things up and calling in the Child Welfare Board and for sending Lidia and Trinity to an even safer location where they could both get needed medical attention.

But once Suzanne arrived, once she was sitting across from Sookie, the Harmony House director waved off her praise.

"Just doing my job," Sookie told her. "Watching out for those who can't always do good for themselves."

Suzanne shook her head. "You do such wonderful work here . . ."

"I'll be happy when my work is done," said Sookie. "When women no longer need a safe place to run to."

"If you ever want the Cackleberry Club to stage a fundraiser for you . . . a fund-raising tea or something . . . just let me know," said Suzanne. "We'd be happy to do it."

"I love that idea," Sookie said with enthusiasm. "Raise some money as well as our profile."

"You're pretty high-profile already." Suzanne chuckled. "You've been in the local news. And with the arrest of Claes Elam . . . well, you'll probably draw even more media attention."

"Tell me about it," laughed Sookie. "We even had a freelance CNN reporter call here this morning. He's busy on a couple of assignments but thinks he can sell them on the Claes Elam story, too. Said he might swing into town tomorrow if he can touch base with some buddy who lives in the area."

"That's big-time coverage," said Suzanne. "Good for you."

"He wanted your contact information, too," said Sookie. "So I gave it to him." She peered at Suzanne. "That was all right, wasn't it? I hope you don't mind."

Suzanne shrugged. "I doubt he'll get around to me. I'm just small potatoes in this thing. You guys here are the real stars."

"THE prodigal owner returns," said Petra, when Suzanne walked in the back door. "You've got a visitor waiting out front."

"Who is it?" asked Suzanne, hoping fervently it wasn't Mayor Mobley or one of his lackeys come to rag on her some more.

"Missy Langston," said Petra. "She showed up ten minutes ago. I told her you'd be back pretty soon, so she decided to hang around. Ordered tea and scones, too, bless her little heart."

Suzanne stepped out into the café, scanned the tables, and caught sight of Missy. Missy waved, and Suzanne waved back then went to her table and slipped into the chair across from her.

"I just heard the big news," said Suzanne. "Looks like congratulations are in order." She was referring, of course, to Missy's new job as manager of Carmen's boutique.

Missy blushed. "I didn't want to say anything yesterday, because it was still kind of a deep, dark secret. But when I spoke with Carmen first thing this morning, she said it was okay to start telling people. I think she's anxious to get a buzz going. At least that's what she calls it."

"A little prelaunch chatter," said Suzanne.

Missy nodded, trying to look enthusiastic.

"I thought Carmen was furious at you because you told me about the missing files," said Suzanne.

"Well, she was," Missy said with a shrug. "But she kind of got over it. Carmen doesn't have the longest attention span in the world. And she has big plans to make her boutique a real hot spot."

"Wow," said Suzanne. "I still can't believe you're going to work for Carmen Copeland." She just hoped Carmen didn't shoot Missy in the back when she failed to sell her quota of Havaianas or hobo bags. Or maybe Carmen wasn't a crazy killer, after all. Just kind of . . . crazy.

"Know what's really wild?" said Missy. "Our boutique's going to be right downstairs from where I am now. Carmen bought the building. So the boutique will be located on the first floor, and she'll rent out Bobby's old law offices on the second floor."

"What about the law partner?" asked Suzanne. "What's his name again? Pearson?"

"I don't know the exact details about closing the office," said Missy. "Probably Carmen made him an offer he couldn't refuse."

"Well, that's something," said Suzanne. "So you'll still be right there next to Gregg and Brett."

"I know," laughed Missy, "which is so cool. We're evolving into style central. Kindred's very own little Rodeo Drive. Oh, hey . . ." She dug into her handbag and pulled out a four-by-six-inch card. "I finally brought you that chocolate chip recipe."

* * *

SUZANNE helped with afternoon tea, then fiddled around in the Book Nook for a while, straightening shelves, doing faceouts on several of the new hardcover books. She let her mind cruise on autopilot so she could muddle around all that had happened.

But the more Suzanne thought about recent events, the more she decided Bobby *had* to have stumbled upon some kind of information about the prison. Or the kickbacks. And he'd been murdered because of it.

So maybe Bobby had gotten hold of some sort of information or proof. Proof that had been contained in the files stolen from his office? Suzanne wriggled her nose, touched the tip of it with her finger.

Or maybe not.

Maybe the files had been stolen, but the information or proof or whatever it was, still remained in his possession somewhere. That's why crazy things were still happening.

Suzanne reached for the phone, dialed Carmen's number.

"Carmen, it's me again."

"Who's me?"

"Suzanne. Suzanne Deitz."

"Oh you." Carmen Copeland sounded colossally bored. Then again, she always sounded that way. Suzanne was starting to get used to Carmen's callous disregard for people.

"I have a very impertinent request," Suzanne told her. "I'd like to look through Bobby's house. The one right here in Kindred."

"What?" shrilled Carmen. "Are you crazy? No way!"

"I'm fairly convinced Bobby knew something and was killed because of it," said Suzanne.

"That's *your* explanation," said Carmen. "Your rationale for pawing through personal property."

"Two days ago you were thanking me for nosing around about Bobby's murder," said Suzanne. "What changed?" She decided that Carmen sounded even more schizo than usual.

"For one thing," said Carmen, "I didn't know you were under suspicion for embezzling a huge amount of money."

"My *husband's* under suspicion," Suzanne reminded her. "My deceased husband."

"Sheriff Doogie already went through that house like a bull in a china shop," sniffed Carmen. "Days ago. So what makes you so smart that you want to take a look? And why should I even trust you?" There was anger as well as hesitation in her voice. It didn't bode well.

"How's this," said Suzanne. "You have a dead husband up in Memorial Cemetery and not a lot of answers."

There was a sharp intake of breath, as if Suzanne's words had been too pointed and painful for Carmen to bear. Then, finally, Carmen said, "Let me think about it."

"Fine," said Suzanne. "But, please, don't wait too long."

SUZANNE collected the empty cups and saucers, put away the oatmeal scones and blond brownies that were left over. Toni had her book club coming in tonight, and one of the women was bringing goodies. So all Toni had to do was serve up glasses of cider.

So . . . a reprieve tonight.

Stepping out the back door, Suzanne headed for Baxter, who was sitting on his haunches, gazing out toward the woods. She'd fed him earlier, but now he needed to stretch his legs. And the farm fields and woods out back were a far better place than their fenced-in, torn-up yard.

"Go for it, Bax," Suzanne told him as she unclipped his leash then grinned as he coiled and launched himself like a rocket.

Suzanne ducked back inside the Cackleberry Club, grabbed an armload of tea towels and aprons that needed laundering, and carried them out to her car. Then she slowly crossed the backyard, heading for the small shed. For some reason, the door had come unlatched and was flapping in the breeze. A breeze that was turning into a cooler, gustier wind. August on the wane, September just ahead.

Suzanne stared up at the evening sky. Instead of a pink gold sunset, low-hanging dark, purplish clouds were bunched on the horizon, heralding more rain. *Good for the farmers,* she decided. *Maybe even good for business to-morrow.*

When she reached the shed, Suzanne hesitated for a moment, suddenly gripped with the sure terror that something was waiting for her inside. Then she told herself to stop being so foolish, grabbed the door, pulled it open, and peered in.

Nothing.

Well, nothing except an old Toro lawn mower, a couple of sawhorses, stacked flowerpots, and some old green garden hose that, in the dim light, reminded her of a coiled snake.

Shuddering slightly, Suzanne admonished herself to be positive. Stop looking for fly specks in the pepper. Stop looking for creepy-crawlies . . . or murderers . . . around every corner.

"Baxter," she called. "You ready, boy?"

She could hear weeds rustle as he bounded through the woods. But he wasn't responding to her call.

Suzanne stepped into the woods, really a small copse of poplars and birch trees, and was surprised how dark it was in there. She put a hand out, pushed back tendrils of sumac and wild grapevine, followed along a sort of path.

Where was that dog, anyway? Now she didn't hear a thing.

"Baxter!"

Feeling slightly nervous, Suzanne pushed farther through the brush. Probably, she decided, Bax was bounding through the outlying field of soybeans, having a ripsnorting good time chasing field mice or hapless gophers.

Just as she was about to emerge on the far side of the woods, her toe caught on something sharp. Pitching forward abruptly, Suzanne saved herself from a nasty, knee-wrenching fall by grabbing onto the trunk of a poplar.

What did I hit? Tree root?

Steadying herself, she bent down and was surprised to see a thin metal rod with a small red flag on the end sticking up out of the soil.

What the heck? she wondered. Then Baxter came running full tilt at her, paws clumped with mud, and she forgot all about it.

CHAPTER 34

ON Wednesday morning, heavy rain had moved into the area once more. Lightning strobed, and rain spat methodically against the windows of the Cackleberry Club. Once again, the place was jammed. Whenever it rained, farmers exited their fields like locusts to find the nearest dry spot that served good food and a strong cup of coffee.

"I need two hash brown nests, French toast, and a short stack of cakes," Toni told Petra.

Suzanne was right behind her. "Veggie omelet for me."

"Suzanne," said Petra, "you want to grab your roasted red peppers?"

"Sure thing," said Suzanne. This morning she'd roasted a half-dozen red peppers on the grill until their skins were blackened and blistered. Then she'd popped them into a plastic bag for about twenty minutes. The skins were easily peeled off, leaving the soft, flavorful pepper meat.

"Should I dice 'em?" asked Suzanne.

"Please," said Petra.

"Hey, guess what," called Toni. She'd gone back out in the café and then come running back into the kitchen again.

"Dede Krauth brought in ten loaves of her killer banana bread."

"Price it and put it on the table," said Suzanne. She loved the fact that they had a network of bakers, pastry chefs, and organic growers who brought in their finest and freshest to sell.

"So . . . what's the magic number?" Toni asked. "Three ninety-five?"

"Four ninety-five," said Suzanne. She watched as Petra scooped up hash browns, created small indentations, then added sizzling eggs and a dab of Hollandaise sauce. "Here are those hash brown nests you wanted, Toni."

Breakfast segued into midmorning coffee and pastries. Then, around eleven, lunch service started to heat up.

"Caribbean Meatloaf, Drunken Pecan Chicken, and a Brie, Pear, and Walnut Sandwich on French bread," said Suzanne. "Plus Cilantro Lime Walnut Salad and Chicken and Wild Rice Soup."

"These are all your recipes?" asked Toni.

"Yup," replied Suzanne.

"Amazing," said Toni. She grabbed the blackboard and carefully printed out the menu. When she hung it back on the wall, a dozen eyes peered up at it, reading, deliberating, salivating.

Just as Suzanne slid a sour cream biscuit onto a plate heaped with cilantro lime salad, Carmen Copeland walked in. She looked dazzling and slightly dangerous in her tightly belted, shiny black raincoat and oversized dark glasses.

Toni sidled over to greet her. "You want a table, honey?" she asked in her trademark sassy manner, one that charmed men but sometimes intimidated women. "Or can we fix you somethin' to go?"

"Neither," Carmen responded coolly. She wasn't the least bit flustered or intimidated.

Suzanne beat feet across the café. "I'll take care of this," she told Toni.

"You betcha," answered Toni with a grin. She knew darned well who Carmen was.

"I take it you're here to see me?" Suzanne asked when she and Carmen were alone.

Carmen inclined her head slightly. "I can't stay. I just stopped by to . . . well, to give you this." She pressed a single brass key into Suzanne's palm.

"For Bobby's place?" Suzanne half stammered.

Carmen gave a tight nod. "You know where it is?"

"Um . . . Penny Hill Road?" Suzanne was stunned. She hadn't been expecting actual cooperation.

"Nobody except the sheriff's been in there since . . ." Words failed Carmen for a few moments, then she pulled it together and lifted her chin proudly. "We may not have had a good marriage," she said in a voice Suzanne could barely hear, "but Bobby was a very good man."

"I know that," said Suzanne.

Carmen's dark eyes glinted. "And that dinner meeting with Lester Drummond you were so suspicious of?" Now her words rang strong again. "He asked me to help plan a *fund*-raiser," she spat out.

"WHAT did *she* want?" Toni asked, once Carmen had gone.

"I think she wanted to be nice," said Suzanne. "But then her true nature got the better of her."

"You mean the mean, cantankerous, spitting black mamba side of her personality came out?" laughed Toni.

"She *is* a character," Suzanne agreed tactfully.

Lunch flew by and, once they finished serving, Suzanne busied herself with organizing the grocery shelves. Half the loaves of banana bread had already sold as well as a couple of jars of strawberry jam and two small rounds of white cheese. She rearranged the display by adding a dozen jars of homemade honey and made a nice arrangement with tubs of apple butter.

Suzanne had one small nook left in the Cackleberry

Club and had high hopes of turning it into a homemade gift boutique called the Velvet Rabbit. For right now, that area was blocked by a large bulletin board hung with homemade ads and flyers. Some flyers advertised firewood, clothing alterations, and fresh sweet corn. One flyer, that had hung there for a while, had Puppies for Sale scribbled out and was hand lettered over with the words Free Dog.

But, hard as Suzanne worked, that darned key Carmen had given her was beginning to burn a hole in her pocket. So once tea service had begun, she quietly slipped away.

BOBBY'S house was located in one of the older sections of Kindred. It was a two-story modified Cape Cod painted Williamsburg blue and surrounded by mature maple trees and at least a dozen Scotch pines. But with rain sluicing off the roof and no lights on inside, the house looked a lot more lonely than cozy.

Suzanne parked directly in front, opened her driver's-side door, and unfurled her plaid umbrella. Then she hopped out of her car, ducking under the umbrella as fast as possible. She strode purposefully to the front door, climbed two low steps, and stuck the key in the lock. As the door creaked open, she called out a tentative, "Hello." Force of habit, even though she knew no one was there. No one had been there for a week.

Shaking raindrops from her umbrella, she parked it, half open, in the entryway. Then she gathered up a pile of accumulated mail that lay helter-skelter on the floor and took a few steps in.

Suzanne's first impression was of dust and dead air. She thought it sad that a home no longer lived in could assume a lonesome feeling so fast.

Locating a light switch, Suzanne snapped on overhead lights. But the place still felt dim.

Okay. Try to get past this morose mood that's come over you and get to work.

Suzanne started in Bobby's home office. It was a small room with French doors, just off the dining room. A contemporary-looking white wooden desk was strewn with magazines, old copies of the *Financial Times,* Post-it notes, and a glass paperweight with some type of fish fossil inside. It also held a Dell laptop computer and silver Tensor lamp. Parked behind the desk was a bright purple chair that looked like one of those eight-hundred-dollar ergonomic Herman Miller designs. Bay windows afforded a view of a pleasant if slightly overgrown backyard.

She set the mail down amid the clutter on the desk, scanned through everything for anything that might be important, then shuffled through the Post-it notes.

Nope.

An old-fashioned lawyer's bookcase stood against one wall; above it was a wrought-iron shelf with more law books. A small credenza stacked with files sat against the opposite wall.

Suzanne wasn't sure what she was looking for, but she opened drawers, pawed through files, opened more drawers. And still came up with . . . nothing.

So what now? Upstairs?

Suzanne walked out to the hallway and climbed the staircase.

There were three bedrooms on the second floor, none of which displayed any distinct personality. Still, Suzanne could tell which one had been Bobby's. It was the bedroom with the nice gold quilt, the coins still scattered on the bureau, clothes hanging in the closet.

She rummaged through the bureau and closet, found nothing, then walked out to the hall and opened the door to a storage closet. It was empty save for a few blankets and some fishing gear.

Pulling open a door at the end of the hallway, Suzanne discovered a narrow set of stairs leading to the attic. The dusty risers also revealed several large footprints. Probably Sheriff Doogie had come this way, too, probing, exploring.

Suzanne tiptoed up.

The attic turned out to be more of a crawl space than anything. In the dim light of a sixty-watt bulb, Suzanne discovered two sets of cross-country skis, more fishing equipment, and a really awful-looking gold love seat with a tuxedo button back. Rain continued to drum on the roof, making the place feel spooky and oppressive.

Back downstairs, Suzanne explored the kitchen, dining room, and managed a quick foray into the basement. It was musty but neat. No major accumulation of junk, no place to really hide anything.

Fighting back disappointment, Suzanne returned to Bobby's office. She sat down in his chair and sorted through his mail again. An American Express bill, light bill, phone bill, and lots of junk mail. She was about to hoist herself up and leave, when she glanced at Bobby's computer.

E-mails?

She opened Bobby's e-mail file, found a dozen or so messages in his in-box. The only thing remotely interesting was a message from josh001@ksbureau.com that said, "Back from Madrid on Wednesday. Will touch base— dinner and drinks, you pay?"

Suzanne was about to chalk it up to another cryptic non sequitur when her eyes fell on Bobby's answering machine. She hadn't noticed before, but the red light was flashing. Bobby had a message.

But hadn't Doogie been here earlier? Wouldn't he have listened to the messages?

Sure he would, she told herself. Unless this was a recent message.

Suzanne's fingers hit the button and, immediately, a crackly male voice said, "It's Josh. I'm back, bro, but I still didn't get that paperwork. You sure it's been scanned and e-mailed to me? Umm . . . call me, okay?"

A low-level buzz strummed in the back of Suzanne's brain.

What paperwork? And who was Josh?

As her heart beat a little faster, Suzanne stared at a collection of photos on Bobby's wall. There was a photo of Carmen posing with a group of authors; she'd just won the Silver Heartstrings Award, the big prize in romance writing. Next to it was a framed photo of a man in hip waders in the middle of a fast-moving stream. Could that be Josh? Was he the same guy she'd seen in the floatplane photo in Bobby's downtown office?

Suzanne walked over to that photo and studied it. Then, for some reason unbeknownst to her, she lifted it off the wall.

Her fingers touched a crinkle of paper.

What? Something stuck behind?

She turned the photo over, saw a folded hunk of paper wedged into the edges of the frame.

She carried the photo back to Bobby's desk and, with trembling hands, unfolded two single sheets of paper. It took barely a second to register that one sheet was a photocopy of a check, the other the back of the check. The amount was in the millions and made out to Dodd Development. The check had been endorsed by Vern Manchester.

Vern? Holy shit.

Suzanne exhaled rapidly, as though she'd been punched. Vern was the one who'd received a kickback, not Walter! He was the one feeling heat from contractors under pressure by the attorney general's office. So Vern Manchester had misdirected evidence toward Walter.

Suzanne stared at the check, feeling a wave of nausea. Her temples pounded; her throat suddenly felt hot and scratchy. Rain continued to pound down outside, battering the windows. The room suddenly felt cold and inhospitable, as though a window was open somewhere. Or a door.

Suzanne lifted her head.

Vern was standing there, hooded eyes glaring at her. She gasped.

"Suzanne." Vern's voice rasped like flint against rock. "Couldn't leave it alone, could you?"

That's when she noticed the gun in his hand.

CHAPTER 35

"VERN!" Suzanne screamed as she shrank back in the chair.

Vern shook his head as though he was supremely disappointed in her. "First Bobby had to snoop, and then you had to go poking around, too."

"I . . . I didn't mean to!" protested Suzanne. She was so stunned, she didn't know what to say.

"You stupid, nosy girl," snarled Vern. "Give me that!" He snatched the paper from her.

As Suzanne jumped reflexively, her right hand came down upon the glass paperweight. She grasped it tightly, then rocketed the thing right at Vern's head. It struck a glancing blow above his left eye, leaving a bright red gash.

"Oww!" he howled, firing a wild shot at Suzanne just as she dove beneath the desk.

Scrambling for a weapon, any weapon, Suzanne came up with a small metal trash can. She hurled it at Vern, grabbed for the telephone, knocked the receiver off the hook. If she could only dial 911!

Vern deflected the trash can in midair, leveled the gun at her, and fired again.

Suzanne's shoulder felt like it had been ripped open with a hot poker. The intensity of pain stunned her, blotted out all else. Howling like a wounded animal, she knew for certain she'd been hit, knew that Vern meant to kill her! In full-blown panic now, Suzanne understood she had to do something. She had to somehow get away, summon help while she still could. Her fingers clutched and grasped at the thing closest to her and hooked the back of the purple chair. Slowly, painfully, Suzanne lifted it clumsily with her good arm, then swung it at the bay window. Glass exploded everywhere, curtains suddenly whipped in the breeze, rain poured in.

Suzanne stole a quick glance at a stunned Vern, then dove through the makeshift hole she'd created. Shards of glass sliced her arms and ripped at her hair. Something cut into her left hip.

She experienced a fleeting split-second moment of flight, then was jarred back to reality when she somersaulted hard and landed on her back. Her feet slapped down on wet grass, the back of her head jounced against the cobblestone walkway that led around from the front of the house. Staring at gray heavens and rain sluicing down, Suzanne felt herself beginning to lose consciousness.

Just rest for a second, she told herself. *Just lie easy.*

No! her inner self screamed. *Got to get away!*

Through a veil of gray, Suzanne crooked her head and suddenly saw Vern's leg appear in the window, kicking wildly at the remaining shards of glass. Then his other leg began to wiggle through. Like a bad nightmare from which there was no escape, she realized he was coming after her!

Suzanne rolled over onto wet grass, trying to get her arms under her, fighting to push herself up. Out of the corner of her eye she saw a blur of motion out on the street. Car? Mail carrier?

Can't tell. Too hurt, too woozy.

Vern had squeezed through the window now and was coming toward her, baring his teeth, holding his gun at eye level. Rain continued to batter down, plastering his white dress shirt against him, revealing the outline of his old-man undershirt.

Suzanne lifted her hands in a gesture that begged for mercy. "You don't want to do this," she pleaded in a hoarse croak. "This is crazy, you'll spend the rest of your life in prison."

Vern waggled his gun playfully, then pointed it directly at her heart. "The next peal of thunder," he snarled, "will drown out the gunshot." He let loose a high-pitched bark and added, "The rain will wash away your blood!"

Suzanne cringed, fully expecting to be jolted by one final, fatal shot. But as rain streamed into her eyes, as a loud boom exploded in her ears, a bright red spot bloomed suddenly on Vern's white shirt!

Slack-jawed and hunched over, Vern gave a stunned look as he seemed to register his wound. Then his eyes rolled back in his head, and he slowly crumpled to the ground.

Whipping her head sideways, Suzanne saw Sheriff Doogie, drenched, grim-faced, feet spread apart on the lawn, both hands clasped around his gun in a classic shooter's stance.

SUZANNE rode to the hospital in the passenger side of Doogie's cruiser as they screamed along at about a hundred miles an hour. Lights twirled madly, his siren blared. Doogie was grim-faced, barking orders into his radio the entire way. When he finally careened into the curved entrance to Mercy Hospital's ER, a team of four white-coated nurses and doctors were waiting with a gurney.

Doogie lifted Suzanne out of the car and laid her down gently.

Her feeling of floating and otherworldness was suddenly replaced by a stab of pain.

A nurse who identified herself as Judy placed cool hands on Suzanne's forehead. "Keep your eyes open, honey, stay with us."

"How bad?" asked Doogie, practically screaming now. "How bad is she hit?"

With practiced fingers, Dr. Sam Hazelet unbuttoned the top three buttons of Suzanne's blouse, pushed it gently aside, and peered at her shoulder wound.

"Hey there," Suzanne said to him, her tongue feeling thick and cottony. "Remember me?"

"Sure do," he said, hurriedly putting a stethoscope to her chest.

"Is she gonna make it?" screamed Doogie. He'd lost his hat somewhere, and gray strands of hair were plastered against his head. Tears welled in his eyes, his nose was running profusely.

"She's fine," Sam told him in a calm, measured voice. "The bullet just creased her. Stitches for sure, and we need to check out her other cuts and abrasions."

"Head hurts," murmured Suzanne.

"Did you hit your head?" asked Judy.

Suzanne managed a painful nod.

"Might need a head CT," Judy suggested.

Sam Hazelet held up two fingers. "How many fingers am I holding up?"

"Two," said Suzanne.

"What day is today?" Hazelet asked.

"Rotten day," said Suzanne. "Wednesday."

He leaned closer. "What color are my eyes?"

She smiled up at him. "Blue."

Another siren screamed at full decibel, and the ambulance carrying Vern Manchester veered in and rocked to a stop beside them. The EMTs scrambled out, unfolding the stretcher bearing Vern.

Sam was over there in a split second. A whispered conversation ensued as he bent over the body, then he gave a quick shake of his head.

"Didn't make it," murmured one of the nurses.

Doogie gazed down at Suzanne. "Ain't that a shame."

IN a room surrounded entirely by fluttering white curtains, Suzanne's wounds were cleaned and dressed by the nurse, Judy, and Tim Dalton, a physician's assistant. No stitches were required, just a few strategically placed Steri-Strips. Then Judy probed the back of Suzanne's hand with a long, thin needle.

"What's that for?" asked Suzanne.

"Dr. Hazelet wanted me to set up a drip," Judy told her. "You've got your choice of cosmopolitan or apple martini."

"What's it really?" asked Suzanne.

"Just something to rehydrate you. Don't worry. It won't take long."

"Then I'm going home," said Suzanne, dropping her head against the pillow.

"We'll see," said Judy.

But whatever it was, pain meds, Valium, or just the saline drip that rehydrated her and restored electrolytes, Suzanne was feeling pretty good some forty-five minutes later. Opening her eyes, she found Doogie standing over her. Somewhere amid the furor, he had dried off and changed into a fresh shirt.

"You're hovering," she told him. "They didn't revise their diagnosis, did they? I'm not going to die?"

"Shit," said Doogie in his gruffest voice, "you ain't even really shot." He wiped at his eyes, gave a huge sniffle.

"Creased," said Suzanne, remembering the blinding-hot pain. "Creased is shot." She reached a hand out from beneath the flimsy white blanket. Doogie didn't hesitate to grasp it and give a warm squeeze.

She looked up at him. "Vern's really dead?"

"Yeah, he is," said Doogie.

"How do you feel about that?" she asked. Even though Doogie was gruff and brusque and blustery, she knew he had a very human side. It couldn't have been easy for him to take a human life.

"Just fine," said Doogie. "It was him or you. An easy choice."

Jerry Driscoll, one of Sheriff Doogie's deputies, tentatively pushed back one of the white curtains surrounding Suzanne and crooked a finger at him.

Doogie slipped away, but was back at her side a few minutes later.

"What?" asked Suzanne.

"All hell's breaking loose out there," said Doogie. "Things are falling into place." His mouth twitched slightly.

"What?" Suzanne asked him again.

Doogie gave a dry chuckle. "You ain't gonna believe this, but Mayor Mobley called. He's on his way over to see you. I guess word's out all over town."

Suzanne rolled her eyes. "You really think the mayor's coming here to apologize? He'll probably just do his usual weaseling then toss me a few crumbs of sympathy."

"Ah, don't worry about it," said Doogie. "I told Mr. Fancy Pants Mayor to cool his heels in the second-floor lounge until I come get him."

"What floor are we on now?" Suzanne asked.

"First," said Doogie, his eyes sparkling.

"You're gonna go get him?"

"Sure I am," said Doogie. "Tomorrow."

SUZANNE was given the go-ahead to be released. But first, Dr. Sam Hazelet stopped by to see her and give her a bottle of pills.

"You know about these?"

She shook the brown bottle, scanned the label. "Darvon. Yeah." They were semiserious painkillers.

"Probably won't need more than a couple," Sam told

her. "Your color's back, BP is normal, you're actually looking . . . very good."

"Thanks, Dr. Hazelet."

"Sam. Call me Sam."

She smiled faintly at him. "Sam."

He threw her a concerned look, then fished a pen from
his white coat and grabbed a prescription pad off a flimsy
metal table. He made a few quick jottings. "If your pain
worsens, you experience dizziness, or you need anything
at all, just . . ." He held the slip between two fingers, twid-
dled it a moment, then handed it to Suzanne. "Here."

Suzanne accepted the slip. "Thanks. I'm feeling better,
though." If he hadn't written out another prescription, she
would have sworn he was flirting with her.

"You don't want to overdo it," Sam cautioned. "Not yet,
anyway." He flashed a grin and then ducked back through
the curtains.

Suzanne glanced down at the slip, wondering what other
magical mystery medicine he'd prescribed for her.

And, much to her surprise, discovered it wasn't a prescription at all. Dr. Sam Hazelet had written down his
phone number.

Blinking rapidly, pulling herself up straight, Suzanne
stared at the filmy curtain that moved faintly in his wake.
She brushed the back of her hand across slightly flushed
cheeks and finally let the smile she'd been holding in spill
across her face.

Well, I'll be . . .

CHAPTER 36

SUZANNE probably should have gone right home. Should have crawled into bed, downed a couple of Darvon, and let the pain pills gallop across her mind. Let herself think about . . . possibilities.

Instead, she persuaded Doogie to drive her back out to the Cackleberry Club.

"Suzanne," Petra cried, eyes sparkling with tears. "Thank goodness you're okay!" She wrapped her arms around Suzanne, giving her an ultragentle hug, then stepped back, as if to inspect her. "You are okay, aren't you?"

"This way, this way," cried Toni. "Sit over here." She pulled out a chair, frantic with worry.

"I cancelled Hooked on Wool," said Petra, "when Sheriff Doogie called to say you were coming."

"And we've got tea and scones all ready," added Toni. She bit her lip, fighting to hold back tears. "How do you feel?"

Suzanne eased herself into a chair. "It's hurts a little, but . . . I'm okay. Now."

Toni grabbed Suzanne's vial of pills and shook them. "Better swallow one of these puppies."

"Then I'll fall asleep," said Suzanne.

"Sleep is what you probably need most," said Petra. She sat down at the table next to Suzanne, while Toni poured cups of relaxing chamomile tea.

When Doogie came stomping in, chattering into his cell phone, Petra poured a cup of tea for him, too. After all, Sheriff Roy Doogie was now a bona fide hero.

"Oh," said Petra, "some guy named Josh called. Said he was a friend of Bobby's."

Doogie put his hand over the phone. "We know about that," he told the women. "In fact, I talked to him."

"What?" said Suzanne.

"Bobby was apparently going to enlist the help of his freelance journalist friend to do an exposé on the construction money kickback," Doogie explained. "Vern must have gotten wind of it."

"So Vern killed Bobby and stole the files from his office," said Suzanne. "The files he *thought* contained evidence against him as well as a few more to kind of . . . smokescreen things."

"Looks like," said Doogie. "I spoke with Carmen Copeland twenty minutes ago and, when I really pressed her on the fact that Bobby might have been on his way to her house the morning he was shot, she recalled that he *had* mentioned something about his scanner being on the blink."

"Now she remembers," said Petra.

"Duh," added Toni.

"So Bobby was gonna grab the evidence from his house, then go to Carmen's place and send those documents to Josh?" asked Suzanne.

"Probably," said Doogie, then started up a conversation with one of his deputies again.

"This is all so weird," said Petra. She tugged at Doogie's shirt. "What happened with Lenore when you went in and searched her house?"

"Lenore pretty near pitched a fit," Doogie told her as an

aside. "And went completely hysterical when she found out Vern was dead."

"So Vern got the kickback," said Petra. "That kind of explains why Lenore's been cruising around town in a Lexus."

"She won't be for long," said Toni. "Repo man's gonna pay her a visit."

"Won't be on the library committee, either," murmured Suzanne.

Doogie talked for a few more minutes, then hung up. Taking a long gulp of tea, he smacked his lips and reached for a scone.

"But how did you know it was Vern?" Suzanne asked. She was still having trouble following the story.

"I stopped in to see Missy just as she was telling you about Dodd Development," said Doogie. "So I asked her about it. She didn't seem to know much, so I decided to run that name through the system, too. Along with those contractor papers you gave me."

"For once the system works," chirped Toni.

"Anyway," said Doogie, "it rang some bells in the state attorney general's office. Vern Manchester came up as CEO of Dodd Development along with information on state zoning permits they'd applied for." Sheriff Doogie gazed at Suzanne. "Besides the fraud and embezzlement with the prison, it looks like Vern had his eyes on your property as well as the Journey's End Church."

Suzanne thought about the lights Reed Ducovny had seen across the field and the little red flag she'd kicked over. Probably, she decided, they'd been out surveying her land at night. Doing it on the QT. Filing for building permits when they didn't even own it yet. "So you were following Vern?" she asked.

Doogie nodded. "Good thing I did."

"Wait a minute," said Petra, outrage building in her voice. "Does this mean Vern also torched the church?"

"I can't prove it yet," said Doogie, munching away, "but it sure points in that direction. Vern wanted to build some sort of strip mall right here along the highway."

"And what about Teddy?" asked Suzanne.

Doogie shook his head sadly. "Must have seen Vern. Came riding by at the wrong time, and Vern assumed Teddy witnessed the shooting."

"Wow," said Suzanne. She put a hand to her head. It was spinning from information overload.

"So Junior's off the hook," said Toni.

"As well as Garland and Charlie Pepper," said Petra.

"And Claes Elam," added Suzanne. "Although he's got his own set of troubles."

"That's for sure," said Doogie. He downed the rest of his tea and stood up. Cocked a concerned eye at Suzanne. "I better get you home." He glanced from Petra to Toni. "Can one of you, uh, women, stay with her tonight?"

"I will," said Toni. "Just let me make a quick call." She pulled her cell phone from her bag, started to punch in numbers, then stopped. "Suzanne?" she said, glancing at her friend. "Are you okay?"

Suzanne's head was tilted sideways and she had a dreamy look on her face. "It sounds like . . . music."

Petra grabbed for Suzanne's wrist to take her pulse.

"Oh no!" cried Toni, suddenly alarmed. "I think Suzanne's slipping down that long, bright tunnel!"

"No," laughed Suzanne. "I really do hear music."

They were all quiet then, listening. "I hear it, too," said Petra. "Singing."

Sheriff Doogie stepped to the window and pushed back a lace curtain. "It's those poor folks from the church."

"What's going on?" asked Toni.

Petra went over to the window and peered past Doogie's shoulder. "Must be their Wednesday night prayer meeting."

Suzanne rose shakily and gazed out the window. From where she stood, she could see members of the Journey's

End Church milling about the soggy, sooty ruins of their former church, trying to make do with a prayer meeting in the parking lot.

"Hope those poor folks can rebuild," said Doogie.

Suzanne continued to stare across the vacant lot at the congregation. Rain pelted down on their heads as they gathered in a semicircle and lifted their voices in praise. Still, they looked like they'd lost their best friend.

"Invite them over," said Suzanne. "Let them have their service here."

"You think?" said Toni.

Petra nodded and grabbed her coat. They watched as she ran through the rain to the cluster of people. She gestured, then pointed back toward the Cackleberry Club. A sea of faces turned and stared at them.

A minute later, church members began filing into the Cackleberry Club.

Suzanne met them at the door. "Welcome," she said, grasping the door frame for support. She was suddenly aware of hands being pressed into hers, lips brushing her cheek, warm words of appreciation.

Toni brought out a stack of tea towels and passed them around so folks could dry their faces. Petra began handing out mugs of hot coffee and tea.

Reverend Yoder was the last to appear in the doorway of the Cackleberry Club.

"Come in," Suzanne told him, warmth resonating in her voice. "And please, have your evening service here whenever you want. Neighbors are always welcome."

Reverend Yoder's lined face was filled with gratitude; tears shone in his eyes. He grasped Suzanne's hands and held them gently in his gnarled hands. "When I count my blessings," he said with a catch in his voice, "I'm going to count you twice."

Favorite Recipes
from the Cackleberry Club

Eggs in Purgatory

¼ cup finely chopped onion
2 tbsp. olive oil
2 cups canned, peeled tomatoes
Pinch of dried oregano
Pinch of chipotle pepper
Tabasco sauce to taste
Salt and pepper to taste
8 fresh eggs

In a large skillet, cook onion in olive oil over medium heat for 8 to 10 minutes. Add tomatoes, oregano, chipotle pepper, Tabasco sauce, and salt and pepper. Simmer 12 minutes until thickened. Break an egg into a small bowl. Using spoon, make indentation in tomato sauce, then slide in egg. Add remaining eggs. Cover skillet and cook 2 to 3 minutes or until eggs are set. Serve with toast or crusty French bread.

Strawberry Spinach Salad

1 bunch spinach, rinsed and torn
10 large strawberries, sliced
½ cup pecan halves
½ cup sugar
1 tsp. salt
⅓ cup white wine vinegar
1 cup salad oil

Mix spinach, strawberries, and pecans in a large bowl. In the blender, mix sugar, salt, vinegar, and oil until smooth. Pour dressing over salad greens and toss until lightly coated. (As an option, you can also add 3 ounces of crumbled goat cheese or blue cheese.)

Cherry Pie Muffins

2½ cups flour
½ cup sugar
2 tsp. baking powder
1 tsp. baking soda
½ tsp. salt
¼ lb. butter, melted
1 cup sour cream
1 egg
½ tsp. vanilla
1 can cherry pie filling (21 oz.)
1 cup slivered almonds, toasted

Sift together flour, sugar, baking powder, baking soda, and salt. Make a well in the middle and add butter, sour cream, egg, and vanilla. Mix together well. Add cherry pie filling and slivered almonds and mix again. Spoon batter into greased muffin tins and bake at 400° for 25 to 30 minutes. Check with toothpick for doneness, then remove tin from oven and cool on rack about 10 minutes before removing muffins. (Note: muffins can be frosted.)

Chicken Pâté Tea Sandwiches

2 cooked chicken breasts, diced
½ cup cream
1 sprig rosemary leaves, chopped
Salt and pepper to taste
6 slices of thin bread
Baby field greens, a few pieces

Place chicken breasts and cream in food processor and blend until smooth. Add chopped rosemary and salt and pepper and pulse again. Spread chicken pâté on bread, top with a few greens, and make into sandwich. Cut off crusts, then cut sandwich diagonally into 4 wedges. Yields about 12 small tea sandwiches. (As an option, you can also top chicken pâté with a dab of chutney.)

Bodacious Bacon Quiche

1 tbsp. butter, softened
9" pie shell
10 pieces cooked bacon
4 fresh eggs
2 cups cream (or half-and-half)
½ tsp. salt
½ cup shredded cheese (Swiss or Gruyère)

Smooth butter over bottom of uncooked pie shell. Add crumbled bacon. Whisk eggs, cream, salt, and cheese together in bowl. Pour egg mixture into pie shell and bake for 15 minutes at 425°. Then turn your oven down to 325° and bake for an additional 35 minutes. Let quiche rest for 10 minutes before cutting.

Corn and Red Pepper Pancakes

2 cups corn (fresh, frozen, or canned)
¼ cup red pepper, diced
¼ cup onion, chopped
2 tbsp. parsley, chopped
2 cups melted butter
1½ cups flour
3 eggs
1½ cups cream (or half-and-half)

Combine corn, red pepper, onion, and parsley in large bowl. Stir in melted butter. Add flour and stir to coat vegetables. In separate bowl, lightly beat eggs, then add cream. Fold egg/cream mixture into vegetable mixture. Cook as dollar-size pancakes and serve with sour cream and salsa. (Or use cooked bacon bits as a topper, too!)

Buttermilk Scones

1¾ cups flour
1 tbsp. sugar
¼ tsp. salt
½ tsp. baking soda
2 tsp. baking powder
6 tbsp. chilled butter
¾ cup buttermilk

Blend dry ingredients together. Cut in butter. Blend in buttermilk to form a loose ball. Divide dough in half and press each piece on floured board to ½" thickness. Cut each piece into 6 pie-shaped pieces. Place on greased cookie sheet and brush with buttermilk. Bake at 400° for 10 to 12 minutes.

Drunken Pecan Chicken

1 chicken, cut into serving pieces
½ cup red wine
½ tsp. dried rosemary
¼ tsp. dried thyme
¼ tsp. dried sage
Garlic powder to taste
Salt and pepper to taste
2 tbsp. olive oil
1 cup pecans, chopped

Arrange chicken pieces in baking dish and pour wine over all. Combine rosemary, thyme, sage, garlic, salt, and pepper and sprinkle over chicken. Drizzle chicken with olive oil, then sprinkle with chopped pecans. Cover dish with foil and bake at 375° for 40 minutes. Remove foil and bake an additional 30 minutes or until chicken is cooked.

Toad in the Hole

1 pkg. pork sausage links (12 oz.)
¼ cup chopped onion
1 tbsp. oil
2 eggs
1 cup flour
½ cup water
½ cup milk

Brown sausage links and onions in skillet with oil. Drain, then place sausages and onions in a 9" × 13" baking dish. In medium bowl, beat eggs well. Add flour, water, and milk to eggs and beat all together vigorously. Let mixture rest for 5 minutes. Pour egg mixture over sausages. Bake in preheated 400° oven for 25 to 30 minutes, or until top is browned. Makes a great breakfast, or serve with a citrus salad for a main meal.

Blond Brownies

1 stick butter, softened (4 oz.)
1 cup brown sugar, packed
1 egg
1 cup flour
¼ tsp. baking powder
⅛ tsp. baking soda
Pinch of salt

¾ cup chopped walnuts
1 cup semisweet chocolate bits (8 oz.)

Cream together butter and brown sugar, then beat in egg. Add flour, baking powder, baking soda, and salt, then stir together. Stir in nuts and chocolate bits. Spread batter in a 7" × 11" pan that has been greased and floured. Bake at 350° for 20 to 22 minutes.

Chicken and Wild Rice Soup

½ cup uncooked wild rice
4 tbsp. butter
1 medium onion, chopped
1 cup celery, chopped
3 tbsp. flour
Salt and pepper to taste
1 can chicken broth (10 oz.)
2 cups milk
2 cups diced, cooked chicken

Prepare wild rice according to directions on package. Melt butter in large pot over medium heat. Add onion and celery, then sauté for 8 to 10 minutes. Stir in flour, add salt and pepper to taste. Add chicken broth and milk, then stir until soup thickens. Add cooked rice and diced chicken and simmer for about 10 minutes.

Easy Sour Cream Biscuits

2 cups self-rising flour
½ tsp. salt
12 oz. sour cream

Mix all ingredients together, then form into a soft ball. Place on floured board and roll out to about ½" thickness. Cut out biscuits using a 2" round cutter. Place on greased baking sheet and bake at 425° for about 12 minutes or until browned.

Egg Tips and Factoids
from the Cackleberry Club

- For baking cakes, try to use medium to large eggs. Extra-large eggs may cause your cake to fall once it's cooled.

- To prevent eggs from getting tough and rubbery, always cook them using moderate (not high) heat.

- Don't want to get stuck with rotten eggs? Then go ahead and test your eggs. A fresh egg will sink to the bottom in a bowl of salted water, but a bad egg will float.

- Be sure to keep your eggs refrigerated. They'll age more in a single day at room temperature than they will in one week in your refrigerator.

- The breed of the chicken determines egg color. Breeds with white feathers lay white eggs, breeds with red or brown feathers lay brown eggs.

- Brown eggs are the "tough guys" of the egg world. They always have thicker shells than white eggs.

Turn the page for a preview of the next
Tea Shop Mystery by Laura Childs . . .

OOLONG DEAD

Coming March 2009 from Berkley Prime Crime!

OVERHEAD branches slapped at Theodosia's cheeks, a crisp breeze nipped and pecked tendrils of auburn hair from beneath her black velvet riding cap. Sitting astride Captain Harley, a dun-colored jumping horse, Theodosia Browning couldn't have cared less as she charged her mount toward the fifth jump in the annual Charleston Point-to-Point race.

This pulse-pounding, exhilarating ride was part of a high-society weekend Theodosia felt lucky to participate in. The Wildwood Horse and Hunt Club, a club she'd ridden with before, had invited her to join them. One of their members, a regular steeplechase rider, had broken his collarbone a week earlier, and she was riding in his place.

And wouldn't you know it? This was one of those amazing October days when the sky was a curtain of cerulean blue and every shrub and tree blazed red and gold.

Starting from the outskirts of Ruffin, where the horsey set mingled with Charleston society over mint juleps and bourbon and branch, the race course snaked alongside a country road, headed into deep woods, and ended at a makeshift finish line some six miles away. It was a challenging course, littered with two dozen tricky jumps that included hedges, logs, fences, and muddy ditches. Heady stuff for Theodosia, who spent much of her time indoors.

Amidst the hiss and burble of teapots and the coming and going of customers, Theodosia Browning served as owner and proprietor of the Indigo Tea Shop in Charleston, South Carolina's historic district. For the past four years, she'd served tea, catered events, and dealt with the challenges of being a small-business owner in a great big, ever-changing free-market economy. No wonder, when it came to riding, she was also a fierce competitor.

Pounding down a long, sloping trail, Theodosia was happy to be far away from the viewing stand, hospitality tent, and inevitable TV cameras. The air was cooler here and the mossy, loamy scent of low-country soil filled her nostrils.

As brush swooshed against her leather riding boots, Theodosia charged toward the always-difficult in-and-out jump. Easing back on the reins just slightly, she tried to gauge her timing. At the last jump, Captain Harley had launched a little early and his back hooves had ticked down hard on the gate. Even though this in-and-out jump carried a greater degree of difficulty, Theodosia intended to take it cleanly.

Bending forward now, Theodosia felt the heave and shudder of the large horse beneath her and squinted intently as the double jump came into view. Her hands slid forward to grasp a fistful of the horse's rough mane to insure she wouldn't get left behind when the big horse launched. Then, forearms aligned with Captain Harley's head, knees gripping the horse's mud-spattered sides, they were suddenly airborne.

Skimming over the first split-rail fence with ease, they landed with a resounding thud that sent clods of mud flying. Captain Harley took one scrambling, bounding stride, then Theodosia felt his muscles gather again as they launched like a giant spring over the second fence.

Leaning back in her saddle, Theodosia prepared herself for the inevitable hard jounce when the big horse touched down. Felt a tingle of exhilaration mingled with accomplishment.

But Captain Harley suddenly stumbled, then lurched crazily, his landing completely off kilter!

Bad landing, Theodosia thought as she was jerked rudely in the saddle, her horse slaloming left, sliding a few feet, then crab-stepping wildly off course!

What happened? she wondered. *Bee sting?*

Theodosia dug her heels into the horse's sides and jerked hard at the reins, fighting to regain control. But her quick efforts weren't enough. Something—some movement she'd also caught out of the corner of her eye—had spooked the big horse once again.

Leaning forward, Theodosia continued to jiggle at Captain Harley's bit, trying to simmer him down.

But Captain Harley, caught in his paroxysm of equine panic, was having none of it. Lips slicked back over long teeth, Captain Harley shook his great head from side to side, tossed his head back, and uttered a shrill, high-pitched whinny that sounded like a banshee's shriek as it echoed through the depths of the piney forest.

He's going to rear over backward, Theodosia thought to herself. And just as Captain Harley flung his head back for the second time and his front hooves churned wildly in the air, Theodosia felt herself beginning to slip backward. Gradually, inescapably, she was going to go down.

Theodosia, who'd been riding practically since she could walk, who'd been in tight jams before, did what any seasoned rider would do to save their own hide. She did a tuck and roll.

Only, in this case, it was more like a sickening, slow-motion summersault. First, Theodosia was staring at blue sky populated by airy puffs of clouds, then she had a view of sloppy mud, littered with pine needles. Back to a quick, dizzying image of treetops, then another terrifying view of dark earth spinning toward her.

Thud.

A rude, teeth-rattling landing jounced Theodosia the full length of her body. As her breath was punched out of her, her head reeled, and a cloud of darkness began to descend. Hovering on the edge of consciousness, Theodosia willed herself to keep breathing, even as her mind seemed to spin like a centrifuge.

Moments crawled by as Theodosia lay huddled on the ground. Captain Harley was long gone, his hoof beats miniature thunder that echoed off the trees, then faded to nothing. Gradually, Theodosia felt dampness seep through her riding breeches, became aware of the rich, arboreal scent of forest floor prickling at her nose. She also felt a sharp stab of pain in her side.

Ribs cracked? Maybe broken?

And a raw, intense throb at the base of her neck.

Dear Lord, not my spine!

Theodosia's eyes peeped open. Landing in a semi-sprawled position, she found herself facing the second split-rail fence. Her nose and the left side of her cheek tingled hotly and she vaguely remembered scraping up against a creosote-coated rail.

Staring at her boots, Theodosia gingerly tried to move her left foot. Though it felt strangely disconnected from the rest of her, the black riding boot bobbled to and fro just fine.

Feeling heartened, she tried the right foot. Again, a moderate amount of success. Deciding she might not be so badly injured after all, knowing she had to get to her feet before another horse and rider came charging through the jump, Theodosia let loose a slow groan and rolled over onto one side.

That's when she saw a fresh spatter of blood tingeing a small patch of grass.

Bleeding? Where?

Her addled mind still wasn't tracking properly. Theodosia peeled off her riding gloves and felt her face. Couldn't detect any major cuts or scratches.

She slid off her riding cap, really a fancy hard hat, and released her mass of curly, auburn hair. She carefully patted her scalp. No dampness oozed, her skull seemed blessedly intact. So far so good.

Then . . . what? she wondered.

Twisting her neck slightly, feeling a rise of panic, Theodosia caught sight of more blood. And finally saw the body. Laying right there in front of her. A woman in a pale peach suit, crumpled horribly and slumped against the split-rail fence.

Theodosia's first panicked thought was that she'd run the poor woman down. Had crashed into her and unwittingly battered her with Captain Harley's lethal, steel-shod hooves.

That's what I saw. That's why Captain Harley freaked out! Oh dear Lord.

Theodosia pulled herself to her feet, staggered slightly, thought for sure she was going to be sick. Then she somehow got it together.

Managing another step, she went down hard on her knees beside the woman.

Is she breathing? Theodosia wondered. She tried to recall the ABC's of first aid. Airway, breathing, circulation.

She touched two fingers to the front of the woman's throat, just above the cameo that was pinned to her blouse, but could detect no pulse. She scanned quickly for some sign of injury, but saw none.

Gently, cautiously, Theodosia pushed the woman's brown hair from her face. The woman's eyes were shut tight; blood smeared her forehead and all the way down to the bridge of her nose. And, there, right between the woman's eyes—Theodosia leaned in closer to look—was a small black hole. The sort of entry hole a small-caliber weapon might make.

Shocked, Theodosia stared into the woman's slack face as the metallic, slightly cloying scent of blood wafted upward.

Theodosia squeezed her eyes closed, forcing herself to breath through her nose, willing herself to calm down. Not to panic.

She slowly opened her eyes and focused.

In the dim recesses of her brain, something about the woman struck her as being strangely familiar.

Theodosia rolled back on her heels and studied the woman again. She noted the thrust of the woman's jaw, her high cheek bones, the spark of diamond studs in her ears. And was suddenly rocked to her inner core.

She knew this woman! Had seen her on TV just the other night. Had exchanged slightly unpleasant words with her a few months ago. Had . . . *ohmygosh, it can't be her!* . . . had dated her brother!

It came to Theodosia in a wild rush of recovered memory, the name popping into her brain with so much force she swore it made a cartoon bubble above her head.

"Abby Davis," said Theodosia, her voice rising as if it were a pleading, crying question. "Shot to death?"

She stared at the woman again as a sick feeling puddled in the pit of her stomach.

Last time Theodosia had come face-to-face with Abby Davis, they'd had a rather public disagreement. And now here she was, lying dead in front of her.

The coincidence, the irony, seemed almost too much for Theodosia.

Nerves on edge, she studied the body again. Noticed there was fresh dirt under the fingernails of Abby's left hand. As if she'd attempted to pull herself along.

Shaking, feeling somewhat repulsed, Theodosia reached out and carefully shifted the body. It rolled over and settled lifelessly into a sad heap. The fingernails on Abby's right hand were just as filthy.

Theodosia lifted her gaze to the bloodless pallor of Abby Davis's face. It was a shocking contract to the cameo that glinted so hypnotically in the fading afternoon sun. Red, blue, and brilliant yellow stones shining brightly.

"What just happened here?" she muttered.

But there was no answer save the faint whisper and sigh of the forest.

Don't miss the next Cackleberry Club Mystery

Eggs Benedict Arnold

When Ozzie Driesden, Kindred's local mortician, ends up on his own slab, the ladies from the Cackleberry Club launch their own investigation. But as friends become suspects, one suspect turns traitor.

Watch for the next Tea Shop Mystery
also from Laura Childs and Berkley Prime Crime

Oolong Dead

A wild steeplechase through the South Carolina low country brings Theodosia face-to-face with a dead woman—and sparks the return of a boyfriend she never thought she'd see again.

And the next Scrapbooking Mystery

Tragic Magic

Design-wise Carmela Bertrand of Memory Mine scrapbook store is tapped to create spooky set decorations for Medusa Manor, a new haunted house attraction in New Orleans. But a flaming body hurled from the third-floor tower might just put a damper on the project.

The Tea Shop Mysteries by
Laura Childs

DEATH BY DARJEELING

GUNPOWDER GREEN

SHADES OF EARL GREY

THE ENGLISH BREAKFAST MURDER

THE JASMINE MOON MURDER

CHAMOMILE MOURNING

BLOOD ORANGE BREWING

DRAGONWELL DEAD

THE SILVER NEEDLE MURDER

"A delightful series."
—*The Mystery Reader*

"Murder suits Laura Childs to a Tea."
—*St. Paul Pioneer Press*

penguin.com

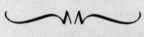
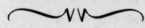